The Commando-Colonel's thoughts were heavy, and she gave the small room but a cursory glance before slipping her jacket from her shoulders and hanging it on the peg by the door. If most of her mind was fixed on her own concerns, she had not abandoned the care which had kept her alive so long in her perilous work. The heavy curtains scarcely began to move before she heard the soft step of a booted foot.

"Varn Tarl Sogan does not crawl to the assault from out of the shadows," she said without attempting to face the intruder.

"Turn," a cold, well-remembered voice commanded. "Move slowly." The woman obeyed. She stood very still with her hands near to her sides, slightly away from her body. He held her eyes. They met his quite steadily. "You do recognize me then," he stated.

For the first time her attention went visibly to the blaster in his hand. It was set to kill. "Have I firmed your resolve to use that?"

STAR COMMANDOS

P.M. GRIFFIN

ACE SCIENCE FICTION BOOKS
NEW YORK

This book is an Ace Science Fiction original edition,
and has never been previously published.

STAR COMMANDOS

An Ace Science Fiction Book/published by arrangement with
the author

PRINTING HISTORY
Ace Science Fiction edition/October 1986

ISBN: 0-441-78041-5

Ace Science Fiction Books are published by
The Berkley Publishing Group,
200 Madison Avenue, New York, New York 10016.
PRINTED IN THE UNITED STATES OF AMERICA

To Andre Norton,
for her belief in this book and her support.

STAR COMMANDOS

ONE

COMMANDO-COLONEL ISLAEN Connor moved briskly along the busy street. She jerked the collar of her jacket still higher in a futile effort to break the bite of the wind.

Damn and bother this never ending dust! It got into her eyes with painful regularity, each time all but eliminating for a second her visual contact with her surroundings. A guerrilla could die in less than half that time.

Her eyes slitted as the grit-laden breeze intensified. She had better take care here. Visnu's sole spaceport might be safe enough for these others hurrying or ambling along its unfinished streets, but if anyone should begin to think she was something other than a planet hopping exobiologist . . .

Once more the air cleared and she fixed her attention on the world around her. There seemed to be little unique about it. The port was typical of any such installation servicing a first-ship colony. The planeting field and complex of associated buildings formed the core from which the few streets radiated. No paving had been done on any of them yet and would not be done for a long time to come, but the structures lining them, squat and unlovely though they might be, were sturdy and serviceable. They were chiefly warehouses interspersed with a few shops and with some light technical or craft industries. Two taverns were located near the core to draw the spacers,

1

and there was a single hotel, her present goal, farther out. The only significant-looking building was the combined head-quarters and residence of the planet developers.

Her expression hardened at the mental reminder of that scum, but she willed her thoughts to turn to Visnu of Brahmin.

The big planet lacked anything yet to be discovered in the way of natural beauty, or even much of fauna, but that dearth of native life forms made her all the more attractive to potential colonists such as this group from Amon presently claiming her. They wanted to work with their adopted world, not dominate her, and they wished to create as low an ecological impact on her as possible. The Commando sighed. They were too fine a people to have been served thus.

Amon was a very old planet, colonized centuries before the advent of the Settlement Board. She was small and poor in resources, and her populace had long since passed the maximum number she could safely support. A strong, disciplined race, they had not permitted the metastasis to continue further. Balance was achieved and their culture saved but at inevitable cost to personal challenge and individual fulfillment.

More and more people sought what their ancient home could no longer provide. A colony was the answer. All knew that, but worlds acceptable for settlement were not common. Amonites had no fondness for the massive bureaucracy of the Federation. Their patience soon wore thin with the slow progress of the Board controlling all colonization activity, and they deeply resented that off-worlders should have so much power over their lives and their choices. When this other group had offered them a planet ready for immediate occupation, they had leaped to make their claim.

Two years had passed since their ships had planeted. They had built homes, planted crops to sustain them and their livestock, and had begun real work at last among the trees that were the focus of their hope and labor. Life was hard as yet, with little ease and constant, body-wracking toil, but conditions were perceptibly improving and would improve more rapidly still once they could begin exporting some of that fine dark wood and marvelously sweet fruit. With luck, that should be early the following year.

Her mouth hardened. So much hope, so much work, and all of it for nothing.

The colony was an illegal one. Her unit had been sent here to investigate it and had secured evidence in plenty that the documents shown to the settlers were false. Visnu had been privately discovered and had never been properly explored or evaluated. Developers had merely moved in, taking advantage of the postwar troubles gripping the Federation, and had falsified the necessary papers and begun transporting the colonists here. The Amonites were completely unaware of that. This, too, she had confirmed, but it would make little difference to them apart from keeping them out of Federation court. Their settlement's fate would be sealed the moment she filed her report, a fate rendered all the more bitter by their very innocence.

Islaen Connor hated her part in all this. By the Spirit ruling all space, how she hated it! Her own Noreen was an agrarian world, a planet of farmers, and she identified intensely with the aspirations of this other people. She identified with their sweat and their sacrifices. She wanted to the core of her being to help them, yet she could not merely lift from here and forget what she had learned. There was too much peril in that.

Sudden fire, deadly as a blaster's bolt, flashed in her eyes. Men, so-called humans, had done this to them! She would have those subbiotics for it! She would crush them, these bloated leeches sucking dry their victims' dreams. The guerrilla officer gripped herself. Raw anger could be useful under some circumstances, but allowing it rein now would serve no good purpose and might lead her to betray herself.

What had happened here was not a common crime, but neither was it unknown. Such activity carried heavy penalty if detected, for an unsuitable planet could bring death to anyone trying to make a life upon her, but it also carried the promise of huge profits to those successful in concealing what they did.

The men directing this effort had believed they would not be assuming any very great risk, not in the few months they needed to remain associated with it. Once the preliminary work was done and the last of the contracted settlers had paid out their resettlement fees, they would be able to withdraw, leaving their bastard colony to rise or fall as it would.

The brown of her eyes darkened, and once more she had to quell a powerful surge of anger. It was a familiar pattern and so too were the consequences. All too many such settlements crumbled, for abandonment usually stripped them of interstellar support. The Patrol did not know to check on their progress and, if some disaster did threaten, no ships would be there to offer aid or take the imperiled colonists off-world. These people were fortunate in the extreme. Sector authorities had grown suspicious of the activity around Visnu.

The settlers would see little cause for rejoicing in that luck. At the very least, they would probably be forced to abandon the colony and see all their work set to naught when the Federation conducted the proper tests. Few planets were suitable for settlement, only those rare ones able to support new intelligent life in synergy with their own.

Islaen scanned those near her on the busy street. She was uneasy this morning, and her hand strayed frequently of its own accord to the blaster resting at her side. There were none of the Amonites present in the crowd, hardly surprising since there was very little to draw farmers into an area designed for the use of starship crews. She would have much preferred it if there had been. They were a hard and just folk, and she would be far less concerned about meeting with sudden violence had a few of them been near.

The guerrilla officer knew she had ample reason to keep on her guard in this gathering. She had no illusions as to her fate if it came to be known that she had been sent to reconnoiter Visnu at the request of the Sector's governor. Developers engaged in such a project could not readily draw upon legitimate spacers, but they paid well and found little difficulty in filling their needs from other sources. Many of those around her were wanted by the Navy or Patrol, by planetary authorities or all three. Few of them, hunted or not, would feel much fondness for Federation officials. They could be expected to react quickly to any agent's presence here. Preoccupied as she was, she could not be oblivious to that.

Suddenly her eyes widened, and only her iron will and war-trained reflexes prevented her from faltering in her step.

That man . . . No, it could not be!

Islaen kept on moving, but his image burned in her mind. For four long years, that one had been the focus of her every thought and effort. She could not be mistaken.

There were differences. That was to be expected, the inevitable result of time and drastically altered circumstances.

Such changes were irrelevant. The body had thinned, but its

strength and grace of movement remained, as had the straight carriage of one bred to the life of a soldier. New lines might mar the strong features, but they remained recognizable. Even the loss of the beard which had once framed his face could not disguise his features.

The Commando knew his racial characteristics all too well, his height, the olive skin, the eyes which were almost the same dark brown as the hair, a trait not common outside the central planets of the Arcturian Empire, not common even there.

Those eyes, intelligent, cold although even now not utterly lacking in compassion, proud still despite the lash of brutal fortune, they above all else betrayed him to her.

The Commando's head raised. She had seen on him what few others in either ultrasystem would have been able to detect, much less to name: the dull shadow of accepted despair. A swift pang of grief and pity had twisted in her own heart in response to it only to be swallowed in a fierce surge of triumph that his spirit should hold unbroken under it. She who had suffered little was showing less courage than this old enemy. She must mend that failing now, or she would be unworthy of facing him again if they were to be pitted against each other once more.

The woman was beautiful, fully as beautiful as any fair toy gracing the Emperor's harem, and so Varn Tarl Sogan's attention was on her when her eyes swept over him. An icy fist seemed to close around his heart as he saw her pupils widen. Was he betrayed?

The fugitive used the excuse her loveliness provided to study her intently. He did not know her, of that he was certain, but ignorance on his part meant nothing. Pale skin and the red gene apparent in the rich auburn hair were common on Thorne, particularly in conjunction with refinement and delicacy of feature such as she displayed. There was no one native to the subjected planet who had not cursed his name with each new day. Few, particularly among those dwelling anywhere near his headquarters, did not know his features as well as their own. Better. Hate had sharpened their awareness of him.

He fought to calm himself. It did not seem possible that she should have recognized him in these radically altered circumstances. Even had she been born of Thorne and been present there during the critical period, he should be secure. Her perception of him was the key.

There was a vast distance between the man he had been and what he now was. Varn Tarl Sogan had wielded absolute power with all the authority granted him by birth, rank, and the crushing force of the Empire he had represented. Defeat had not dispelled that air of command; his inbred discipline had upheld him during the withdrawal. Neither his grief at the fall of the cause he had served nor his crushing certainty of the fate awaiting him had become apparent to his closest aides, much less to the masses cheering their departure.

The spacer Varne Sogan was another being. If he bore features characteristic of the Arcturian race, as much could be said of countless others, whole planetary populations and many of the mongrels bred in the starlanes, men who might carry the blood of a dozen or more systems in their veins. His clothing was that worn by the latter group, no longer the scarlet uniform with its insignia of rank and courage. The short beard that had once framed his jaw was gone, eradicated so that its shadow might never betray him. Hardship, pain, and this purposeless, furtive existence he was doomed to endure had lain their more subtle brand upon his face and body.

How could one who had known him in that old life name him now? Besides, it was hardly reasonable to imagine that anyone could recover so quickly and completely from such a meeting. Will and art did not work so far.

The dark eyes glittered cold and hard as they looked back into the past. No, that most assuredly was not true. Thorne had taught him something of what the combination of control and wile could accomplish.

The planetary Resistance had been strong even before the Federation had sent in Commandos to aid its fight. After their arrival a frighteningly efficient army had emerged. Its warriors had harried the invaders frequently and hard, sometimes with crippling success. Their losses had been heavy, but nearly all had occurred during the active course of their missions or in their immediate aftermath. They had never given themselves away by any show of sudden fear or furtive air although they must have come into unwanted contact with the Empire's soldiers numerous times during the course of the occupation.

Treason had never played any great part on Thorne. Security had been extremely tight from the start, and the Resistance had dealt swiftly with the few who had attempted betrayal. Prisoners had surrendered some information, but each individual's knowledge was limited, and most had succeeded in slaying themselves before they broke, many by ingenious means. In every case, their captors had been taken utterly by surprise despite their efforts to thwart suicide attempts.

His mouth hardened into a grim line. With such a people, anything was conceivable. If she was one of them and if she had fought in their cause, she could indeed be expected to have such command over herself.

His own course was clear enough. It disgusted him, but he ignored that. He had little love for his life, but the Empire's cruel gods had decreed that he must continue in it. So be it. Live he would and live in freedom. This was a savage universe into which he had been thrown, and he must act savagely now to preserve himself and his liberty in it.

Jake Karmikel parted the green dust drapes. The heavy curtains had done their work well, and already a thick layer of fine gray sand had accumulated behind them although he had occupied the room for less than a week. The spacers using this hotel were of a kind who resented any intrusion into their quarters, even that of cleaning services, so provision had to be made to keep the fine sand from invading the chamber itself while it was occupied. The usual chill wind was blowing, and he wondered absently why the damp of it did not do a better job of keeping the grit down.

The Commando-Captain's attention switched suddenly from his surroundings as the one he had been watching for turned the corner onto the street. He studied her closely, frowning slightly. The indefinable steeling that always came on her at times of crisis in a mission was with her now. He hoped it was no sign that complications had arisen to trouble their current assignment. Everything had gone smoothly thus far, and the unit fully expected to be off-world again within another week.

Jake wanted off-world badly. This was his last Commando assignment. Once the team's reports had been logged and they had undergone the final debriefing, he would be free to pursue at last the lifeway he had always wanted, that of a trader and explorer ranging the wild planets of the rim, perhaps discovering worlds. . . .

Would Islaen Connor be with him? She had promised to give him her answer when they returned to base, and for this reason, too, he was anxious to get back. He had waited for her so long.

It was an ill sign that she had not accepted him at once, but he was not really overly concerned. She had little choice if she were to have what she herself desired.

The stars had gripped the brown-eyed Colonel, too, the stars and the Navy. With him, she could retain her rank and Commando affiliation, work as a troubleshooter and occasionally as a Federation diplomat, a delicate task at which she excelled, while also engaging in full exploration activities. Alone, she could expect no more than sporadic missions such as that on which they were currently engaged, and even those would grow rarer as she inevitably rose in rank. The Commandos were little different from the Regular service in keeping their very senior officers bound to base.

She could not achieve her hopes by demobilizing as he could. He was a trained pilot with several years' experience behind him, well able to bring a ship through the dangers inevitable to rim voyaging. Islaen was not, and men willing to lead the life she desired, to assume the responsibilities it entailed, and to deal with her as she would have were not readily found. He himself had agreed to maintain a tie with the Commandos only as an inducement to draw and hold her.

His blue eyes lowered to the sill as the woman disappeared into the building. Once he would have scorned the thought of accepting a wife who came to him as a matter of convenience, but time had a way of altering a boy's pride, of teaching compromise where total victory was not possible. Islaen cared deeply for him. He knew her well enough to be certain she would make a success of the relationship, whatever her motives for entering it. They had already proven they could live and work well together. All that was more than sufficient to induce him to take less than he might have wished for in a wife, in order to gain her.

TWO

IT TOOK BUT a few minutes for the Commando-Colonel to reach the third floor level, the topmost in the squat building where their quarters were located. She knew Jake would be awaiting her report and went directly to his room, knocking on the door and simultaneously giving signal upon her transceiver.

The red-haired man admitted her without delay. His eyes searched her face. "Something's happened?"

"Perhaps." She found herself reluctant to discuss her glimpse of their old enemy. "It'll require some study before I can answer that." That must suffice for now, Islaen thought. She had no will to bring further misery upon Sogan, not unless he had come to merit it.

Karmikel gave an inward sigh of relief. All appeared to be going smoothly; whatever had touched her interest seemed not to be connected with their mission on Visnu.

The large brown eyes fixed on him. They were as soft as he had ever seen them. "You deserve better from me than I've given you, Jake." The man's heart went dead within him, but he responded lightly. "How so, Colonel?"

"You honored me with the offer of your hand. I should never have held silent so long before saying I can't accept it."

"We're good together, you and I," he said slowly, "and we

9

want the same things. It's not even that you'd lose stature. I'm
well enough aware of your abilities that I'd let you retain command. What can possibly hold you?''

"Comments like that last, for one thing!" The woman got a
grip on herself. It was the difficulty of the interview and not
his words that nettled her. She must hold control now and not
permit this to degenerate into an argument.

"I like you, respect you and your abilities, love you as a
comrade and a friend, but I don't feel toward you as I should,
as I must, toward the man I would take for my husband."

"That might come with the living. We of Noreen aren't
given to sudden rushes of passion."

"We're trained to know ourselves and to accept what is in
us as well." she said, and then sighed. "I can't use you, Jake.
I won't degrade you by taking all you are offering merely to
accomplish my own ends."

Karmikel turned away from her. "Is there any man alive
who can touch your heart, meet the standards it has set?" he
asked after a moment, his voice thick with bitterness.

"Maybe. Maybe not. I only know I grieve because my cold-
ness has brought you pain. It's my own failing and none of
yours, and you shouldn't have had to suffer because of it."

He made no answer to that, and she left him after a few
seconds of awkward silence.

Islaen went slowly to her own room. Both her spirit and her
thoughts were heavy, and she gave the small room but a cursory glance before slipping her jacket from her shoulders and
hanging it on the peg by the door.

If most of her mind was fixed upon her own concerns, she
had not abandoned the care which had kept her alive so long
in her perilous work. The heavy curtains scarcely began to
move before she heard their rustle and then the soft step of a
booted foot.

"Varn Tarl Sogan does not crawl to the assault from out of
the shadows," she said without attempting to face the intruder.

"Turn," a cold, well-remembered voice commanded.
"Move slowly." The woman obeyed. She stood very still with
her hands near to her sides, slightly away from her body.

He held her eyes. They met his quite steadily. "You do

recognize me, then. I was right about that. You are of
Thorne?"

"No, although my likeness to her people was in a great part
responsible for my coming to know you there. It was necessary
that we should all be able to blend well with the populace."

Sogan started visibly at that. "A Commando?" he asked in
amazement; although he realized fully half the personnel serving in the Federation Navy had been female, it was difficult to
believe they had been numbered among the tough guerrilla
fighters.

"Commando-Colonel Islaen Connor. I led the penetration
team on Thorne for the better part of four years."

"And the Resistance with it?"

"Of course."

For the first time, her attention went visibly to the blaster in
his hand. It was set to kill. "Have I firmed your resolve to use
that?"

"You fought well for your cause. I should not have spared
you then, but I bore and bear no hatred against you." The
weapon did not waver. "I have less liking now for murder
than I did upon entering here," he told her gravely. "If you
were to live, what would be your course?"

"None with respect to you, most probably. You're free to
make your life where you will in the Federation."

He laughed coldly. "You seem to forget . . ."

"I forget nothing! Your name's not on any list of those for-
bidden to enter here. It certainly doesn't stand amongst those
monsters who would be incarcerated or executed if they were
found within our borders. As for your own people, I should
hardly be inclined to inform them that they had failed to
butcher you."

"And those comprising the Federation?"

"There are always the bitter, the intolerant," she admitted.
"I wouldn't broadcast your race or the part you played in its
cause, but, beyond that, you have nothing to fear from us as
long as you keep reasonably within our laws." The woman
studied him speculatively. "You wouldn't have been eager to
draw the interest of any authority down on yourself. I think
I'm not far wrong in believing you've been very circumspect
these last few years, Admiral."

"I no longer bear that rank!"

"No. I'm sorry for my stupidity in laying it on you." Her eyes looked into a black distance. "That was one of the greatest triumphs of injustice in all the War and all its aftermath."

Once more, he stared at her. The ice in her tone was that of interstellar space to one suddenly bereft of ship and suit, implacable and all the more terrible for its utter lack of passion. Slowly, the former Arcturian officer lowered his blaster. "I choose to believe what you have said."

Islaen drew a deep breath and released it again. "Praise the Spirit of Space for that. I had no desire to kill you." She moved her right hand slightly to reveal a glimmer of metal at the wrist.

Varn nodded almost imperceptibly, as if to himself. "A knife?"

"Spring sheathed. You saw work done by its like on Thorne."

"All too often." He was silent only a moment. "It appears I was the one under threat, not you."

The fair woman shook her head grimly. "Not so. You would have died, aye, but I should have perished as well. There was little hope I could have avoided your bolt. I was determined to wait until you were actually firing before I struck."

He inclined his head toward her in the manner of a lord of his race before one royally bred. "You have my gratitude, Colonel Connor. You were a worthy foe in war and are even more worthy in yourself." Islaen smiled a little bleakly. "What of you, Sogan? Will my name and rank become known here?"

"No!" The reply came swiftly and emphatically. His dark eyes swept instinctively to the screened window. "Varn Sogan has no comrade on Visnu who would be betrayed by my silence."

He found her gaze fixed intently upon him when he looked to her once more. The man frowned. "Do you doubt me?"

"No." She hesitated, then spoke swiftly. "I don't know what your connection is with these people, but even if you are under contract to them, I'd advise you to sever it as quickly as possible. When those in charge here finally bolt, as they're likely to do very shortly, you could be swept up in the turmoil that will inevitably result. Whether the Patrol comes early or not there will be severe trouble on Visnu. I don't want to see you trapped in it."

"I shall not be. I only flew in a single cargo and have been paid for that. Had nothing happened, I should have left in a couple of days. Now, I shall heed your advice and go as soon as I can ready my ship." A shadow passed over his features. "There can be little rest for me here now that I know another on Visnu is aware of the place I once held."

He gave her formal salute and stepped behind the curtain from which he had emerged and through the open window it concealed.

Islaen Connor slowly walked to her bed and sat upon it. She was shaking, not visibly but within herself. The past had hardly returned, but if it had, more was to be expected of her than this.

She forced herself to review dispassionately the two ultrasystems whose fates had been so tragically intertwined, as if she were scanning the highlights of a history tape. She hoped the cold, hard facts would make Sogan's betrayal and breaking seem necessary, for the man certainly had not merited his fate.

Both ultrasystems had developed simultaneously, ever growing in knowledge and power, expanding from star-system to star-system, colonizing wherever they found planets to sustain them. Their methods of accomplishing that spread were very different, the philosophies guiding them as distant as the space separating their mother planets.

The peoples of the Federation, both the seed of Terra and those they found among the stars, had been cursed so long by the need to battle would-be conquerors and those who played the tyrant that they had developed a deep love of personal freedom and, at long last, the wisdom to see the strength inherent in diversity. Terrans and their offshoots, exoterran humans, mutants, and races rising from entirely separate roots all found places and welcome in the Senate and the system it governed.

Planets joining with them did so voluntarily. Those unwilling to do so were left to themselves. Surplanetary affairs were handled by local rulers, ultrasystem personnel intervening only when off-worlders or interstellar law was involved. This system was not perfect, but those few attempting to move against any planet, Federation member or nonmember, were quickly crushed and severely punished.

The Empire had followed a drastically different course. Its people were warlike to a degree never found even on pre-space Terra. Eventually one group succeeded in dominating the rest. Having subjugated all their homeworld, they might have fallen to the more subtle force of luxury, but fate was kind to them. Science progressed more rapidly among them than had been the case on most Federation planets, and by the time their mother planet had been broken to their will, the challenges of space and the stars were opening before them.

Islaen shook her head, no longer able to completely hold to her assumed detachment. So many facts streamed through her mind, and to turn real thought upon them was to expose an infinity of horror.

The Arcturians were valiant, disciplined, utterly dedicated to their cause, but they carried their old ways with them to the stars—including hatred for intelligence cased in any form not closely resembling their own. Ever victorious, they carved out a vast empire at the heavy expense of those they found before them. They ruled sternly, though, by their own lights, justly. All power lay with the fighters, the mighty hereditary warrior caste, and all others existed only to do them service.

The two ultrasystems had come into contact at last, as was inevitable with such vital cultures ranging and spreading throughout a single galaxy. Their relationship was uncomfortable from the beginning. Such violently opposed philosophies could not but clash, but both strove to avoid open conflict, knowing any war between them would have to be long and awesomely costly.

The leaders' efforts were in vain. Federation people could not watch other populations exterminated or reduced to servitude. Whatever their governments might desire, some groups moved to save threatened neighboring planets. Finally, one such rescue led to the destruction of an Arcturian starship.

That had happened years before her birth, but it began the war which had clouded all her youth, the war which had touched even peaceful Noreen and had turned farmers—and one farmer's daughter—into soldiers.

Both ultrasystems had their militants, those who clamored for conflict, for destruction in the place of seemingly endless and useless talk. That faction was strong in the Empire and held their ruler's heart if not, at first, his will. They used the news of the attack and the destruction of their vessel very effectively, and soon they had gained their aim. The Federation and the Arcturian Empire became belligerents in the direst struggle ever to rend the galaxy which had nurtured them both.

She did not try to suppress the shudder that coursed through her. The millions left dead, the countless billions of lives shattered and disrupted, that was beyond any one person's comprehending, but the dying and the suffering she had witnessed was more than sufficient to permit her to appreciate the nightmare of the whole.

The Colonel compelled herself to continue with her self-imposed review.

While both ultrasystems had been serious in their efforts to avoid war, neither had been so naive as not to prepare to meet it. Each believed itself ready, well able for offense and defense, but the Empire proved far more capable when the time of testing arrived. Arcturian armadas swept through Sector after Sector as if unopposed, seizing those planets it desired either for their strategic value or for the resources they possessed. It was several years before the battered Federation Navy could stem that advance and begin the infinitely slow process of driving the invaders forth.

The woman's great eyes glowed. Stem it, her system's forces had, broken and bleeding though they had been at that dark hour. It was at that point, when the first glimmering hope brushed the embattled Federation fleets, that High Command had devised a plan for intensifying the surplanetary phase of the War.

The great conflict would be settled in space between the mighty armadas, but if invasion troops could be destroyed on the planets they had thought to utilize as bases, or pinned there, if supplies and essential service installations could be wrecked, and if intelligence could be gathered, much help could be given toward inclining the balance in the Federation's favor. To this end, an ancient form of Terran warfare was revived, and the Commandos were born.

The pick of all the Navy, the soldiers accepted for this service were trained to operate in small units either to conduct laser-quick, devastating raids and then flee back into space or to penetrate a fallen planet and there establish themselves to harass the invaders. Their success was phenomenal, for their form of fighting was utterly alien and unsettling to the invaders, and they functioned under such conditions and in such constant peril that they became the most famous and feared unit in either Navy.

The guerrillas usually found on-world help. Federation people and those of sister planets who had remained independent of the ultrasystem were alike both in their love of their homeworlds and in their pride in the lives they were winning for themselves. They were not the stuff of which docile servants were made, and when their planets' official defenses crumbled, they quickly united in underground organizations to continue the battle against their foes.

Many were remarkably successful, and with Commando aid became even more so. Invasion fleets were actually driven from a very few worlds and on a great many were reduced to near impotence, at least with respect to the help they were able to divert to their increasingly more heavily pressed comrades in space.

A grim shadow passed through Islaen's spirit. Some planets had paid a terrible price for that success. Few Arcturians had much respect for the civilians they were finding so inexplicably difficult to dominate, and invasion commanders dealt harshly with restive populations. A handful, despairing of ever gaining complete control over their charges, had burned off rebellious planets. That had not happened often, for it gave the victory, albeit a most dark one, to the Federation. The Empire did not invade worlds for which it had no immediate need, and the cinder left behind after burning was of no more use to them than to the life it had once supported.

The Commando-Colonel's head raised. Not all Arcturian leaders had been of that ilk, and not all fighters against them had been forced into such ultimate sacrifice.

Thorne had been among the more fortunate of the Empire's victims. Though part of the Federation, her pre-space populace had requested noninterference so that their culture would be able to develop naturally, but they had permitted the establishment of a small spaceport. They were humane enough and were willing to bend so far to accommodate emergencies arising in their well-traveled but planet-poor Sector. Thus, they had been aware of the War from its outset and had heard something of the fate of worlds and peoples swallowed by the Empire's forces.

Thornens lived in strongly built towns populated by kinship groups. They neither liked nor trusted anyone outside of their own clans and those with which they intermarried, but they were a race of traders and appreciated the need for cooperation and interaction when circumstances demanded. Intrigue was also as much bred into them as was the need to breathe oxygen, and the War had scarcely begun before they had started organizing themselves against the eventuality of an invasion. They had gone so far as to import weapons to equip themselves to meet interstellar foes. When the Arcturians did come, easily blasting away the spaceport's few heroic defenders, a full-blown, fairly well armed Resistance was ready to oppose them.

So good was that movement and so successful that her unit had been forced to prove itself several times over before being permitted to join forces with it.

Thorne had no cause to regret that union, Islaen thought. They had worked well together, and there had been no negative vote when she had been named commander over the whole war effort scarcely six months after Commandos and Thornens had entered into partnership.

By rights, they should have driven the Arcturians clean off-world. They would have done so had they been pitted against any other officer, but Varn Tarl Sogan was not a man to be forced from his post.

Admiral Sogan was one of the Empire's most brilliant commanders and a war prince of a house connected with the Emperor's own. He was not a man to whom occupation duty would normally have been assigned, but Thorne was important. This was a key Sector, and she was the only planet in this part of it. Control of her, of the base she would provide, was essential for any Arcturian fleet hoping to operate there for any prolonged period of time.

Sogan had been a deadly foe. He was smart, determined, and he did not share the inability of so many of his brother officers to think unconventionally, as a partisan, when the occasion demanded. It was all the Resistance could do to keep his forces too occupied with dealing with them and protecting their precious supplies to take part in the increasingly more bitter struggle in the starlanes. They could not neutralize the invaders.

The woman shook her head. Had the War not turned so decisively against the Arcturians, keeping reinforcements and matériel from reaching him with any regularity, her Thornens might have failed altogether. Sogan was that good.

The war prince had fought with all his people's singleness of purpose and cold calculation, and anyone connected with the Resistance could expect little mercy if taken by his forces. But he never descended to atrocity, nor did he permit any excess to those serving under him. Unlike most of his kind, he did not despise his opponents, considering them to be warriors in fact, whatever their birth. He had soon concluded that brutal measures would serve more to stiffen their resolve than weaken it, a conclusion he welcomed. Butcher work went sharply against both his nature and his sense of honor. Because of this, although the people of Thorne hated him, they respected him as well.

Their hatred changed in the end. The Empire's last, mighty thrust was broken at Cornith, and with its failure, the Arcturian cause was lost. Three months later, the Emperor surrendered.

Defeat shattered the mind of Sogan's commander, though none recognized his madness at the time. He directed his subordinate to move swiftly, before any treacherous order to lay down arms could reach him. Thorne was to be burned off and with it every planet in the Sector which had directly or indirectly given support to the Federation's cause.

The Resistance leaders and their guerrilla comrades, who had full access to the Admiral's headquarters, had been stricken numb with horror.

There could be no thwarting that sentence. Help could never reach them in time, and there was nothing they could do in their own cause. It was the huge, space-moored battleships which would carry out the order, and those they could not touch. They would be able to warn the Federation forces, thereby sparing other worlds from meeting their fate, and they could avenge themselves on some of the Arcturian personnel while they remained on-world, but Thorne and every living thing upon her was doomed.

They had accepted the inevitable when the impossible oc-

curred. Varn Tarl Sogan incinerated the order sheet he had received and closed himself in his quarters, telling his aides of
the capitulation and stating that he was not to be disturbed for
any cause save an imperial communiqué. There he had waited,
alone with his despair, until the official command for a quiet
and honorable surrender was delivered to him.

Islaen's heart still trembled at the enormity of the thing he
had done, that stark violation of Arcturian law and the warrior code he revered. She and all those standing with her in
that cramped spy chamber knew what the decision had cost
him and knew the price he would be forced to pay if any of his
own should ever learn of it. An Arcturian soldier who
disobeyed a superior's order merely died. An officer . . .

Her eyes closed.

Sogan had in due time surrendered his fleet to his Federation counterpart, and the rest, well, that was history, grim,
bloody, and, to her mind, utterly evil.

THREE

COLONEL CONNOR SAID nothing about her meeting with the former Admiral when her comrades assembled some hours later to discuss the progress they had made. There was an air of satisfaction on all four. They settled themselves comfortably in their commander's room, Islaen and the two men claiming the chairs, Babaye Llyne lounging casually on the bed.

The latter's light blonde hair was bound in the tight braids of a female spacer, and a case of navigational charts lay near her hand where she could reach them quickly should anyone enter the room.

The Colonel had deemed it best to divide the unit into two parts during their stay on the planet. She and Jake assumed the roles of planetary biologists who had stumbled upon Visnu while on a study tour of this section of the rim. Babaye and Tomas Dyn took the part of the crew carrying them, living aboard the *Meteor* as was the practice of spacers even on the most luxurious of the inner-system worlds. Although the unit lived and worked as two isolated pairs, they could meet easily for private speech. It wasn't strange for a crew to come to their passengers' more roomy quarters to discuss scheduling and future course.

In actuality, they did touch upon those topics this time.

Their work on Visnu was nearly complete, and all of them were eager to set the time for their departure. Here, there was some disagreement among them. Islaen maintained that they had more than sufficient evidence and wanted to lift immediately, while her companions, particularly Corporal Dyn, always the most cautious and methodical of the four, wanted to wait a few days longer.

Sound arguments supported both positions, too many for the Commando-Colonel merely to wield her rank as a means of deciding the matter. All were deeply involved in discussion when a sharp knock fixed their attention on the door.

None had been in line with either it or the window. They moved still farther back as their leader signaled Tomas to admit their visitor.

Islaen Connor felt herself tensing. Even before she saw the heavily cloaked figure, she guessed who the intruder was.

Varn allowed the cowl to slip back from his face as the door closed behind him.

"Sogan!"

He did not know from which of the two men that hissed whisper had come. The expressions of all three strangers were ludicrous with surprise, or would have been had their grip on their weapons been less sure and determined.

The auburn-haired woman gave her comrades an amused glance. "You might as well hear what he has to say before you burn him."

The Arcturian's eyes swept the walls in a significant manner before fixing on her. He said nothing.

She smiled in appreciation. "Speak freely. We made sure there would be no eavesdropping before beginning our own discussion. Why have you come to us?"

"To bring you warning. Your mission is known or at least partially guessed, although you are believed to be Patrol agents, not Navy personnel." His head raised a trifle. "It was not through me that they learned."

"No, that would not be your way. You wouldn't have any reason to come here if it were the case. The others'd take care of us without need of your making contact with us again."

"They will act, Colonel, and soon."

"What do the developers intend?" Jake demanded.

"A tramp spacer, and one not even in their service, would hardly be admitted to their councils. I cannot even say whether they share their employees' knowledge, although doubtless they do. The news is all over the spaceport.''

''Their wisest course would be to pretend ignorance and just allow the spacers to take care of the matter,'' Babaye Llyne said slowly. ''There are those here well able for that work.''

The Arcturian nodded. ''So do I reason. Some of this rabble can poorly afford to come under serious Patrol scrutiny. They have been talking and want you eliminated quickly. There is no contact to speak of between life in the port and that of the colonists, and so the disappearance of a small, unconnected party such as this one could be easily arranged with no one's ever becoming the wiser.''

Jake's blue eyes narrowed. ''All that's true enough, and we're grateful for the warning, but why should you risk yourself by giving it?''

''Perhaps I do not want the garbage out there accomplishing what all my command could not. Perhaps I feel more akin to you than to those others. My motives are quite irrelevant. What is important is that you depart from Visnu at once.''

''I'm rather curious to know how we gave ourselves away if not through you.''

''One of the crewmen aboard that freighter which planeted yesterday morning recognized you, Commando. He said he had seen you on Beta Gary a couple of years ago.''

Jake's lips pursed. ''Aye, that's more than possible. We pulled a raid on some black marketeers there who had made a grab for a shipment of Navy weapons. It was a quick sweep, and I was the only one to actually planet.'' His eyes clouded. ''I seem to have betrayed us all.''

''Not entirely. Only you and Colonel Connor are actually suspect, she because no true biologist could be unaware that you are but playing a role after all this time. The others are seen as no more than common spacers, props for your mask, although they are to be terminated as well as a precaution.''

''Don't forget yourself. You're likely to be judged guilty by association for coming to us, whatever reason you give for it.''

''I was not seen.''

The other man raised a brow. ''You've kept your self-confidence, Admiral.''

Sogan did not bridle at the use of his former title this time. ''I have learned to move unobtrusively since we last encountered one another.'' He turned to Islaen. ''Is this not so, Colonel?''

She laughed softly. ''It is. At least, no one appears to have detected your previous visit to me.''

Karmikel's head snapped up. ''What . . .''

For the first time, the trace of a grin softened the line of Varn's lips. ''I came here this morning to kill her. Obviously, I altered my plans before fulfilling them.''

''Whatever about that,'' Islaen broke in hastily, ''we all owe you our thanks. May the Spirit of Space go with you.''

''Fortune be with you as well. I fear if she is not, you will never lift from Visnu, forewarned or not.''

Karmikel checked the hall outside, then carefully resealed the door again before turning to his commander.

He did not attempt to conceal or rein his fury. ''Why didn't you tell us he'd been here?''

''Because it had no relevance to our mission,'' she replied calmly.

''No relevance!''

''I did say there was something which would require study, but I realized that would be unnecessary once I had spoken with Sogan.''

''His coming to kill you was a great testament to his character,'' Jake told her sarcastically.

''I failed to completely screen my recognition of him, and he panicked.'' She shrugged. ''It was easy to talk him out of it. There's no evil in him.''

Fire suddenly flashed in her dark eyes. ''Why do you challenge me? Have I ever misread any being, ever failed to name a traitor or clear an innocent man, ever failed to know our enemies in war or in our more recent work?''

''Easy, Islaen,'' Babaye drawled. ''We'll all die fast enough if we start taking things too much for granted. What about his part in what's happening here?''

''There's no heavy guilt on him. He claims he's not so much as contracted to the developers, and I tend to believe him. He most assuredly has no part in any of their plottings. I should have detected some hint of that either the first time or, even more strongly, now.''

''You didn't pick up any of the hostility this morning?'' Dyn asked.

The Colonel shook her head. "I was uneasy and felt the need to keep my blaster within quick reach of my hand, but that's all." She flushed slightly, feeling her failure. "I was preoccupied and so might have missed much, but I believe there was little to detect at that point. News such as this spreads fast, and faster still the decision to do something about it. I am certain Varn Tarl Sogan knew nothing of it when I spoke with him earlier."

"I don't know," he replied doubtfully. "That ship he mentioned has been on Visnu since yesterday morning."

"A fact that makes me think the developers do know and have permitted the news to leak into the ranks so that events might be started on their rather predictable course."

"It wouldn't be easy to prove that."

"Do you imagine we're dealing with fools?—It could also be that the spacer didn't see Jake or fully place him until a few hours ago. Memory can tease before fulfilling its purpose."

"My credits go with your first suggestion," Babaye told her. "Whatever he says, Admiral Sogan did risk himself in coming to us. It would be a pity if we failed to capitalize on his warning."

"We'll do what we can to profit by it," the commander promised grimly. "The outcome lies with fortune.

"You and Tomas, return to the *Meteor*. Look a bit disgruntled, as if we vetoed your will. You are not suspected, or were not, and should be allowed to pass untroubled, but if that has changed any you might be allowed to get farther if we seem not to be too friendly.

"Wait one hour, then lift whether we be there or not. Get off-world at once if you detect any trouble in the port or if any preparations seem under way to board you. Make report to Horus on our beam as soon as you have won free, then head for home. Jake and I will go to ground and wait for the Navy."

FOUR

BABAYE AND DYN left the hotel. Commando training, the need to ever place mission before their own and their comrades' lives, had held firm. They had not protested against their orders although both realized the two officers' chances would be slim if they were forced to remain behind on Visnu.

They walked briskly along the street, noting the clumps of men gathered there. They had the look of idlers, but there were too many of them for that, and their eyes followed the Commandos just a little too intently.

The Corporal scowled as they passed uncomfortably close to one such group. "We should lift and let them have all the time in the universe for their exploring."

"Ah, they pay well. A couple of more days on this hole won't really matter . . ."

It seemed an eternity before they finally gained the *Meteor* and set her screens in place.

The pair went swiftly but carefully through their security check and then hastened to prepare the vessel for space and the rigors of a sudden lift. That done, they sat for a time ordering their notes and ever more intently watching their monitor screens. If nothing went amiss, their comrades should be joining them within the next quarter hour.

"It's hard to believe, isn't it," Tomas asked abruptly,

breaking the almost total silence that had fallen between them, "Varn Tarl Sogan's rising from the dead like that?"

"I thought the past had come again for a moment there," his companion agreed.

"It's odd that Islaen kept the matter so close."

"Not really. She said his presence here is incidental to our mission, and she can hardly be blamed for not wanting to expose him."

She turned on him almost savagely. "Nor do I wish to expose him!"

"Peace, Babaye. Sogan remained human throughout the War and paid heavily for it. Do you imagine I want to see him suffer again for the same cause?" Whatever answer she might have made him was silenced by a series of flashes which suddenly flickered on the right monitor.

Blasters!

A blinding glare filled the screen. They were forced to jerk their faces aside.

"What in space . . ."

"Never mind! Let's get the blazes out of here!" Even as she spoke, the woman was throwing herself into the pilot's chair.

As soon as her companion had followed suit, her fingers streaked across a series of buttons on the control board, first activating the *Meteor's* space seals and then giving her the command to lift. A moment later, the pressures generated by the fast-rising starship clamped down upon them.

Islaen was just settling her combat pack on her shoulders when the Captain returned with his own. She glanced at him. "Ready?"

He nodded. "Lucky we've made a habit of traveling beyond the port. They'll think that's what we're about now. Maybe."

"Fake biologists have to act like real ones, you know." The woman gave him a wry smile. "At least our ruse didn't fall apart because we failed to play our part accurately."

They waited a few minutes longer to give their companions time to secure the *Meteor*, then left their quarters.

Islaen felt the change in the atmosphere as soon as they stepped out onto the street. There was no missing the fact of their danger now.

So much emotion! She first marveled that her companion received no trace of it and then envied him because he could not; this was darkness only, and no being should have to endure the uncleanness of it.

The Commando leader realized she had been wise in choosing to make her move at once rather than waiting for night to give them cover. They would not have been granted very much more time in which to act. Their enemies, too, had been waiting for the others to leave and get well away, knowing it would be easier to overpower two than four.

When would they strike? That was all important now. While she and Jake remained on what passed for the streets of this part of the port complex, they were ready victims. The low buildings both confined their movements and provided shelter for snipers, while their stark, flat facades offered little cover to the fugitives. The street, too, was empty of parked vehicles, bare of anything which might serve them as a shield.

Their chances would improve if they could make either the planeting field or, failing that, the rough area beyond. They would have a reasonable hope of fighting in either place and of concealing themselves if they could not reach the ship, especially as the evening advanced and darkness came to cover them.

Her heart was pounding against her ribs in a heavy, slow rhythm painful to endure, but she kept her expression casual as she seemed to engage her companion in light speech. If they appeared to be at ease, unsuspicious of their peril, they just might be permitted to go on. That would seem to be to the attackers' advantage; their demise could be concealed so easily out in the wilderness or, if necessary, so easily explained. . . .

No, the restlessness and anger were both growing stronger. She had lost this part of the gamble.

Even then, neither face nor body altered. She forced her lips to retain their smile as she whispered the warning to prepare for battle. If they were to have nothing else, she was determined that they should at least retain the power of surprise when the time came to strike.

Her blaster was in her hand, discharging in short, rapid bursts. A gasping scream answered its first flash, but she concentrated on those still in the field against her and did not hear it reach its aborted climax.

Jake was shooting as well, each of his bolts counting even as did his commander's. His body twisted like a snake's with his efforts to make himself an elusive target.

The speed and accuracy of the Commandos' defense broke the initial force of the assault, but their respite was short-lived, scarcely a couple of breaths' space. Their opponents were tough, the veterans of many a spaceport fight and some of more than a single murder. They knew that both numbers and terrain were with them, and they were not ignorant of the dangers inevitable to attacking Patrol agents, as they believed these two to be, and then permitting them to escape. They drew back, out of that portion of the street where their intended victims were still confined and began to pour in bolt after bolt against them.

The pair separated—the force of the fire coming at them compelled that—and endeavored to sell their lives as dearly as possible since it was obvious they could not be preserved much longer.

Islaen snapped off another shot. They were fortunate none of the spacers had taken to the upper windows and roofs. They would both have been felled already had that been the case. Their enemies must have realized it as well, but access to the warehouses was not easily gained.

All that was but a token nod by fate, irrelevant save that it would allow them to take a few more of their opponents with them. The attack could not have occurred at a worse location, and its outcome would not be postponed much longer.

A cry of mingled grief and anger broke from her as she saw Karmikel crumple. He rolled toward the wall opposite her but did not move when he struck against it.

Jake . . .

Islaen had blocked her receptors at the fight's start, knowing that raw hate and lust for death pouring in from their opponents could interfere with her reactions in the battle. She was spared the experiencing of her comrade's death, but the sense of irreparable loss burning inside her would have been no sharper had she felt his fine mind vanish from the existence they knew.

Her bolt raced back along the path of that which had felled her comrade, and she saw it find its target with fatal effect. The woman felt no satisfaction. Soon, her body would be lying beside his.

Screams. Her head jerked toward the place from which they had come. No blaster strike elicited that kind of agony!

A wall, no, a cone of flame was boiling down the street,

white fire of such intensity that it incinerated anything coming
too close to its fury. Her eyes could not bear the sight of it for
more than the fraction of a second necessary to feed that much
information into her mind.

Islaen cast herself back, throwing herself against the building nearest her. That searing doom did not fill all the space
between the structures flanking it. A pathetically narrow lane
remained free on either side. Perhaps she could survive the
heat of its passing, escape with relatively light injury.

She gave no thought to her enemies. A blaster brought an
easy death. This . . .

There was nothing to fear from the renegade spacers. Like
the Commando-Colonel, they were either cowering against the
unyielding stone or had fled up one of the cross streets, those
near enough to escape that way. A couple, finding themselves
in a doorway, tried to force their way inside, but the time left
to them was too short; they would not have been able to
manipulate the latch even had it been unsealed.

The heat was already intense. The fireball was being pro-
pelled by some sort of vehicle—that much was apparent now-
—but she could not see through the glare to discover its nature
or the source of the flame itself.

She cringed. Another second, and it would be upon her!

The fire vanished, quenched even as it reached the place
where she was. A flier braked to a stop. Its grim-faced driver
kicked the door open.

"Hurry!"

"Varn!"

She dove for the machine. Scarcely had she leaped into it
than it shot forward again, once more preceded by its blazing
shield.

The Arcturian thrust something into her hands. Dark goggles. There were two pairs, their straps slightly tangled. She
quickly freed one and pulled it into place over her face. She
sighed with relief. The heat was still nigh-unto unbearable, but
at least she could see clearly and without pain.

Sogan, his own eyes screened, gestured toward the blaster
she still grasped. "Get ready to use that. They will be at us as
soon as we pass the cross street."

So it proved, but the guerrilla officer fought as effectively
from the racing vehicle as she did on foot, and those daring
enough to strike at them were compelled to stay back out of

prime range for the few moments needed to bring them past that first danger point.

There would be others, and soon they would have to face more than antipersonnel weapons. Only the shock and terror of Sogan's sudden attack and the speed of it had saved them from that even this long.

The former Admiral was no less aware of their peril than was his passenger. He made a sharp right onto the next street, which led to the actual planeting field, demanding more and still more speed from the racing engine.

The spaceport was before them.

Too late! The ship he sought was lifting!

Varn glanced once at the woman. There was no time to try for his own vessel. He jerked at the controls. They must get away from the field, from the port altogether, before their deadly screen vanished. The fuel must be almost totally exhausted. . . .

The cone of fire held for another three minutes, then it flickered, sputtered a thin shower of sparks and clots of fire, and was gone. He raised his goggles and looked bleakly at the place where it had been. They must depend on speed now, and their opponent in this dire race was Death.

FIVE

THE TWO FUGITIVES did not despair. They had come far before losing their chief weapon, and they had left such chaos in their wake that they were safe for a while. Those of their enemies still capable of taking action were forced to control the conflagration they had begun or risk seeing the spaceport, and with it their starships, utterly annihilated.

The first of the settlers had come to Visnu only two years previously, and it was not necessary to travel far from the center of the port complex before all sign of human intervention vanished.

The Arcturian kept their speed high, near the vehicle's maximum rate. Once the situation in the town became less critical, parties would be sent out in search of them. They would have to go far and conceal their trail well before they could count themselves secure.

He dropped altitude until they were skimming only a few feet above the ground instead of high over Visnu's forest. A single, small, rapidly moving vehicle would not be readily spotted through the thick canopy of the trees. That cover was well worth the intense concentration required to keep them from slamming into one of the trunks.

Hour after hour passed. The flier broke into the open, the

narrow strip that marked the edge of the great, high plateau in whose center the Amonite settlement was located. Varn forced more speed from the laboring engine, sent the machine diving down, down toward the promised cover far below.

They sped over a series of rough, relatively barren rises, then pierced the treetops and leveled off again as they neared the ground. The man allowed their speed to drop back to its former rate. He realized his work was going to be harder. The trees were more closely set here. Their foliage was lusher, enough to reduce the amount of light reaching them. It was not going to be an easy task to avoid them all. It would not have been had he been entirely fresh, and already he was bone weary.

Sogan's jaw tightened. There was no help for it. He had chosen to involve himself in this, and it was now his task to carry the work through.

He glanced at the forest around them. It was vast and somber, comprised of massive, gnarled trees, each surrounded by a circle of roots arching up from the ground like the legs of titanic spiders, joining with their parent trunk ten to sixty feet in the air. Had those trees been set any closer, it would have spelled disaster for the fugitives but fortune was with them. The fit was tight, but the flier was just slender enough to pass between the huge trunks.

His face and body were drawn and rigid with tension. They had room. He kept telling himself that, reassuring himself, but he knew too well that any relaxing of care on his part, any error in judgment, would erase that advantage. Their course was of necessity erratic in the extreme, and at this speed, any mistake at all would send them slamming into one of the trees. The result of that would be almost certain death for both of them.

It should not come to that. He was skilled with machines, and this one should not fail him despite the fact that it had not been designed for such work.

The flier was a personnel carrier, long and narrow in shape with a blunt nose and conservative wings flanking the drive exhaust in the rear. The four wheels were large but were so set into the undercarriage that scarcely a quarter of their surface was exposed to view or to the drag of the air.

As was to be expected in a first-ship colony, it was no luxury craft. The front seat was narrow, a close enough fit for them and an extremely tight one for a couple of big men. The seat behind it was smaller still. The rear section formed a cargo area sufficiently large to hold gear and supplies for several days' absence from the settlement, enough time to map out and establish a new farm site.

The flier was outfitted for work on the cool plateau, not for this swamp, and it had neither a self-atmosphere nor even so much as basic climate conditioning. Sogan cursed that last lacking more and more bitterly as time wore on, but he knew the region itself was more responsible for his discomfort than any mere failing of his equipment.

This place gnawed at his morale. The damp which had characterized the port was here as a deadening humidity that brought the sweat out on his body until his clothes were dark with it. There was no wind, no movement of air at all. So thick were the trees and so closely set that they would have entirely baffled the efforts of the most violent gale. Everything was hot and still, permeated by the heavy, rich smell of luxuriant plant growth.

"They showed sense in setting the port on the plateau."

"Aye," his companion answered almost absently. She, too, had been studying their surroundings and liked them no more than Sogan.

"This has the look of a swamp," she remarked abruptly. "Even now, the soil is muck in some spots. We'd have been in trouble long since if this were a surface vehicle. In a wetter year or at a different season, these ways could be entirely impassable to anything on the ground." Her brows drew together. "I wonder what that might mean for the colonists?"

He shrugged. "Nothing. Why should it mean anything? They are not down in this hole."

"I read what little is known about Visnu. Most of the land is low like this. Changes here could well affect what higher ground there is. Swamps are notorious for breeding things, microlife and larger species—usually detrimental to human welfare, to put it mildly. There have been no studies to indicate what might come crawling out of here if conditions altered a bit."

The other looked swiftly upon her. "So much concern for the vermin back there?"

Her head snapped up. "The bulk of Visnu's populace consists of victims, not killers," she replied coldly. "Then, too, there is always the very slim but ever-present possibility of some new plague arising on an unstudied world and spreading to systems far beyond its birthplace."

"I stand corrected, Colonel."

Both fell silent after that, and nearly half an hour passed before either of them spoke again. Islaen was annoyed with herself for having allowed her anger to take her tongue. She owed this man much, and she needed him. It behooved her to be politic in her behavior toward him, not arrogantly self-righteous.

Besides, how much was he to be blamed? The training given an Arcturian war prince was not likely to instill much consideration for a small band of squatter tree farmers. He had probably not even thought of them at all when he had spoken. She, herself a product of an agrarian society, instinctively gave them her sympathy and had overreacted to his comment under the lash of her concern for their safety.

She glanced at her companion's set profile. "I haven't thanked you for pulling me out of there."

For a moment, the stiffness remained, then he sighed, and his head lowered a trifle. "Thank me later. I may have only brought you to a slower and considerably more agonizing death." He wiped his right hand against his knee to take some of the sweat off it. "It is growing dark, and we should have come far enough, but I dislike stopping here. . . . There must be some end to this accursed forest!"

They could not go on much longer without lights, and those would betray them to any searchers coming out this far.

"Try going northwest," she suggested. "When we were planeting, we spotted what looked to be a ridge system extending out from the settlement plateau in that direction."

Sogan gave her a quick look of admiration. "I see why you Commandos succeeded as you did. Very well, Colonel, let it be as you suggest. We have no other goal before us."

SIX

VERY LITTLE LIGHT remained by the time Varn at last noted a rise in the terrain. Once their ascent began the character of the land changed rapidly. Before they had climbed four hundred feet the swamp-born forest had given way to one of more conventional type—tall, straight trees, none spectacular in girth, most of them crowned with leaves of the gold-green color which marked the greater part of Visnu's vegetation.

They had ascended to about a thousand feet when the guerrilla officer called a halt. The trees were widely spaced with heavy thickets of lesser growth between them. They could no longer see well enough to maneuver without lights, and to activate those would be to broadcast their location through the ragged canopy.

Both remained within the vehicle for several minutes, carefully surveying their surroundings for potential threat. At last, Islaen opened the door. She shivered as the wind, heavy with the evening's chill, bit at her.

"It's a luxury to feel cold again."

"Aye, though we shall probably not consider it so for long. You think we are secure here?"

The woman nodded. "No one followed us. Even were I wrong about that, it'd be exceedingly difficult to spot us down

37

here unless we get careless." She glanced about the vehicle.
"Do you have any supplies with you?"

"Some. I bought a store of food as a cover for having the
flier with me."

"Perishables?"

He nodded. "Aye. It is what a spacer would be expected to
choose when on-world, is it not?"

"It is. We'll use those first, then."

"You?"

She smiled and touched the pack she had just swung to the
ground. A Commando's combat gear was frequently his life,
particularly on sparsely populated worlds. Guerrilla fighters
were trained until teaching became instinct to keep hold of it,
whatever chaos surrounded them.

"Common rations, I'm afraid. Nothing very tasty."

"How is it that you could have so much with you? Was this
not an undercover mission?"

"Why not? A biologist doing field work would be expected
to rough it on occasion." Her eyes sparkled. "She probably
wouldn't have some of the things that are in here, but I just
didn't bother calling any attention to those."

"Doubtless that was wise," he remarked dryly. The Arcturian reached into the back of the flier. He rummaged through
his supplies and brought out two packets without looking at
them. He handed them to his companion. "You have a pluto-
nium disk, I presume?"

"Of course."

"Excellent. At the least, we shall not be forced to devour
these cold."

Islaen gave a mock shudder. "Please! That would be terrible for morale." She glanced at the labels. "I'll take this
one." Without thinking, she added, "You can't abide sea-
food."

Varn stared at her. "How did you know that?"

She laughed. "Sure, I just about lived with you for four
years."

"What do you mean?"

"Our headquarters adjoined. Passages connected them,
complete with watchposts so good that they required no
Federation improvements at all. We kept them monitored continuously, so we naturally came to know you and your staff
quite well."

The former officer's face tightened. He strode away from her.

She followed after him, cursing her insensitivity. "Admiral . . ."

"I feel so stupid," he whispered. "So many of my men died on Thorne, and it was my own words, my own criminal carelessness that slew them."

"No! I'm the stupid one for boasting as I did."

He struggled mightily with himself to chain the emotion ripping him. At last, he sighed. "You were not boasting, Colonel. You were but speaking. Your pride is not such that you would use anyone so, or I read you very badly."

The woman, too, struggled to master herself. He did not need a display of what she was feeling now. "Varn, don't judge yourself. It wasn't your fault. The Empire never studied the denizens of the worlds it invaded. How were you to know that intrigue was as natural to the people of Thorne as currying an angora steer was to me? Their hidden ways were truly cunning and at the same time, of too primitive a nature to be detected by your sensors. We took care to use very little advanced equipment ourselves."

The great eyes caught his. "You were successful against us, too, despite all our knowledge. Resistance movements on other planets, Commando-led or purely local, utterly defeated their worlds' invaders or fought them into ineffectual little pockets in far less time than we were active on Thorne. It was the War's end that brought about your capitulation, not any direct effort of ours."

"You saw to it that my command was able to do very little to influence that outcome," he reminded her.

"All the same, you remained a deadly threat to the Resistance and to the Federation Navy in that Sector right until the end. No one could appreciate that more than I, who had the responsibility both of containing your forces and bearing the brunt of any outbreak you might make."

"You are a generous enemy, Colonel Connor," he said after a moment, "more generous than we, than I, would have been had I faced you like this from the place of the victor. . . . I do ask that you leave me for a while. You have opened things to my knowing which both my mind and my heart must meet, or I shall ever be a coward in myself."

Her head lowered in acquiescence. "As you will," she murmured as she withdrew from his presence.

Islaen Connor sat on a tall stone set conveniently close to the front of the flier. The machine was still equipped with its strange weapon, and her eyes were fixed on it, sometimes seeing it, sometimes looking beyond its physical presence.

It was a simple enough device, merely a large canister of the fuel used in many of the smaller service-type ships strapped to the nose with metal cable. Its rigid hose had been extended so that it projected well beyond the vehicle itself, and the firing cord had been drawn back to the driver's side and manipulated by hand.

Her eyes were focused on it now. Simple it might be, but it was ingenious as well, worthy of any Commando's invention. Any Commando daring enough to put his thought into practice, she amended mentally. It required no small amount of nerve to release all that violent heat so close to the fuel supply of the vehicle in which one was riding.

There had been peril even in assembling the thing. Such canisters and hosing were normally handled strictly by automatics. The stuff was not terribly volatile in itself, but it was horribly corrosive and would rapidly have eaten its way through the heaviest gloves—and then through the flesh and bone beneath them, had the smallest spill or leak occurred.

A chill touched her as the screams of those the flames had felled rose up in her memory. It did not help to acknowledge that this terrible weapon had saved her.

It was terrible, aye, in the manner of the death it brought, but not costly in terms of human life. Stark fear and the utter, unopposable power of it had kept potential assailants back, away from them, during most of their flight through the port. She and Jake had actually slain more during their own brief battle. . . .

Her eyes closed, and she looked hurriedly away. That loss would not be dismissed quickly.

"I am sorry about your comrade." Varn's voice was soft and gentle. She looked up, a smile of gratitude instinctively lighting her tired features.

"Thank you."

"I would have brought him out had he lived."

"I know," the woman responded gravely. "You had two extra goggles with you."

There was a tremor in her voice, and his fingers brushed her arm. "This one, he was more than a subordinate to you?"

Islaen nodded. She struggled to choose words which would not betray the depth of her pain, that or allow it an opening to sweep her. "A friend. A very close friend. We entered Basic from the same planet. It was his encouragement and more often his taunting that got me through parts of the training, Regular and Commando. How many times since he gave me my life, I couldn't begin to number."

Her voice wavered. "This was to be Jake's last mission as a Commando. Neither of us realized how true that would prove." Her face twisted before she could master herself completely. "I suppose we shouldn't permit ourselves close friendships in our work."

"You would be something less than men if you did not. Or women," he responded gravely. "We of the Empire pride ourselves on our hardness, and we are no cowards in battle, but we have never isolated ourselves from our comrades."

"That would be cowardice in itself, I suppose. Jake . . . Jake wouldn't have wanted to see me yield to such fear."

Sogan smiled. "No one could ever lay the lack of courage against you, Colonel Connor."

The woman drew a deep breath to completely steady herself and compelled her tone to grow lighter. "Islaen. Commandos have a dislike for formality over extended periods, and fate has decreed that we're to be comrades for a while."

His dark eyes remained somber. "I have a given name as well, although you seem but little inclined to use it. I have heard it on your lips only twice, once in your danger and once in my pain."

The Federation officer flushed. "I should apologize even for that. You're not a man with whom people may take liberty."

"More knowledge from the past?"

She frowned. "A little, perhaps, but chiefly instinct. There's something about you which forces one to keep his distance."

She sighed to herself. That invisible barrier had deepened a thousandfold since she had fought against him on Thorne, and she shuddered in her heart at the thought of all which had worked to bring its thickening about. Neither humankind nor fate itself had been good to this man.

SEVEN

BRAHMIN, VISNU'S SUN-STAR, was well above the horizon when Islaen Connor woke the following morning. She saw that her companion was already up and gave him a cheerful greeting.

The Arcturian returned it and came over to the flier on whose front seat she had spent the night. "You slept soundly, Commando. I should have thought you would have been a bit less trusting of me. After all, some would say I had reason to bear a powerful grudge against you."

"You'd not slay in the night. Such work would be repugnant to you even if grim need demanded it."

Varn made her no answer. His look was strange, and she cocked her head to one side. "What's wrong?"

"You are so certain of yourself. Have you never misread a man?"

"No. I have a gift there. It showed during Basic, and the life I've led since has honed it sharp."

His expression hardened, and he seemed to move away from her without actually doing so.

Her chin lifted as a flush of anger rose to color her cheeks. "I'm a mutant and, thus, one to be despised? Perhaps, Admiral, but the Resistance on Thorne had cause in plenty to bless me and my power. Several wretches your kind had corrupted through fear or greed came to well-earned ends because of it.''

The next instant was one of battle for Varn Tarl Sogan although no altering of face or stance betrayed that turmoil. ''I meant no discourtesy,'' he finally said. ''Old custom is difficult to break.''

''Aye, injustice does keep a tight rein,'' she replied sourly. ''What is our next move?''

The Commando checked her ill humor. After all, she herself had been so uncomfortable with her new-found ability that she had never mentioned it to her superiors. Why should she expect more from him?

''Make a permanent camp. We might as well settle in properly while waiting to get picked up.''

''How long will that take?''

''Two weeks if the *Meteor* got through. Three if she didn't.''

''The Navy will come even without summons?'' he asked in surprise.

''That was arranged before our voyage to Visnu. We were given a certain span of time in which to work. If nothing negating the need for action reached headquarters by the end of it, the landings would commence.

''You see, investigations of developers' activities have come to a sudden halt before when supposed squatter colonies have vanished. There might be the danger of that happening here —or there might be none—but the chance could hardly be taken with so many lives at stake. At the same time, the mobilization of such a raid is costly, disruptive to any innocent community on which it descends, and it strips too much power from the defense of the rest of the Sector. That's why Navy help was asked and my team was sent in to gather intelligence. Commandos know how to gain information, and our reports carry considerable weight.''

''Would not the lack of report be taken to mean you were lost?''

She shook her head. ''Only that we were prevented from giving it. Our skill at surviving in unpromising situations is acknowledged. It'd be assumed that at least part of the unit would make it.''

She studied him somberly. ''Provision has been made to

take us off whether the *Meteor* returns or not, if that's what you're asking."

"It is," Varn admitted, then he scowled. "You well know it, of course."

"No. How could I?"

"You have just said you can read thought." Islaen frowned. "Not thought. Feeling. Instinct. Emotion. And only when powerfully emitted. It's hard to explain, but be assured that the workings of your mind do remain your own."

The Arcturian concealed his relief. "How will we know when your people come if we stay buried out here?"

She raised her left arm to reveal the tiny instrument strapped to the wrist. "A signal on my communicator. I'll then broadcast another telling them to wait for us."

"Most efficient," he told her. "I hope the call comes soon. I disliked Visnu's spaceport, and I care even less for her wilderness."

The woman laughed. "We're one in that! It should be better higher up, at least psychologically. Check out the flier while I make sure we don't leave any signposts behind us."

The Commando was not long at her task when she heard her companion snarl an oath in his own language. She hurried to the vehicle. Sogan was sitting at the controls, glowering darkly.

"What's wrong?" she demanded.

"We appear to have a malfunction. It will not start."

"Is there any fuel?"

He glared at her. "Am I a fool! Look at the gauge. You may know something about functioning in the more forsaken reaches of the universe, but the handling of machinery is obviously not one of your strengths."

Arrogant bastard! Islaen Connor barely managed to control her anger. Adding a mental expletive in her own language, she shrugged and walked away.

When she turned and saw the Arcturian beginning to unfasten the cord binding the empty flame thrower to the flier, her annoyance vanished. Was he working too fast in his anger? The seal on one of the extension links of the hose could easily have ruptured during the shaking the crude system had been subjected to yesterday.

She returned to him. "Let me help, Varn. I do know enough to be able to take your orders."

He looked up. "No need. This should be a quick job."

"You still might need a hand. Something could be fractured."

The man turned from his machine again, this time in surprise. There had been concern in her voice. Did she fear for him?

He smiled. "Do not worry, Islaen. I have no wish to see my hands burned through. There are no leaks. You may well believe that I looked for them before starting."

The woman nodded. She gave an inward sigh of relief. She should have realized Varn Tarl Sogan would not have been so careless as to take on a hazardous task without showing caution. His survival in a new and hostile environment was proof enough that he knew how to take care of himself.

It was some time before Sogan came in search of Islaen. He found her well downslope of the place where they had spent the night.

"You might as well relax, Colonel. The guidance system is shorted. A combination of too much heat and too much speed, I suppose. We were incredibly fortunate that it kept functioning as long as it did."

"You can't fix it?"

He shook his head. "It is a major job. I could do it if I had the equipment and parts, but not with the little I have on hand now."

She sighed. "A pity. We'll miss it."

He frowned. "What do you mean?"

"We can't stay here."

"Travel on foot will be very unpleasant," he cautioned, "not to mention that it could be highly dangerous as well."

"So could remaining in this place. Look down there." The Commando-Colonel pointed to a heavy tangle of growth which had sprouted up in the semishade of a half dozen widely spaced trees.

Sogan's eyes narrowed as he studied it more closely. It required no woodsman's training to recognize that the entire thicket had suffered recent severe trauma. A great, wide swath was completely devoid of vegetation, and much of the greenery on either side of that had been broken down, or sheared off, and partially stripped of its foliage. Both the dark soil and the wilting vegetation glinted with an odd, silvery sheen in the bright morning light.

"Some local creature?"

She nodded. "I fear so. Slugs and sluglike animals are fairly common to the universe. Mostly, they're quite small, but Amazoon boasts a few species that grow to forty feet or more."

"This thing seems to be a vegetarian," he ventured.

"Maybe. Maybe not. Nearly all the really big kinds are omnivorous."

"Why did it fail to come after us if we were of potential interest to it?"

"That I don't know. Perhaps the scent of the flier threw it off. Machines are still unknown out here. Then, too, the slope's a bit too dry. Slugs prefer moisture."

"Very well, Colonel. I agree that we must move. Which way do we go?"

"Back toward the port, I suppose. The nearer we are, the easier it'll be to connect with the Navy now that we're without transport of our own. I know of a good cave on the plateau where we can hole up in near comfort. We'll just have to be more careful than would've been necessary out here about attracting unwelcome attention."

She frowned then. "The trouble is, there'll be no avoiding the swamp. The rises between here and the plateau are separate entities. We'll have to descend each and leave it completely to seek the foot of the next. That'll mean a lot of very rough trekking, or I badly misjudge Visnu's lowlands."

Islaen's gloomy prediction proved all too accurate, and the hours which followed were a waking nightmare for Varn Tarl Sogan. The forest of spider-trees, as he named them in his mind, was indeed a swamp, and the soil from which the great trunks and their attendant roots arose ranged in consistency from unpleasantly slippery to nearly liquid slush.

The latter portions, in truth nearly all of the miserable road, would have been impassable to him had it not been for his companion. She was able to look at the seemingly featureless quagmire around them and find in it patches of more solid stuff. Thus they went on, covering the wettest areas step by slow step until they once more reached firmer ground.

By watching her closely and taking great care to put his feet exactly in the place she just vacated, he managed to follow her, a progress aided by a spacer's lightness of movement and natural balance. Gradually, Varn began to discern for himself some of those safe spots which had at first been utterly invisible to him, but that increasing awareness of his surroundings filled him with no false sense of security. He knew all too well that if some cruel slash of fate should separate him from his companion, he would be hopelessly lost and very probably dead before even a single hour had passed.

Temperature and humidity both increased drastically, seeming to treble with each slow-passing hour. Long before Brahmin reached her zenith, it was only will, stubborn pride, and hatred for this place of mud and heat that kept him on his feet and moving forward.

Somewhat to his surprise, he realized that the Commando officer was faring little better than himself. No, she fared worse. She had by far the greater skill, but her strength was patently not the equal of his. There was no slumping of her straight form or unsteadiness in her step, but weariness and strain maimed her too-white face beyond any disguising.

His respect for the woman deepened as time went on, not so much for the courage she displayed or the strength of her resolve, both of which he assumed in one of her history, but for her more conscious use of self. Islaen Connor would not founder, whatever her weariness. She knew herself and managed her resources so they sustained her and would continue to sustain her, however painful the effort.

He liked, too, her patience, for there was no question that he was holding her back, her patience and the way she accepted her own mishaps with no bridling of bruised pride. He suffered more of the latter than she, of course, more slips on the wet ground, more stumbles over or into the exposed roots, but he, like the woman, bore these accidents silently, giving thanks to his own harsh gods that all were but minor annoyances. He was no more blind than was his companion to the potential for disaster in such an environment.

They broke their journey at midday. Islaen hauled herself

up onto one of the lower roots of a spider-tree. Working her
way along it, she finally sat straddling it with her back resting
against the trunk. Sogan joined her in another moment. He
started to unseal his pack, but the guerrilla's hand stopped
him.

"No. Let them be. They'll spoil all the quicker for being exposed in this greenhouse."

She pulled a couple of small, cello-wrapped packets from
her own supplies and gave one to him.

"Try this."

He opened it and looked without enthusiasm at the narrow
wedge of deeply corrugated chocolate-brown concentrate it
contained. But Sogan was hungry after his morning's exertions. This was scarcely the first time he had sampled survival
rations, and he didn't hesitate before biting into it. For a moment, the wafer felt dry against his tongue, then his mouth
was filled with a rich, creamy liquid.

His companion laughed at his expression. "It was perfected
during the last couple of months of the War. Very handy in
situations where potable water might be in short supply. The
flavor could stand some improving, but one can't have everything."

"We never had anything as good."

"Neither did we in a practical sense. It came out too late to
really benefit us. Even now, this is still reserved for use in such
work as ours. It'll be another year or so before the formula's
released for general marketing." They finished eating in
silence and rested a few minutes longer before sliding from
their perch. They resumed their seemingly interminable
march.

Varn found the going more difficult than he had earlier
despite the break and the food he had taken. Maybe it was
because there would be no further respite until that time,
hours distant, when they reached higher ground once more,
but a deadly discouragement settled over him. It lowered his
already poor tolerance for the heat and humidity, the heavy,
motionless air, and the stench ever rising out of the muck at
their feet. It threatened to affect his progress as well, but this
he would not permit. His will was still sufficient to maintain
the care and speed of his going despite the weight of depression and weariness he bore.

Will and pride. As long as the woman before him could continue moving, he would not give over.

Two hours passed. The Arcturian did not falter during that time, nor did he suffer significant mishap, but growing exhaustion and inexperience ate at his powers of concentration and coordination as the fuel of his makeshift flame thrower would have eaten into his flesh. He would not be able to continue much longer.

His companion made a small spring to reach her next stepping place, balancing herself with the aid of a low root growing conveniently nearby. Because all that was in him longed to remain in place, he lashed himself into following after her.

The step he took was poorly judged and too hasty. His foot missed the top of the hummock the woman had just left. The side on which it came to rest would not support his weight. It slipped and, despite his efforts to regain his balance, his leg went completely from under him. He crashed heavily to the right, striking what passed for the ground before he could so much as thrust out his arms to break his fall.

"Islaen!"

There was terror in that call. This was not as the mud he had encountered before in like incidents, noisome and filthy only. It was deep here—the Commando had warned that they might find it so in places. He shuddered to think how deep it was, and it clung to him with an almost conscious tenacity. He could not rise from it. No, worse, his every movement only drove him the deeper into its embrace.

The woman whirled about. Even as her eyes found him, she realized what had occurred.

"Flatten yourself out more! Swim!"

"I cannot!" he gasped. "It grasps me too tightly!"

She was deadly calm. Varn must come out of there within the next few minutes or be sucked under. He was powerless to help himself. All aid must come from her.

It was not a hopeless situation, but its outcome was dependent upon several factors beyond her control. If only this root on which she leaned would prove as strong as it appeared . . .

She swung herself up on it and inched her way along, traveling as rapidly as she dared on its narrow surface, until she had gained a point as near as possible above the trapped man.

"Varn, reach up a hand to me. Take hold of mine."

He battled mightily to free his right arm. It was near the surface, and he succeeded at last. Islaen stretched as far as she might until their fingers met. He grasped her with the eagerness of desperation.

Her mouth was dry with her own fear. Sogan's struggles had cost him heavily; only his head and a little of his shoulders remained above the mud now. Sogan despaired even as he clasped the woman's warm fingers. She had succeeded in stopping his descent, but nothing more. She was powerless to draw him forth.

"It is no use. You do not have the strength to bring me out."

"No, but this root is strong enough to hold us both. I'm braced on it. Here, take my other hand and use me, my arms, for a rope. Pull yourself up."

As she spoke, she grasped the circle of wood more tightly still with her legs and reached down with her left arm. Aided by the support she was already giving him, the man was soon able to free his other hand. In another moment, he had joined it, too, with hers.

"Excellent," she told him. "It's much easier balancing myself this way. Start climbing now. You've broken some of the mud's hold. Don't give it a chance to settle back again."

The next minutes were ones of wrenching agony. Varn Tarl Sogan had never before demanded such effort from his body. He did not know whether or not it would be able to meet his need, and he was not at all certain the Commando was equal to the task. Those two slender arms and the shoulders behind them must surely snap under this strain.

His human lifeline held sound and firm, held and even added to the force of his own fight. The muck's grasp broke so suddenly that he almost sprang from it. Once he found himself free, he was not long in scrambling up to safety.

Varn lay gasping there for long seconds while the knowledge that he still lived flooded through him in a wonderful wave. At last, he struggled to sit up. His perch was more stable than he had imagined, and he relaxed secure in his spacer's balance.

The sight of Islaen's face drove the new-born feeling of well-being from him. One look was enough to tell him something of the ordeal she had undergone.

"I have hurt you!"

"No. I'm pulled a bit, bruised, but not actually injured. It'll quickly pass."

That might be true enough, but he could see that her hands, her arms, even her legs were trembling not with fear, but in the manner of muscles strained beyond their ability. "Here, rest against me. Let me support you. Do not try to hold on any longer yourself."

Islaen settled back, half resting against Sogan. She could feel his heart racing, the aftermath of his exertion and fear. After two days fighting for survival, it felt good to have his arms around her. Slowly, she allowed herself to relax enough to lay her head against his chest despite the mud covering him.

The fugitives didn't move for some time, until Islaen felt they were enough recovered to continue. She sat up, taking her weight back upon herself.

"I suppose we'd best go on," she said. "I'd like to get out of at least this part of it as quickly as possible, and we've lost a lot of time already."

"Are you sure you are ready?" he asked doubtfully.

"I am." Islaen sighed as she wiped a semidry glob from her cheek. "I just wish whatever gods rule Visnu would provide us with some means of getting this stuff off us. I don't fancy spending the next week or so coated in it."

EIGHT

VARN SILENTLY AGREED with his companion's last statement as he started to follow her once more. He had hated the noisome mud from their first contact with it. The thought of being so thoroughly covered with it irritated him almost beyond bearing.

He did not have to suffer for long. Scarcely had they begun moving again than it started to rain, the first either had seen on Visnu. The downpour was extremely heavy, and because the air was so still, it dropped straight upon them with no slope or change at all in the character of its fall. Its weight and force were such as to almost drive them from their feet.

A few minutes after it had begun, they were forced to halt again and take to the roots; the way before them had become so covered with water that the ground was no longer visible. The two fugitives sat together in silence, miserably hunched up in a futile, instinctive effort to keep some of the rain from pouring quite so freely down their necks and chests. Everything was still. Only the steady, soft hiss of the falling water and the rustle and creaking of the vegetation through which it passed gave evidence that they were in a physical universe at all.

The cloudburst stopped as abruptly as it had begun. Very shortly almost every sign of the deluge was gone. Islaen stared

at the ground. She could not believe so much water could
possibly have been absorbed by soil already so wet. When she
gingerly lowered herself to test it, she found that it still held
her. She called to Sogan to try his greater weight on it. He
complied with some inner reluctance; his first encounter with
the mud had not left him eager to meet its embrace a second
time, but he too found that it seemed to bear him up well. He
tried a few more steps and nodded his readiness to go on.

"Colonel," he said suddenly.

She glanced back over her shoulder. "Aye?"

"I shall thank you to make no more petitions to the gods of
this place." A welcome smile touched his face.

She laughed. "No fear of that, Admiral!" The woman
shook her head as if in dismay. "They are generous in their
response. Perhaps it is because no sentient life rose up here to
address pleas to them and they find they like a novelty."

His mood sobered. "Take care, Islaen Connor," he warned
gravely. "We of Arcturus' systems have learned not to mock
the gods."

"Aye, yours are a hard lot, are they not?" A smile brightened her face. "Noreen's are mild, gentle, noted for tolerance
and good humor." She gave a little laugh. "I suppose they
must be with such a mad populace to give them homage. Ah
well, this brings us no nearer our goal. Let's begin, Admiral."

Neither the heat nor the humidity had lessened, the former
officer noted unhappily as they continued their march. He
very much feared they had not seen the end of the rain.

That prediction proved accurate, and they were forced to
stop twice more before the afternoon had aged into early evening.

He was glad of these delays even though their footing deteriorated after each episode. He was tiring fast now, a weakening only intensified by the need to continue to maintain, aye,
and increase his vigilance and care of movement. A grim
shadow darkened his haggard face. If he were weary, the Federation woman must be well-nigh spent, and if she gave way,
they were lost; he would never be able to bring them out without her guidance.

He saw her stumble and because he was close by her, inten-
tionally so, he caught her arm.

Islaen accepted his support for a breath's space but then

disengaged herself again. Trailblazing was her task, and Varn had need of his own strength.

"Thanks."

He studied her closely, uselessly since she had anticipated his scrutiny and had made her face a mask. "How are you doing?"

"All right." She made a wry face. "I can't say this is the sort of thing I favor most in my work."

"Perhaps we should make some sort of camp for ourselves, maybe on the roots."

"Comrade, I may not enjoy slogging through this swamp," she told him tartly, "but I'm quite capable of doing it."

"Sorry. I intended no insult."

Unconsciously, her fingers reached out to brush his hand. "I know that well." Her brow lifted a fraction. "You surely don't think me so sour as to read offense into everything I hear?"

"Not sour," he replied seriously, "but the ways of our people are very different. Three years in exile have not been enough to permit me to feel entirely certain amongst you." He smiled gravely. "Men of the type I have come to know have died for giving unintended insult."

He should have said men he had observed, he thought. He could claim no real knowledge of any of them. Since he had been stripped of his rank and his old life, he had avoided contact with others as much as possible: The little he had been compelled to permit was with the spacers and those servicing their needs on the outer rim of the Federation ultrasystem. Many of them were fugitives as he was and were equally eager to remain apart from their fellows. He had never in all that time met with the like of Islaen Connor, one who in his mind was fully equal to all he had been—a ranking officer, and that of her Navy's most elite division, noble in herself, whatever her birth, a fair woman possessed of humor, courage, compassion, and a depth of soul he ever more greatly longed to probe.

A flush darkened his skin. She was all that, a thousand times more than that, but she was also the wielder of a power which gave her much information about the thought-ways of those around her. He had no wish for her to become aware that he entertained any such interest. That knowledge could only give her more than a little concern, tied to him as she now was. She bore and had borne quite enough already without having to assume that weight as well.

He had his own pride to consider, too, and a code he had
not abandoned with the stripping of its privileges. Circumstances no longer permitted him such desire, and it was weakness only and worse to dwell upon that which could not be
honorably attained.

He studied her surreptitiously but carefully. There seemed
to be no change in her, however speedily covered, and he
relaxed somewhat. She had apparently not detected the
unwelcome turn of his mind. Maybe it had been of too fleeting
duration for her to have discerned it, or maybe she was merely
too preoccupied with their present concerns. She gave every
appearance in her behavior of trusting him, and so might not
be spending as much energy as she normally would in screen-
ing him. He could not know that for certain until he had
learned more about this ability of hers, about its scope and her
manner of utilizing it, but he believed himself safe for the moment.

Varn put that thought from him as well. Right now, he, too,
had more immediate matters before him. Once more, he
looked upon the woman, this time softly. He was tired, so terribly tired, and he knew it must be worse for her, whatever her
courage and the strength of her will.

"I still wish we might rest, for my own sake as much as for
yours."

"So we would had conditions remained as they were at their
worst, but the way really has bettered, you know. We weren't
able to walk so closely together during most of the day. The
ground is far less wet under foot, for all the rain we've had.
I think it's beginning to rise as well, although the slope's
scarcely perceptible as yet. Haven't you begun to feel it, too?"

He pondered a moment. "Perhaps, or perhaps it is but your
suggestion playing with my memory." He forced his body to
straighten. "Let us press on."

Maybe it was only because the Commando officer had
called his attention to it, but the Arcturian noticed an ever-
increasing improvement in their footing and in the nature of
the land through which they moved. Another hour passed before he actually relaxed. He had seen the spider-trees grow
smaller and more widely spaced for some time, but only now

did he observe the first of the tall, straight varieties which replaced them at higher elevations.

A weight seemed to have lifted from Islaen as well. She walked more lightly now, as if she were just beginning her day instead of having spent hours in grueling labor. She knew they would soon be free to rest, and, indeed, he was fairly sure she was seeking a good campsite rather than trying to cover additional ground.

They should be able to stop soon. The trees were fine and dense, the soil firm under foot, pleasant to walk upon, the air cool. Even a few patches of the thick, low growth which had characterized the rise where they had passed the previous night had begun to put in an appearance here.

Islaen appeared to be completely oblivious to her surroundings. The very opposite was the case. Her every sense probed the treelands around them. She had been uneasy that morning and had grown steadily more unsettled until her nerves had become so taut that she could have screamed. A world this lush with vegetation should be equally rich in animal life, yet they had seen no sign of anything, however tiny, since leaving camp this morning. Where were the creatures which should populate Visnu?

She frowned. Where, indeed, were the plants? The growth around them was thick, but such a climate demanded still more of an infinitely greater variety. What was wrong here?

A high-pitched buzzing noise snapped her out of her reverie. In the moment of hearing it, she dropped to the ground, her blaster seeming to appear in her hand. She listened intently but could detect nothing; the rustle of her falling had silenced the faint disturbance which had roused her.

She had gotten a fix on it. Slowly, cautiously, the Commando began inching her way toward the thicket from where she thought the noise had originated—if there had been a sound at all. She was beginning to lay it to imagination and exhaustion.

There it was again, and much louder, the same buzzing. There was no great volume to it, and she did not think the creature making it was a very large one. It was confoundedly hard to spot. She was right at the thicket now, and still she could see nothing. Suddenly, the woman came to her feet. "Oh, you poor baby!"

* * *

Varn Tarl Sogan dropped down beside the Federation warrior. He, too, drew his weapon, quickly but not with the speed Islaen had displayed. His mouth was dry, and he could feel his pulse begin to race. What had troubled her?

The Arcturian did not attempt to follow in her creeping advance; he did not have her skill in such work and could too easily betray her approach to whatever lay concealed in that thicket.

The tension left her as abruptly as it had come. She rose quickly with all the fluid grace he had come to anticipate in her movements and rapidly penetrated the shrubbery. He saw her bend as if to examine or pick up something and then rise again.

He moved forward himself although he neither relaxed nor holstered his own blaster. It was only when he had almost reached the place that he heard the buzzing which had caught his companion's attention. Curious now, he, too, forced his way into the tangled greenery until he reached her side.

The woman's hands were lifted nearly to her face. They were cupped, and it was a couple of seconds before he saw what she held. It was an animal, one of the enormous insect tribe by the look of it, large, better than eight inches long, and seemingly bigger still in her small hands. The body was thick in proportion to its length and brilliantly striped in orange and purple-black. It looked covered with a thick coat of hair. Six pairs of legs supported it, and stumpy, clear wings beat furiously above each of these. Three antennae started from the black head. A short, barbed projection extended from the hindmost tip of its abdomen. Although the wings moved so rapidly that they were but a blur to the human eye, they appeared to be powerless to lift the creature from Islaen's hold.

She looked up at his approach. "A bee," she explained, "or something close enough to bear that name for want of a better. It's a bit stunned. Probably banged itself against one of these trees during that last downpour."

"What are you going to do with it?"

"Try to revive it. Noreen was alive with bees. We'd often find ones like this and had great success in bringing them around." After that, the woman gave her attention to her strange little patient. She began blowing strongly and steadily into its face, trying to keep a constant flow of air directed at it.

Varn watched this procedure with growing concern for several seconds. "Be careful," he warned sharply at last. "Such things are often venomous, and one that size could inject a large dose. Humans might have little or no tolerance for it."

"Aye," she agreed, "but I love bees. I don't have the heart to just let it die, as it must if it can't take to the air again. I think I can depend on my knowledge of its kin in other places."

"And if you err?"

"My reflexes are quick. I should be able to avoid its strike." Islaen shrugged. "If not, my life's not essential to any current mission that I should fear to risk it."

"It is essential to the continuation of mine!"

She looked up. "I would not discard it lightly. I wouldn't hazard it in the first place if there were more than the faint outside chance of danger. You'd deny this creature its life?"

"No," he sighed, "nor you your wish. Besides, there is no peril. It recognizes that you would help it and is grateful for that aid." Islaen kept blowing patiently. Suddenly the bee rose out of her hands and disappeared from sight amongst the trees.

The two continued on, each silent and thoughtful. The countryside did not encourage speech. The ground was dry, but it was rough, and the slope on it was now uncomfortably perceptible. Soon, they were climbing for a fact, seeking footholds and gratefully utilizing the support provided by the close-set trees.

They went on without further pause for another couple of hours until the evening began to show its effect upon the sky. At last the Commando raised her hand in a signal to halt. She stretched her weary limbs and looked about her.

The campsite she had chosen pleased her. It was a small clearing fully screened by trees, comparatively level, and freshened by the waters of a lively stream bounding across its northwest corner. It was the little river which caused her to choose this place, although they might have gone on a bit farther. They had gained considerably in altitude over their high point of the previous day, and she thought free water might become somewhat scarcer nearer the top, aye, and the cover sparser.

"Do you have any objections to spending the night here?"

"None whatsoever," the Arcturian replied without quite

masking his relief. He eased his pack from his shoulders and
seemed about to sit down beside it.

"Not yet, Comrade. The light won't hold much longer.
Strip and examine yourself for parasites. There's no telling
what we might have picked up down in that mud. I'll do your
back when you've finished with the rest."

He frowned at the command in her voice. Islaen saw his
look and arched her brows. "You may know something about
the functioning of machines, Admiral, but wilderness survival
technique is obviously not one of your strengths."

The man stiffened and glared at her. Then, to her surprise,
he laughed heartily. "That was well merited! Very well, Colonel. Since you are the more expert of us, I readily yield you the
right of command."

The Federation officer chuckled as she moved a little away
from him. Walking to the stream, she undressed and bathed in
the cold water after first checking it for life forms. She knew
he must be as glad as she for the chance to wash the mud from
himself and his clothing; the rain had cleared much of it away,
but a lot still remained, a great deal too much for either of
their liking.

The examination she gave herself was of necessity a careful
one. She did not permit herself to hurry through it despite the
cold of the air on skin wet from the bath. She dressed again in
clothes fresh from her pack and returned at last to her companion.

Varn had finished as well and was partly clothed. His tunic
lay on the thick, green carpet at his feet. It was sopping wet,
and the water ran from it into the ever-eager root systems of
the little creeper plants that were Visnu's ground cover at these
higher elevations.

"Any luck?" she asked.

He shook his head. "No. Very poor hunting altogether.
You?"

"Nothing either." She shivered. "Let's finish up so we can
see about shelter and some dinner."

Islaen frowned. She sensed discomfort in Sogan and knew
that he was reluctant to begin this last phase of the examination. Her lips tightened. No, he would not be anxious to display his back to anyone. She steeled herself, determined to
spare him response on her part. "It shouldn't take too long to
find out if you've missed any passengers."

He yielded without protest. The woman shuddered in her heart when he complied. No portion of clear skin, however small, remained to be seen, only a deeply corrugated mass of scar tissue, so much that it seemed more like a grotesque shell than human flesh. How had he not been crippled by such treatment? He must have endured the agony of exercising almost continuously while that was forming, she thought, and even then, it was a miracle he had retained his full motor capacity. The muscle tissue had been shredded right in to the bone. . . .

There was no delay or hesitation in her movements, whatever the shock the sight had given her. The search required more time than it should have, for that roughened skin provided many sites where small creatures might lurk, but she conducted her hunt calmly and efficiently.

"All clear," she told him when she had finished, then turned and began unfastening her own tunic. She slipped it off and tied it about her waist by its sleeves. She felt ashamed of her own unblemished body after what she had just seen but again gave no indication of her discomfort. "Your turn, Admiral."

The Arcturian was quick and thorough in his scrutiny, but despite his seriousness of purpose, he was very much aware of this woman's beauty. He could imagine that glorious, fair body shimmering beneath a layer of pale blue or sea green butterfly silk and knew that beauty such as this, beauty which was to him faintly exotic, would have been a rare jewel even in the Emperor's harem. Like his companion, he concealed what he felt. Honor would not permit him to discomfort her under these circumstances. He had no wish to cause her that at any time . . .

She was handling herself well, he thought absently, neither making a display nor huddling in upon herself. It was no trial to work with one such as this.

When she was fully dressed, the Commando set about constructing a shelter for the night. She was nearly certain it would rain again before morning and saw little sense in sitting out in the weather like a pair of drowning rats. Besides, they had had a brutally hard day, and even if the next was easier, they would need the best rest they could get to be fit to meet its challenges.

Varn was determined to aid her, even if all he could offer

was brute strength. He proved to be a far greater help than she had anticipated when she had accepted his offer. He was not a man who bridled under instruction or hesitated to question where he did not understand, and he was very quick to learn. Soon he was able to do good work in the cruder part of the construction. They were under shelter well before she had imagined they would be.

The Arcturian frowned when he discovered his companion would not close the lean-to they had made. "The breeze is cold now, and the night will put more of a bite into it," he said.

"True, but it might be best that anything drawn into this clearing by our scent should also smell and see our fire."

He was silent a moment. "That I had not considered. Is it wise to risk one, though?"

"Here, aye. This place is actually no more than a hole in the woods. It can't be seen from any other slope, and I'll make sure that it's enough under cover that no sign of it can be spotted from the air. The trees'll do the rest."

She shivered as an unusually sharp gust bit into her and looked sympathetically at her companion. He must be frozen in his still-wet clothes. "It'll be to our good to get warm again and to knock the water out of our things. There's no air drying at all with the humidity this high."

NINE

SOGAN HAD HIS doubts about starting any kind of fire in a country this wet, but Islaen proved more than able. They were soon sitting before a cheerful blaze. He eyed the food warming in its embers. "Are those portions not rather generous?"

She shook her head. "The perishables won't hold much longer in this climate. We'll do better to make good use of them now rather than let them spoil." She smiled. "Enjoy the feast while you can. We'll have the last of it tomorrow morning, and then it's rationing for us."

"Suppose our stay is a long one?"

"We should have enough. If not, quite a number of these plants are edible, and nearly all the water is potable even without treatment, though I shouldn't really care to skip that precaution. Jake and I made use of the time we had to spend beyond the settlement to do a bit of testing on the chance that the information might come in handy some day."

He sighed. Her words had reminded him of the purpose behind this trek of theirs. It had retreated to the periphery of his awareness under the pressure of their more immediate trials.

"Once we are rescued?" Varn asked. "What happens then? Will the result really be worth all this? You will have saved the settlers from possible disaster, but they will have been delivered into another."

Her face turned hard. "Aye. It will be worth it. The evidence my team gathered will jail those misbegotten so-called developers, maybe for long enough to discourage others of their kind from trying the same game. I'll glory in having a part in that."

The anger left her again. Their food was ready by then, and Islaen took it from the fire, giving Sogan his share. Both of them ate quickly at first, eagerly, since they were hungry, and then more slowly as the sharp edge wore off their appetites.

"It tastes better done this way than by disk," he remarked.

"Everything does. The old, slow ways really are best for a great many things."

Sogan made her no reply. He seemed to sink into his own thoughts and then to study her. The look he bent on her was none too pleasant. She had built the fire and cooked their food. She had, for all practical purposes, constructed their shelter. She had guided them all this day. She had hauled him out of that mud when he had been clumsy enough to fall into it. . . . Muttering sharply in his own tongue, he tore his eyes away from her and fixed them on the merrily dancing flames.

Islaen glanced at him, startled. "What's the matter?"

"This is not the life for which I was bred," he snapped sourly.

"And I was, I suppose?" she demanded testily.

"You do well enough in it."

The woman glared at him. "I do what I must! I've probably confirmed your original opinion of me, but I assure you, we of Noreen do live on a slightly higher technological scale than this, lowly farmers though we be!"

Varn stiffened but the response he had been about to make died unvoiced. She was not angry. She was hurt. His eyes lowered and raised again. "I am making a poor showing of myself, am I not? Merely because I am weary and feeling just about totally useless, I lash out at my companion without any cause whatsoever."

The Commando's expression softened, and he knew without her having to speak that she had forgiven him. He still steeled himself. She had a right to hear the rest of it. "An Admiral knows when and how to give way to his navigators, his mechanics, his gunners, but I have not dared to trust anyone since I made the decision which brought about my disgrace. I am finding it hard now to put myself so completely into your hands."

His eyes held hers for a moment before dropping in embarrassment. "It is illogical and entirely my own failing, but there it is. I am sorry I am so weak as to allow it to turn my tongue on one who has proven herself to be nothing if not a friend."

"If apologies are in order, I should be making them," she replied softly. "I'm supposed to be a diplomat, and here I jump down your throat for a chance remark." She shook her head ruefully and gave him a half smile. "Nothing like a day slogging through a swamp to bring out the worst in my nature."

Sogan did not reply to that. "Warrior. Federation agent. Diplomat. You have many talents, it would seem."

She shrugged. "You find the ones you need, I suppose."

They lapsed into companionable silence.

"What brought you into the Commandos?" he asked suddenly, "or into your Navy for that matter? Are the women of your homeworld inclined to war work?"

She smiled and shook her head. "On Noreen? No, not at all, nor the men either. We're farmers. But to answer your question, our women remain with their homes, tending their dairy and fowl and the kitchen and ornamental gardens."

"You were conscripted?"

"No. The Federation rarely had to resort to that, even on inner-system planets where ease might have emasculated the old virtues. Even then, the Federation would never have violated the cultural mores of the member worlds. There certainly was no need for such measures on Noreen. Our race is an old one and was noted for its hatred of would-be conquerors from its earliest history back on pre-space Terra."

"You were more or less unique among your sisters, then?"

"Aye. The rest left the fighting to the men."

"And you? You did not like the place your culture gave you?" The woman looked into the flames, smiling softly. "I was quite happy as I was." She gave a little sigh. "There were three of us, my two brothers and myself. We felt the family must be represented in the great War effort, but Tam had just begun his physician's training, and Will, well, my parents were on in years, and his help was needed. Noreen is a low-tech agrarian world, you see.

"I volunteered to go in their stead since I had no such claims on me, but they just laughed. They decided to draw lots to see which it would be, and I insisted on being part of it.

"I should have been refused again, I suppose, had my mother not intervened." Her chin lifted a little. "She's a very quiet person and rarely ever asserts her opinion, but when she does, everyone in the family leaps to comply."

Sogan laughed. "I well believe it! There is a lot of her in her daughter, I think. She asserted herself this time in your favor?"

"She did that and then again when I won—or lost—the draw. She saw to it that the result was honored."

The man sighed, and she looked at him. "What's wrong?"

"I was just thinking on the differences between your ultra-system and mine. Neither you nor your brothers would have been given the opportunity to serve with the military, much less rise to a position of command, had you been Arcturian. One must be born to that right amongst us."

He shook his head. "To judge by what we learned of Federation personnel, we may have robbed ourselves of many an outstanding officer and of even more fine warriors."

"Perhaps," Islaen replied slowly. "I do prefer our way both logically and emotionally, but I must also grant you that your warrior caste is, in truth, a breed apart. Even the strongest hatred could not deny what you were able to accomplish in battle and in the planning of it."

He smiled at the compliment. "Well, you have explained how you came to be part of your Navy, Colonel, but not what drew you into the Commandos."

"Jake Karmikel did. I took the test in response to his taunting. No one was more surprised than I when I was accepted. I'm not exceptionally powerful or athletic, and I knew full well that side of it is a major part of a guerrilla's work."

"I have seen what you can do!"

She looked at him, surprised by his vehemence. "Aye, I'd learned even at that point how to handle myself, how to compensate for my weaknesses. They told me later that this was a strong factor in their choosing me. Also, I scored well in other areas."

Sogan thought to himself that he could name some of those,

and that the scores she mentioned so casually must have been extraordinarily high.

"Areas that served you well on Thorne?"

"Aye, they did, especially the bent I seem to have for diplomacy. That should have been the most difficult part of all. Thorne's people are not an easy race to know, and they are extremely reluctant to work at all, much less closely, with anyone not of their immediate clan—but I actually enjoyed it. They're a fine, warm people beneath their suspicion."

"Even I sensed that, I suppose, though it was their courage and the skill with which they conducted their war that won my admiration." He saw the wince she failed to mask. "You are thinking that admiration cost me dear?"

She glared at the fire. It seemed but a cold shadow of that burning inside her. "We should have moved faster."

He shrugged. "What could the Federation have done? It was an internal matter, and you had agreed in the treaty you signed to refrain from interfering in the like."

"The Federation be damned!" she snarled fiercely. "My unit could have gotten you out of there. We would have, had your judges not ignored your usual appeal process and set the execution to follow almost immediately upon sentencing."

"I waived the right of appeal. It would have but prolonged my agony and shame and the shame of my kin. —By all you hold sacred, woman! What would rescuing me from my immediate fate have accomplished? I lead the life of a fugitive now. Where in either ultrasystem could I have gone had I fled?"

"To Thorne," she answered simply.

He glared at her coldly. "Has Thorne such reason to regard me with love?"

"Aye. You forget, we, my unit and the Resistance, knew what transpired in your headquarters, in your private chambers. We held silent at first to protect you, but when your own aide betrayed you and you confirmed his accusations, we made sure the populace and Federation High Command knew the full story as well.

"Understand this, Varn Tarl Sogan, Thorne had many heroes. The most of them were her own offspring. It was but natural and logical that they should strive with all that was theirs to win her freedom and their kin's and their own. You who were no part of her gave her and every creature dwelling

upon her now and in time to come their lives at enormous risk
to yourself, and then you paid the full price for your humanity. You above all others would be welcome and honored
there."

"They are a noble people, and even such a reception as you
describe would not entirely surprise me," Sogan said slowly
after a long silence, "but surely, Islaen, you must realize that I
could accept no part of it. I came to Thorne as a conqueror. I
could not return there as a supplicant."

"No." She sighed. "No, I guess I always knew that." Her
eyes raised to his.

"All the same, Thorne's people granted you citizenship in
their gratitude, and, as a result, you have full citizenship in the
Federation. Had we brought you out of that prison, the Empire could not have reclaimed you."

"It might still have slain me."

"You are tough enough in yourself not to have needed more
than the chance to live," she replied evenly. "You've proven
that."

He looked at her somberly. "Are you forgetting that my
guilt was real?"

"Guilt?—Set aside sparing the Spirit of Space only knows
how many planets in that Sector. You saved your own fleet
and your Empire's honor as well!"

"I violated my commander's direct order. It was for that
reason that I was condemned."

"For disobedience to a man judged hopelessly insane both
by your own people and by our court when we claimed him for
atrocity trial?"

"If I had known that, if I had had even the shadow of a
suspicion about how matters really stood, everything would
have been different, but I had no idea of it. I had seen him in
person only a couple of months previously, and there was no
sign of trouble on him then. It must have been the shock of the
defeat and surrender that pushed him over."

Varn sighed deeply and looked away. "He had been a fine
man, Islaen, a good commander and a brilliant officer." He
faced her once more. "No one suspected his state of mind at
the time of my trial, certainly not the judges who condemned
me."

His expression hardened. "It might have made no difference if they had. The fact of my guilt remained unaltered,

and he was not the only one with the need to vent disgrace and frustration and grief for losses rendered worthless by defeat. I provided too good a channel for that to be dismissed lightly."

"Your people are a savage lot!"

"My people are human! They were bleeding, and if they turned the weight of law instead of what you consider to be justice on me, well, there have been times in plenty when some of your own have responded to lesser hurt with even greater cruelty. I have little cause to whine. I acted fully knowing what I did, and if I had wanted to protect myself, I should have slain my aide instead of imagining I could keep my true orders from him."

Her eyes fell. "I'm sorry. I don't blame you for regretting what you did. . . ."

The man shook his head. "No. I regret some of the consequences . . ."

Memories rushed on him of the consort and concubines who had embraced their daggers under the weight of his disgrace, his children who had been slaughtered to erase the corruption of his seed from the race.

Sogan forced those blood-stained images from his mind. To dwell on them, to give them any opening at all, was to risk plunging himself into a fatal spiral of despair. He made himself speak evenly.

"Thorne is a brave, vital world. What would have been accomplished by burning her off and an unknown number of other planets after her until the last of our ships had been blown out of space by your Navy?

"Arcturians do not fear to die or to bring death, but mark me, Colonel Connor, neither do the most of us love slaughter for its own sake, no more than do the most of the Federation's people. What else would that sick vengeance have been? There was no helping the Empire's cause. That was lost. We did not even have the right to strike against you save in defense of our lives since the Emperor had officially surrendered.

"No, what I did then, I should do again if the choice were once more before me, even if I should have to endure the same punishment as a result." The man said no more. He stared into the fire, seeing in the low flames and bright embers and curling smoke pictures of that darkest period of his life.

"How did you escape them, Varn?" Islaen asked softly.

He shrugged. "I do not know. I suppose they did not even

bother to check whether I still lived when they dumped me into that lifecraft and set her adrift.

"She saved me. She was old, but her support systems still functioned and maintained what remained of me until I was pulled out of Dorita's space. I myself was aware of nothing until I regained consciousness in the hospital there."

The woman frowned and then started. "Dorita!"

A chill went through her soul. That had been an incredible voyage with an incredible rescue at the end of it. He had passed undetected through a great part of the Empire and through most of the Federation, through their wildest and most nearly uncharted Sectors, right to the outermost edge of the vast galaxy. Dorita was the sole colony there, the only outpost of Federation life or, as far as they knew, of intelligent life of any sort. Had his course swerved only a very little in any direction . . .

Her thought was easy enough to read.

"I still do not know whether to thank or curse the gods for that rescue, but it was obvious that they had willed me into that place and willed the continuation of my existence in this realm, and it was mine to do what I might to maintain it.

"I did not intend that it should be as a prisoner or as one doomed to inevitable and imminent assassination. I decided as soon as enough of my mind returned to make thought possible to maintain my freedom and whatever shreds of dignity as still remained to me.

"Dorita is apparently a polyglot colony using Basic as its binder language."

She nodded. "It's a mining camp really, not a permanent settlement, at least not yet. The populace is drawn from all over the Federation."

"I pretended to have less awareness than I did until I learned something about my situation. They had identified the make of my ship, of course, but believed me to be a victim of my people rather than one of the Arcturian race myself, and I adopted that role, feigning faulty memory until I was able to develop a satisfactory history."

The woman frowned. "Why didn't you change your name instead of choosing a variant of it that would be no disguise at all to one even slightly suspicious of you?"

"I had no choice. I had given it to those tending me before I had regained enough wit to guard my tongue. Fortunately, neither did I have full control over my ability to speak, and my words were only partially distinguishable. They did not recognize the significance of what I said."

She nodded. "You were lucky there. What happened then, after you'd gotten something of your strength back?"

"The Doritans bought my ship. She was both a curiosity to them and excellent shuttlecraft, for which they had a real need."

His mouth twisted. "They felt sorry for me and gave me a good price for her, enough to get me off-world and to pay for a wreck-class derelict.

"I acquired the *Fairest Maid* as soon as I reached Zora. Since I am knowledgeable about a vessel's workings—such skill is required of the Empire's officers—I was not long in restoring her to spaceworthy condition."

A grin formed upon his lips. "She is more now than her appearance would indicate." The surge of pride animating him faded again, and he continued in the same dull tone in which he had spoken from the beginning of his narrative. "I took up the life as well as the guise of a spacer and have maintained myself and my ship that way ever since."

Islaen made no immediate comment, and when he glanced at her, he found her looking at him through eyes as brilliant as back-lit amber. "You were never sentenced to death," she said, speaking so softly that he scarcely heard her words.

"I was ordered flogged through the fleet, receiving maximum lashes on each vessel," he retorted coldly. "Even at the War's end, the Empire was possessed of a large number of ships."

"But you were not actually condemned to die," the woman persisted. "I know this much about the soldiers of the Empire, they are not slovenly in the performance of their duty. If you had been slated for extermination, your death would've been verified before you were cast adrift."

The Arcturian straightened a little as the significance of what she was saying reached him. "I have been living in needless fear. No assassins would be sent after me if it were learned I still lived. My degradation might actually serve as a source of amusement in some quarters."

"Not degradation, not if you don't make it that. Varn, a life of incredible brilliance lies before you for the taking!" She ignored his humorless laugh. "You'll have to keep up your guard, right enough. The War brought too much suffering, and I wouldn't trust a large part of a great many populations to respond honorably to the presence of any Arcturian, but even with that danger, all this vast universe is yours.''

Islaen found herself describing for him the life she so strongly desired and could not now hope to gain. ''You have the ship and the skill and the strength to range the starlanes alone.''

''That last is more the product of despair than of strength,'' Sogan said evenly, but he could feel his pulse quicken; his companion's excitement and belief were powerful, and, despite himself, he was responding to them.

He steadied himself, willed his mind to quieten. The last thing he needed now was worthless hope. ''Do we dare sleep without a watch?''

She accepted his wish and merely shook her head emphatically. ''No. It was different in the flier, but this little shelter wouldn't stop much. One of us'll have to be ready with a blaster, just in case.''

''You do not trust Visnu very much?''

''That I don't, nor like her very much.'' The Commando frowned, marshaling her uneasy thoughts. ''There's too much and too little. We've discovered incredibly few signs of animal life. Where are the tiny common things? Why aren't there more larger ones? Why is this wet, rich soil so bare? There are only the trees in most places, and that's not right. They don't block enough of the light to account for such barrenness. Only fairly high up on the slopes do you find much in the way of undergrowth or ground cover, and even that's oddly confined, like survivor colonies slowly regenerating to claim former territory.'' The furrows deepened between her brows. ''What happened here, Varn? Was it some rare disaster, or is there a pattern of destruction active on Visnu?''

''That I cannot answer, Colonel. I would that I could. Your questions are too accurately put to work for my comfort.''

She sighed. ''Perhaps we should be glad there's so little animal life, or at least so little taking interest in us. There are all too many places in the universe where we'd be digested by now.''

The man smiled. ''That bee was anything but hostile. It had no intelligence to speak of, of course, not as we use the term, but it took a kind of comfort from you. It certainly was not moved to eat you."

Sogan stopped speaking. He turned gray-white, as if death had laid its hand upon him. His eyes looked through her into some hell newly opened and gaping before him. "They were right. They were wholly right. I am a pollution upon the universe."

"Varn, what's wrong? What's happened?"

"I knew what that insect felt. I was inside its mind, or it . . . it was in mine."

"If that be true, you are gifted . . ."

"How so gifted? By some random stellar ray? Some accursed and most properly concealed mixture in the bloodline of one or both of my parents? By the tie between them? Their fathers were brothers and arranged the match to hold the wealth of their house intact. Such is acceptable among us but is rare because of the acknowledged danger. If that be the cause, I have paid the price of their risk."

He came to his feet. Islaen bit her lip, but she kept her voice hard. "I'm empowered in a kindred if not the same manner. Is it that I'm an object of loathing to you, something to be maintained, and that unwillingly, while the need for my skills remains and then gladly discarded?"

"No . . . It is not the same." He turned completely from her, stared out at the blackness beyond their tiny fire. He started to walk toward the darkness.

The woman thought her heart must leap up to close her throat. Such was the state of his mind that he was unreachable by reason. Even her goading anger had failed to rouse him. If he were permitted to wander out there now, while his too slight wilderness skills were numbed and his racial instincts reigned supreme, including, presumably, that which praised suicide as a worthy alternative to disgrace and loss . . .

She had to stop him! Even if she cared nothing for him, even if he was not here in this wretched place because of her, she would have had to help him. It was not in her to abandon any man to such pain, much less Varn who had already known so much.

The violence of one passion might burn out another. There was a desire upon which she might work. If there was cost to her in rousing it, so be it. That must be borne.

"Varn, come back to the fire. To me."

He faced about. Her voice had altered subtly in a manner observation and well-nigh forgotten training had taught her. She herself had half risen. She looked up at him with eyes aglow, lips slightly parted.

The Arcturian gazed upon her a moment, then deliberately, grimly, casting away all that remained within him of self-worth, he returned to her. Why not? He wanted her, and nothing else remained for him now. Even she realized that and expected no better from him. He would have this much, and then he would die. He caught her up, kissing her roughly as a man might one of the hired toys of the ports both his pride and his fear had driven him to shun.

Her tunic loosened easily. His hand closed on her breast as he drew her closer to him. Islaen's body tightened at his touch despite her effort to hold herself still, and she had to wield every fiber of her inner strength to control her urge, her need, to fight him off.

He felt her stiffen and relax again by the force of her will. So, Islaen didn't want this. She was sacrificing herself. Sacrificing herself for him. Sick with disgust and shame for what he had so nearly done, Sogan flung her from him with an oath and once more faced the night outside.

Neither of them spoke while he did battle with what drove him and that which had given it rein over him. His shoulders squared. "You have nothing to fear from me."

His voice was thick, but it was quiet, as were his eyes when he again seated himself beside her. He saw that she had set her clothing aright. "I must thank you, I suppose. It is fairly obvious what you did."

The woman's eyes had fallen. "I had to try it." She looked up suddenly. "I'd never just use you . . ."

He smiled faintly. "It seems to me that you were in the greater danger of that."

"Perhaps, yet I knew you are who you are."

"Aye. I am that."

"Varn, stop it! Where's the wrong in possessing yet another sense, in being able to understand your fellow creatures a little better and a little more directly?"

"In itself, perhaps nothing, but no other of my race can do so." He shuddered. "We have a hatred of mutation. Even knowing to our sorrow how the mutant races fought for the

Federation, yet still we despise them. There is no logic in it, yet its hold is powerful in a manner I cannot expect you to comprehend."

"Pain and fear are comprehensible," she said softly.

"You can read so much?" A new shame rose up to stand by the old. "You can feel it?"

"I—know what you endure. I don't know your thoughts. If I did, I might be able to make some answer to them."

He took a deep breath. "My thoughts are not against you or the power you have."

She nodded. "That I know, Varn Tarl Sogan. I felt your distaste when you first learned what I could do. It's not present now and was not present even when you were emitting so strongly before. We're sensitive to criticism of ourselves, I guess, or I'm overly sensitive to it. I'd have picked that up."

He nodded slowly. "Can you still trust yourself with me?"

"Of course."

"Let me take the first guard, then."

"Aye."

She hesitated. "You've endured much today."

"In body and in mind. I badly need time to think. Will you grant me that, Colonel?"

Islaen nodded. "Take what you need." She lay down, curling herself into a ball for warmth. Varn had not misread the signs when he had said he thought it would be cold tonight.

She had no doubt about the wisdom of leaving the watch to him. No matter how deeply his thoughts pressed upon him, the former Arcturian officer would not allow himself to be oblivious to any threat approaching their shelter.

Varn watched the Commando for a few minutes. The little of her face not hidden by the spider silk blanket she had pulled from her pack was already relaxed in deep sleep. So peaceful, he thought. How could she release herself thus on this world she mistrusted—or in his company at all?

His face tightened. He had treated one he respected in a manner that would have been unacceptable to a warrior in the lowest service level in all the Arcturian Navy. Even half-mad, how could he have debased her as he had, aye, and debased himself? He had never found it necessary to use force against any woman.

Need was the answer, of course. It had not been true passion driving him but the despair of utter self-loathing, that, and the stark necessity of countering the turmoil boiling within him by whatever means possible before it warped his mind. Islaen had recognized his trouble, his peril, and had given him his release.

His olive skin darkened in a flush born of shame and anger. How could he have surrendered to himself so completely, he who had exercised strict control over himself from the time he had reached his sixth year? It was a lapse he could not pardon despite his understanding of the conditions which had given rise to it. How the woman could do so at all lay almost beyond his comprehension.

His eyes stayed on her, their expression quietening until it was both somber and tender. He wanted her right enough, but in the gentle manner in which he had always known women.

He frowned. No, not that, either. If he and Islaen Connor were ever to join, it would have to be in full, genuine partnership, after the way of so many Federation cultures. Anything less was unthinkable with a woman such as this.

Sogan sighed then and put the thought from him. That was not likely to ever come to pass. He might be free of the fear which had haunted him these three long years, but little else had changed. His life was not one he could imagine any other sharing willingly, much less this lovely former foe with all the dark memories of his kind that the War must have left to her.

Besides, it was now his to guard, not to dream. The Commando had carried the responsibility for their safety through all this weary day. She had surrendered it at last to him, and he was determined that he should not fail her. He steeled himself. He possessed little in the way of woodcraft, but it seemed that some sort of mental talent was his. Let that be put to the test to see how it might be made to serve their present need.

TEN

THE MAN'S TOUCH woke Islaen suddenly near the end of his watch. She sat up, her blaster already in her hand. If there was not quite fear on him, he was radiating a strong and active concern.

"What is it?" Her lips formed the words without the aid of voice although he had not signaled the need for silence.

He moved closer to her, instinctively she thought. His answer came softly. "Hunger. It comes from many separate points all around us. And above," he added with a glance at the flimsy covering shielding them from the night. "There is fear, too, of the fire, I think. That seems to be holding them at bay."

"Set your blaster to broad beam. If they dread fire, and most wild things do, that should in itself be enough to drive them back." Her eyes flickered toward the roof. "They're very light and probably very small as well, or that wouldn't support them."

She chewed her lip thoughtfully. "I had considered taking to the trees for the night . . ." She shook her head even as she spoke. None of those around them were large. The trunks were slender, as were the branches. Doubtless, many of them would offer good support in an emergency, but she had no fondness for the thought of passing a night in one of them. For one thing, they would get no sleep, and that they needed.

The living wood might hold up their weight readily enough, but they would have had to guard their balance constantly. To doze on one of those narrow branches was to crash down to the ground, and that lay a dizzyingly far distance from the lowest of them. Besides, she had anticipated no danger. . . .

The Commando had planned for trouble, though, any of the kind she had believed likely to develop in such a place. Their shelter was open, easy to escape, and was set close to the forest—indeed, no part of the small clearing was far from the trees—but now Varn reported that they were surrounded. Would they be able to win through to the branches if flight became necessary? Would the trees provide refuge at all?

"What's out there?" she asked.

"There is no way to tell. I have no previous experience with and no knowledge of the fauna of this place."

"What about numbers?"

"A multitude, too many for the counting. That much, I can declare for a fact."

"Intelligence?"

He shook his head. "None worth the mentioning. Or I think none. . . . I can find nothing very much beyond the existence of life and hunger when I reach for any of the individuals, yet when I withdraw a little, there is . . ." He paused, groping for words. "A disembodied blur seems to remain, like the after-taste of a thought."

Sogan drew his hand across his eyes. "It is eerie beyond describing. Perhaps if I were more familiar with such communication, more comfortable with it, I could tell you more."

"No. Go on. You're doing fine. I'd say we're dealing with some kind of intensely integrated herd or hive animal. Theory indicates that many such species are supposed to possess a sort of collective intelligence although the individuals might have little or none themselves." Islaen grinned suddenly. "It looks like you may just have proven that for the entomologists."

"I would as soon forego that honor and let them find their own proof!" He frowned. "Seriously, there is nothing even vaguely resembling thought in what I am receiving."

"No, just an instinct sufficient to allow the colony to function effectively. No more is needed." Her expression darkened suddenly. "I may have done us great harm today by aiding that bee."

"Not so. None of its like are out there. I would have recog-

nized that touch. Besides, we should have heard them coming."

The woman stared at him an instant, then laughed. Of
course! She of all people should have realized that a swarm of
such creatures could never have made its approach in silence.

"How long have they been here?"

"Not long. I cannot say exactly. I know so little about this
. . . power of mine. I have been sweeping the night as it were,
but it is difficult to control, and the concentration is very hard
for me to keep up, and I have been forced to rest frequently.
They were out there when I tried it a few minutes ago. I
learned what I could from them and then woke you."

Tension was open in his voice for a moment. He mastered it
again in the next instant, but he could not quell what was firing it so easily. Sogan felt instinctively that there was great
danger in these strange, subintelligent touches he was receiving, and the longer he maintained the contact, the stronger his
fear became. Soon he would be fighting blind terror.

If the Commando was aware of his discomfort, she gave no
sign of it. "Any change in their attitude, their transmissions,
since you first sensed them?" she asked.

"None." The Arcturian looked at her curiously. "The
sending is extremely strong, almost overpowering. You are
picking up none of it?"

Islaen shook her head. "Nothing at all. My gift is with our
own kind, and even at that, it's very limited."

"Do we try for the trees?"

"No. As long as the fire and lean-to hold them at bay, we're
better off clinging to them, especially since we have no idea
what's out there. But let me know at once if there's any alteration at all, any difference in mood, any increase in excitement
level or in hope."

He nodded slowly. "As you will."

The woman sank into her own thoughts for a moment. She
had spoken decisively—in truth, there was nothing else to be
done—but she felt little confidence. Varn's transmissions were
in themselves enough to throw her. He was not a man to give
way to panic, but it was gnawing at him.

A wave of fear swept through her as the reality of their helplessness gripped her mind. A guerrilla preferred, needed, to
move her own fate, to control it at all times, and she knew they
were effectively trapped here, sitting out a siege.

Their besiegers? They were apparently small, present in number, fearful either of them or of their fire, and *hungry*. Only Sogan would be able to tell if that hunger would eventually overcome their dread.

She looked at him sharply. "You'll be able to maintain the contact?" she asked in sudden doubt, remembering his earlier words.

"With no difficulty whatsoever. Those things hungering for us out there in the night are a powerful stimulus, I assure you." His voice became bleak. "I only wish I could have been a more capable watchman either with woodcraft or with this strange skill of mine. Perhaps then we might have had some warning and been able to escape out of here, or at least know now what we are facing."

"Never mind. You did better than I would've. There's no noise, no disturbance, and there probably was none at their approach. If it were up to me, we'd suspect nothing until we walked outside to meet whatever is there come morning, or saw the first wave marching—or scuttling—in to us."

She saw his body tighten even as she felt his fear swell. "Already?"

"No. Your pardon, Colonel. It is unpleasant in the extreme to find oneself regarded as a food source."

"I'm scared, too, Varn," the Federation woman said softly as she moved closer to him. "I know too much, and I'm blessed with a powerful imagination. I wish you could feel it."

Sogan smiled as he slipped his arm around her. "We need not actually share thoughts to share humanity, do we?" She rested her head against him, letting that serve as her answer.

They remained sitting thus through what remained of the night, silently, ever listening with ears and hidden sense for any indication of movement beyond their shelter.

The man straightened abruptly. "They are leaving!"

"What! Why?"

"I do not know. Need of some sort, but no fear."

They had their answer in another ten minutes. They heard a pattering sound, intermittent at first, then steadier until it became a full downpour. "They don't like rain, apparently," Islaen remarked.

"No. I wonder how long it will last?"

She shrugged. "Who knows?" She turned a rather wan smile on him. "Sleep now."

Varn looked at her as if she had gone mad. "As likely as not, they will be back as soon as that rain stops, which it might at any time."

"We still have the fire," she reminded him, giving mental thanks to Noreen's gods that she had set it well back, out of danger of accidental drowning. "It might be discouraging enough to move them to seek more convenient prey once the weather clears."

"Maybe," he answered without any conviction, "if that collective intelligence of which you speak can make so complex a judgment."

"Instinct can do much. After all, the feeding of any large hunting colony does require some capability for judgments. They've wasted a lot of time on us already."

She straightened, as if steeling herself for battle. "We're likely to have to move fast tomorrow and maybe keep moving quickly. You'll have to be rested for whatever comes."

"How will you know if they return?"

"I'll wake you if the rain starts to slacken at all. In the meantime, this watch is mine and the time of rest yours."

Varn yielded after that and lay down as his companion had done earlier, wrapping himself in her abandoned blanket. He closed his eyes and willed his body to relax, resolving to rest as much as possible; he very much doubted any sleep would be possible. Exhaustion is a powerful soporific, however, and he was well spent in spirit, mind, and body. A welcome oblivion closed in over him before he had completely settled himself.

ELEVEN

A DULL, GRAY version of Brahmin's light filled the lean-to when the woman's hand drew Sogan back out of his retreat. He sat up. He was fully alert but still decidedly tired, and the damp and cold had gotten to his back so that he was stiff in his movements. More than stiff. He had to school himself tightly to give no open sign of distress whenever he tried to move. If the Commando officer was aware of his discomfort, she gave no indication of it.

"The rain's lightening. Anything else going on?"

He closed his eyes and sent his mind out in search of those others. It obeyed him with surprising ease, and he thought it ranged farther than it had been able to go the previous night —rest and practice both seemed to help there—but to no avail. "Nothing. They are not around."

"Good. Let's eat quickly and get out of here. I want to be as far as possible from this place when it dries." There was a new tension on her this morning, detectable in both voice and manner. He looked sharply at her and then went to the mouth of their shelter, to which her eyes had flickered as she spoke. His breath caught, and he stood perfectly still for a long moment, allowing the sight before him to register fully upon his mind.

The gold-green creeper plants which had carpeted the ground the evening before were gone. No trace whatsoever re-

mained of them on the wet, black soil. The trees themselves
were all right, he saw after one instinctive, half-terrified
glance, at least in their upper stories, but the lower trunks had
been cleared of sucker shoots. The spaces between them were
free of undergrowth. There were no thickets now to impede
their progress. Of it all, a few young trees were left, stripped
of their leaves but he thought they were likely to regenerate
others and, thus, survive. He hoped so.

His attention returned to the ravaged clearing. The ground
had an odd, rumpled look, and he stared at it, puzzled and not
a little troubled.

The woman had been watching him. "They got the roots,
too."

"What can have done this?"

"Horde creatures are common in the universe. Many are
vegetarians, but you say these were interested in us as well. . . .
They did know we're animal?"

He shuddered inwardly, remembering vividly that vast hunger. "Aye. That realization seemed to excite them the more."

He saw her go to the rough pack they had fashioned for him
before quitting their first camp. "Dare we delay for food?"

"Aye. I don't like taking the time, either, but it's best that
we do while the rain's still heavy. Human bodies need fuel,
unfortunately, and we may not be able to stop for a long time
once we do start moving." She had been readying their rations
even as she spoke, using her disk rather than the slower natural fire, and now handed him his portion.

"Where could they have gone?" the man wondered aloud
as he wolfed down his share.

"To higher ground or lower, or perhaps they're still here,
under our feet, in some sort of dormant state."

"It could well be the latter," he said after some consideration. "It would explain both their very quick disappearance,
at least from my mind, and my inability to raise them again
now."

"Is there anything else around?" she asked suddenly. "In
the trees, maybe? Can you reach so far?"

"I had not thought to try!" He forced his mind out, searching . . . "Aye! Not a great deal, but, aye! I have several
touches, all wary, all waiting, some ignoring even hunger."

"Slow things, unable to move quickly enough to be sure of
taking advantage of even this long rain?"

"That I cannot answer. There is no stark fear."

"The ravagers are underground, then, and will stay there for the time being," Islaen said decisively. "Let's go."

"But where? In what direction?"

"Away from their line of march or at right angles to it, whichever suits our own purpose the better. Any horde great enough to do all this in a single night isn't likely to detour very far for the sake of two relatively insignificant sources of meat, however patient they might be when chancing upon us. Whatever happens, we'll stick to the trees. Our safety's there, apparently, to judge by the other touches you've received."

They broke camp quickly after that, but not in such haste that the Commando failed to carefully conceal all sign that they had ever been there. Nature might threaten them, but it was still to their own that they must look for their greatest peril.

Both were silent as they left the blighted region. The destruction of life was so complete within it that they were reminded of devastation wrought by man's warring.

This was more frightening, though. There was something uncanny at work here, something elemental, primal. Before it, civilization's veneer peeled back within them. Thus must their first forebears have stood forgotten eons past on the worlds where their races had evolved.

The sight of the lean-to roof had deepened the chill gripping them. It was just barely intact. The greens forming the sloping roof had been chewed down to the wooden supports and the wood itself showed the sign of heavy abuse, as if by many sharp teeth. The humans within had come perilously close to meeting with their besiegers last night.

They relaxed after they had traveled a short distance. The area of destruction proved to be small, although awesome enough in its own right. The ravagers had marched in a column several yards in width, taking everything edible in their path, but sparing what grew on either side of it.

The pair broke away from the trail after noting its general direction. Fortune was with them, and they were not forced to detour at all from the course they had originally set for themselves.

They kept a strong pace, almost as fast as their instincts demanded. The ground was good, rugged but not extraor-

dinarily difficult now that they had rested. Only rarely was it
necessary to slow down for more than a few yards, and more
infrequent still were the occasions on which they were forced
to scramble or to actually climb. Much of the trouble they did
have was the result of the slipperiness and mild instability of
some spots, the legacy of the recent heavy rains.

The weather remained nasty. The dampness of the night had
descended into a seemingly endless heavy drizzle that had long
since soaked their garments through to the skin, rendering
them all the more vulnerable to the chill and the bite of the
wind.

Sogan blew on his hands to warm them but said no word
against the cold. Soon their descent would take them into the
thicker part of the forest where the breeze would be broken.
All too shortly after that they would be in the swamp once
more. If their experiences of yesterday proved any example of
what they could expect for today, it would be heat that they
would have to endure then. To his thought, that was by far the
more crippling.

Despite his present discomfort and the unpleasant anticipation of that to come, the Arcturian's spirits rose as they put
distance between themselves and the campsite. There was no
sign of trouble now. The few contacts he made when he sent
his mind out questing were all distant and unconcerned with
the two humans.

That his companion had said little since they had set out did
not trouble him. He had not felt inclined for speech himself
and assumed her thoughts were running along lines similar to
his own.

He erred there. Islaen's heart was heavy with a weight that
doubled with every step they took toward the marshlands
below. She had hated that region, feared it, knowing as she
did enough about such places to appreciate their threat. What
she now experienced was something different, less reasonable,
less controlled and therefore less controllable, almost a mindless terror. It was taking well-nigh the whole of her will to keep
herself outwardly steady and moving toward that deadly, wet
world where the very soil all too often was a trap. Fear had so
dried her mouth and throat that she could scarcely swallow,
much less trust herself to speak.

She had reason to dread the swamp. She all but knew now

what she had only sensed yesterday, that it concealed a peril even more ghastly than imagination had made it, small agents of an awful death . . .

If only Jake Karmikel were here! The ache of her loss swelled at the thought of him until she was sure it must consume her. Now more than ever, she knew how much he had been to her, how much she missed and would miss him. His good, solid, proven strength would have dealt with a great part of this terror and his sympathetic humor with most of the rest, as she in her own way had so often eased his fears. They had been together so long, knew each other so well . . .

Her eyes closed for an instant. And if this trial proved too much for her, she might even have given over the burden of command to him for a while until she regained her strength. Islaen tried to take hold of herself. She couldn't do that with Varn. He was unfamiliar with wilderness conditions, and he was already bearing a great deal for her sake. If only Jake . . .

The woman forced the memory of him from her mind. Soon, once this was over and she was free from the press of responsibility, she would be able to give herself over to her grief, mourn Jake as he deserved and her heart demanded, but for now, she must concentrate on the task before them. Her accursed panic was already draining her dangerously, too much to allow room for any other debilitating emotion. She *must* shake it.

Her face was drawn and white with the strain of the inner battle she fought, a struggle further intensified by the nagging fear that she might not have the strength to conquer herself when the ultimate test came.

A wave of horror swept through her so intense that she was forced to pause a moment to steady herself once more. It passed, but a new worry assailed her. Perhaps she could muster the courage to go in there and to remain hour after agonizing hour, but how in the name of all space was she to conduct herself as she must, to guard and guide them both?

They did not have much farther to go. Only a few specimens of the upland trees were now visible in the surrounding forest and those were of poor quality. The spider-trees and other distinctly lowland growth had claimed supremacy, and already the soil was wet and sticky and slippery enough that they had to slow their pace.

The Commando drew a deep breath and pushed on with an

energy that forced her companion to quicken his own step.
She had faced danger before, and she had faced fear before.
This mindless dread was a more formidable foe than its
logically based namesake, but she was determined not to let it
gain complete command over her.

"Islaen!"

The woman had already seen what had put the horror into
Sogan's voice. She stood paralyzed, staring at the incredible
thing that had risen up before her, not believing what her
senses told her even while they fed the information into her
stunned mind. Nothing like this could exist outside the imagination! It was a serpent, huge and glorious, possessed of all
the power and terror that were the mark of its kind.

The body was easily the width of her own, but so long that
the creature was extraordinarily slender and graceful. Deli-
cately shaded vertical stripes of green and silver emphasized its
length. The markings drew together on the face to form a
blunt arrow that highlighted the shape of the head itself.

The latter was broader than most of the body and seemed
less finely wrought. The mouth was large with strongly mus-
cled elastic jaws capable of accommodating prey wider than
itself. The eyes were dark and deeply set. They were fixed to
look forward, granting the binocular vision so useful to a
hunter. They had a penetrating gaze that was yet not an expression.

The jaws gaped open. The fangs were shorter than she had
unconsciously anticipated, but that was only a matter of degree. Knives smaller than these could bring death, even without the potent dose of venom each one of them could probably
deliver.

No, that was wrong. A creature that large had no need of
poison and, thus, was not likely to possess it. That mighty
thing would scarcely require constriction; most of its prey
could go down whole.

All this flashed through her mind in the instant of her
sighting the great serpent. Fear and full knowledge of her peril
rose even more quickly, but she was powerless to act. The
creature was possessed of no hypnotic power like that of
Fairie's dragons, but she was held as effectively as if she were
hard caught in one of their spells. All the primal horror her
kind had ever felt for the powerlords of the reptile kingdom
welled up from her mind's nethermost recesses in one swift,

all-encompassing rush that engulfed her every sense and power. She could move no muscle either to flee or to bring any weapon to bear in her defense.

Weapon?

The woman would have laughed hysterically had she been able to force the sound from her paralyzed throat. What possible use would a knife or a pitiful little antipersonnel blaster be against an opponent the like of this?

The slender, beautiful body glided nearer and stopped again. It rose higher and still higher above her. Its head swayed slightly as it prepared to descend and engulf its waiting victim.

Suddenly, the motion stopped. The serpent lowered itself and slid away from her. It crossed some six feet of muddy ground and began to flow up the trunk of a large spider-tree. Islaen watched, entranced, until the last glimmer of its body vanished from sight. That broke the spell holding her. She shuddered convulsively, then shuddered again.

Arms came around her, supporting and comforting. "Easy. It is gone and will not trouble us again."

The woman sank against him, but then shame and disgust filled her and she pulled free. "Draw your blaster and turn it full on me. Yours is the right."

Sogan stared at her, stunned by the deadly purpose in her voice. She had meant that command. "For what cause should I execute my comrade?"

"I could have slain you by my freezing."

"Are you a goddess that you must always react well or courageously? I did not either at the height of my power or during my climb to reach it, and it was for no such failing that I was condemned, however intolerant my race may be of weakness."

There was anger on him, and he gave it rein. "You degrade me, woman. You have borne with my limitations patiently. Is it because you see me as a child or a mental defective and yourself as a being so superior that you are permitted no shadow of failure at all?"

She started to hear that. "No, not so!"

The man checked his fury, and his manner softened. "Then accept your life from me, Islaen Connor, as I have accepted mine from you since you became my guide and guardian in this wilderness."

Her head lowered. She allowed him to draw her to him and pressed her face against his breast. There was comfort in his hold and a gentleness surprising in one of his history and strength.

The Federation officer remained thus cradled just for a moment before drawing away from him again. Her face was still starkly white, but the eyes had lost the look of ultimate despair they had worn when she had demanded her death from the Arcturian.

What had happened to her, she deserved. She owned that now. She had been guilty of a monstrous vanity in believing that her will was sufficient in itself and able to maintain her through any blow, whatever the circumstances. She had been guilty of far worse in acting upon that grossly unrealistic belief. By retaining command when she knew herself to be unfit, by concealing her difficulty from her companion, she might all too well have slain them both. Noreen's gods and those of Visnu were greatly to be praised that nothing worse had come out of it either for herself or for Varn.

She straightened with an inward sigh. The former Admiral had proven himself the better of them. It was now hers to swallow whatever shreds remained of her pride and place the right of decision in his hands before her terror betrayed them a second time.

Islaen Connor started to speak but held her peace. She had realized in that moment that there was no longer any need to do so. What she felt now was a reasonable appreciation of potential peril, not the blind panic-dread of the last several hours. That serpent might not be the worst thing Visnu had to throw against them. Indeed, she strongly suspected it to be so far from that as to be relatively insignificant, but the meeting with it and her survival had broken the tension within her. She was free to face this world as she had faced all the many others she had known since first venturing from Noreen.

Sogan saw the change in her expression. "You are all right now?"

"More right than I've been since we started off today."

"The dose of what you feared?"

She nodded. "Something like that, I guess." The woman cocked her head, watching him curiously. "You said you gave me life. What did you do?"

Varn looked embarrassed. "I told it you were not good to eat."

"You what?"

"I had no weapon fit to fight it, but I was receiving its intention so strongly that I reasoned I might be able to transmit to it as well. I concentrated on countering its appetite for you, or instilling the idea of poison." He shrugged. "It believed me."

She laughed at his obvious discomfort. "You're marvelous! That was one really brilliant stroke!" Her lovely face grew serious, her tone thoughtful. "It's a wonderful gift that you have, being able to interact with other species."

"I assure you, it is no great joy to experience oneself and one's comrades as potential sources of sustenance. It is a blow both to the ego and the nerves."

"Truly, but you felt the bee's gratitude as well."

"Aye," he agreed. "That was nice."

Islaen sighed. "I can only pick up very strong human emotions or passions. Just about all of those are dark, to say the least. Anger is probably the best since that's at least frequently justified."

He smiled "You would not say that if you were not a virgin, Islaen Connor."

She flushed once, then colored again in anger. "Was I so clumsy last night?"

"Clumsy? I fell to your snare like a half-intoxicated menial!—Reason declares that you must be a maid. You could not have spoken as you did just now had you known a man and he you in the manner of male and female. The fires thus roused are strong, Islaen, and there should be nothing dark in them. There is nothing dark in desire, either," he added gravely after a brief pause, "provided it be honorable and no prelude to force."

She nodded. Both Jake and Morris had desired her . . . Her eyes lowered. "You're right, of course. It might have been different had Morris Martin lived, but when I had to assume command in his place, I couldn't afford the complications such involvement might bring, not with two men in my own unit and several more with whom I had constantly to deal in the Resistance leadership. In truth, I was just as happy this was so. Noreen's code is strict in such matters, and I'm not one to cast my beliefs aside easily."

Varn Tarl Sogan watched her averted face. So beautiful, he thought, able and yet strangely vulnerable. He was very glad this was her answer. Such a woman did not love lightly, and she could be damaged, badly damaged, martyred, if she gave heart and body unwisely. And the very idea of her being casually taken, used as a plaything, filled him with anger. To quell it, he spoke quickly and with rather more daring than he had intended.

"It would be glory to make love to you, Islaen, and to feel your body sing with mine, but that could never happen without your full willing in every aspect of your being." He caught himself and forced a grin. "I would also say this is hardly the time or situation for such experiment."

"Not by a far shot!" The woman found that she had to check a note of regret from creeping into her voice. There was a power in this man that even Morris had not possessed. Her eyes twinkled suddenly. "One thing for sure, you've certainly succeeded in taking my mind off that serpent."

He turned to the place where it had vanished from their sight. "I should never have imagined such a thing could be capable of climbing, much less at that speed."

"At least a few kinds can wherever similar species are found in conjunction with trees or cliffs."

"But the size of it! And its weight!"

"The spider-trees are big, too, don't forget, much sturdier than any of their highland counterparts, and the serpent itself may not actually have been that heavy. If it's adapted for an arboreal existence, it could be all powerful muscle and very light bone, maybe with a skeleton almost completely hollow or sporting large pockets of air. I've seen that on several other planets."

The dark eyes had returned to her. "You know so much," he remarked gravely.

"I—I have an interest in such things . . ."

The Arcturian laughed. "Gently, Colonel. I know full well that you do not boast. Your fascination with the natural realms of the galaxy is quite apparent."

"It's high time we were pressing on through *this* natural realm," the Commando said decisively. "Is there anything about to hinder us?"

Sogan listened intently with his mind. "Nothing."

His mouth hardened. "I would I were as quick to give warning when something is."

"No more of that!" Islaen sighed and walked a little distance from him. She came to a root three feet from the muddy ground and seated herself on it. She reached out her hand to her companion. "Come sit by me, Varn. I want to think."

He took her hand and allowed her to draw him down beside her but said nothing while the woman remained deep in thought.

She raised her head at last. "Varn, I don't know much about this power of yours. I don't even know all that much about my own. One thing is certain, though. It's a talent, and like every other talent, you've got to work with it to develop it. It'll take time and a lot of effort before you'll be able to use it with any real skill." She paused, nibbling at her lip as she struggled to present her conclusions logically. Sogan was at least listening, and she thought some of his frustration and feeling of failure had lifted a bit. If only she could raise it altogether, this false guilt he was putting on himself . . .

"I think our two gifts may be somewhat similar in the principles guiding them. If so, it'll be quite impossible for you to always concentrate on the transmissions around you. Sure, you wouldn't be able to do anything else; you'd probably wind up in another bog hole before you'd walked a hundred feet."

"What am I to do, then?" he demanded in exasperation. "Spot checking seems to leave a great deal to be desired."

"What I do. Train yourself to leave your receptors open while you're going about the general business of living. It's like a ship. A spacer doesn't really notice her while everything's normal, but let an unfamiliar rattle start up or an unusual trembling, or silence come where there should be a hum, and an alarm sounds inside him. Train yourself to listen so. It is, after all, but another sense, albeit a unique one."

The man had straightened while she was speaking. "You are right, Colonel. That might well be the answer."

"Just take your time. Don't tax yourself. After all, even at considerably less than your full potential, you're still giving us a lot more information through your power than we'd have without it."

"That also is true." A smile touched his lips. "You argue well, Colonel Connor."

"It's a skill necessary to the rank," she responded dryly. The Commando got to her feet. "We'd best get going."

She set out at a brisk pace. They had lost time which must now be made up, yet it was a delay she could not resent. She had benefited herself, and if her suggestion to Varn bore fruit, the aid he could give them might prove invaluable. Besides, there was no true need for speed, since she did not anticipate nearly as long or as difficult a passage today. Or was there? A shadow darkened her eyes until they appeared black. Danger could arise from more than one source. She forced that thought from her mind and grimly fixed it on the work before her.

TWELVE

TIME PASSED SLOWLY as they labored through the seemingly endless swamplands, but Sogan was relieved that their progress did not have to be purchased at such grueling cost as yesterday's had been. They stayed at a higher altitude, and Islaen told him they would probably not have to remain in the lowlands as long. She expected to reach the base of the plateau well before dark. If luck were with them, they could give a good beginning to the ascent of its lower slope before darkness forced a halt. By the following night, they should be in their permanent camp.

He hunched his shoulders as yet another squall of rain fell from the leaf-hidden sky. The cloudbursts were less crushing now, and they were not forced to stop each time one began. This was fortunate, as there seemed to be scarcely a few minutes respite between the downpours, and each of them lasted longer than those preceding it.

He hated it, this rain that only added to the breathless misery of the swamp and churned the already wet ground into a quagmire. He thanked the Empire's hard gods that they had not been forced to contend with this volume of water the previous day. However Islaen would have fared, he had no illusions about what his own performance would have been; he had scarcely been able to keep going as it was.

He was doing better today. The way was easier, of course, and that accounted for much of it, but still, he believed himself to be surer of foot and quicker of eye. He had taken some of that hard experience to heart, making it his own. Perhaps he would have been better off if it was less true. He would surely have been easier in his mind. With the need to concentrate solely on his movements lessened he was able to study his companion, not merely as his guide but in herself. More than once, he thought he detected a shadow, a dark pensiveness on her.

What troubled her? She claimed to be free of unreasonable fear, and so he must believe this heaviness to be born of concrete cause. Some personal matter released to rise to her conscious mind with the physical easing of their journey? Perhaps. There was a great deal more to her life than this single series of moments. She might be mourning her slain comrade, this Jake Karmikel whose close friendship she had owned. She surely had a right to those thoughts, whatever their source, without his interference.

Despite his acceptance of that fact, he could feel worry rising sharply within him. While they remained together in this wilderness, everything that was of concern to her was perforce of concern to him as well. At last, to keep himself from jumping at mental shadows, he set himself to the task of trying to deduce the cause of her difficulty, using what he knew of her and of her mission on Visnu as the base for his search.

All this while, the Arcturian kept trying his power as Islaen had suggested. His success was not total, especially not at first. He felt the strain of wielding his mind in this fashion and was forced to withdraw into himself and rest fairly frequently. However, passive listening was dramatically easier than active seeking, and he found himself the recipient of a remarkable amount of information, more than he could properly evaluate. His lack of knowledge concerning Visnu's wildlife, any wildlife for that matter, was crippling him far worse than his unfamiliarity with this strange, newly awakened sense of his.

He was amazed by the number of touches he received. The swampland might not be rich in life by the standards of other planets, but it existed in far greater frequency and variety than one with his untrained eyes would have deemed possible.

There was a tension in every one of those contacts, not fear, but more a wariness, an expectation. He described it to Islaen but had to say that he could find no immediate cause for it. Their own presence did not seem to be setting it off, nor was any specific predator that he could detect. It could well be that this was the normal state of wild things which must ever live with the cycle of feeding and hunting and being hunted. Islaen could give him no answer; she was no more familiar with their thought-ways than he was.

Varn Tarl Sogan made himself content with that answer, but he maintained his vigilance, often breaking the pattern of reception with more purposeful searches. While any trace of unease remained, he was determined to hold himself on the alert. Never again would danger come on them because he was slow with the warning. That he vowed to himself and, on his soul, to his companion.

One point he did note. The rain might be in a large part responsible for maintaining the swamp and, thus, the creatures living in and about it, but none of them had much liking for it. The tension rose at the beginning of each new downpour and did not ease again until well after the final drops had fallen.

The change came without signal that he could detect. The man stopped almost in his stride, hissing a warning to the woman as he did so.

Fear, and very sharp.

The source was near. He saw it, a long, dark thing oozing its way along the ground, leaving a shiny, silvery trail behind it. This was only some thirty-six inches in length, but he recognized it by its track as being akin to whatever had caused the damage to the thicket during their first night in the wild.

It reached a root and began slithering up its underside. The man suddenly realized there was motion all around them! He saw a small serpent glide up a trunk to his right. His eyes caught a fluttering movement along a branch, although he was not quick enough to discover its source.

His mind told him much more. Whatever creatures had been on the ground were hastening toward the leafy canopy far above. Quickly and tersely, he described the situation for the Commando-Colonel.

Her eyes swept the area around them. "Is the fear great?"

He shook his head. "It is mostly anxiety. Only these slugs

and a couple of other things are actually afraid.''

"They are presumably slow movers or slow climbers as well. Is the reaction localized?"

"It holds for the full of my range. Admittedly, that is no very great distance, but I must assume it extends somewhat beyond as well."

"Maybe a goodly distance beyond."

"Do we run?"

"We climb." The brown eyes fixed sharply on him. "Are you able? We'll have to get to the lowest branches."

"I find I am able for many things."

She studied the tree nearest her critically. "This should do. The trunk isn't too thick. I'll go up first and then drop a rope down to you. You should be able to get to it and then use it to help you from there." While she was speaking, she had unclasped her belt. She now slipped it from around her waist and fastened the things it had been supporting to her pack. That done, she cleaned the mud from the treads of her boots so they would have the maximum possible grip. "Hoist me up as far as you can onto this root. I'll go from there myself."

He grinned, forcing himself to tease her, in order to lift some of the tension gripping her, gripping them both. "I thought you could climb."

She read his purpose and answered in kind. "Why climb when I can get a lift? Besides, I don't want to get my boots dirty again."

He lifted her, then pulled himself up beside her. He had not reached her side before the woman had clasped her belt around the trunk. Using it for support, moving it ever so slowly upward as she advanced, she began the dizzying ascent to the branches. Higher, ever higher, she went with agonizing slowness while fear swelled within him. She had gone too far now but nothing like far enough. If she lost her grip . . .

She was up, straddling the branch which had been her target. A rope came down. It did not nearly reach the ground, but if he fell before reaching it, he might still hope to try again.

"Varn!"

No more delaying. He had prepared himself as the Commando had done while he had been watching her. Now he began his own ascent. His technique was clumsy compared to the woman's, but he thought that he could make it, just barely make it. Balance was difficult to maintain; the strain on the muscles of his arms and shoulders, his legs, was incredible. He marveled that one so slight had been able to do this at all.

The rope was before him. Carefully, very carefully, he reached for it and, using one hand, drew the wide noose at its end about himself. It was with a rush of relief that he fastened it and set the knot so that it would not draw in any tighter under the shock of a fall. If he slipped now, the strong cord and the tree to which it was bound would let him drop no farther than this point.

The remainder of the climb was no easier, but the security provided by the rope helped. It seemed a remarkably short while before he hauled himself onto the branch behind the Federation officer, catching hold of her small, firm hands to steady himself.

He had his balance in another moment, but still, he had no liking for their perch. It was firm enough, but frightfully narrow, and it seemed to him that nearly any shifting of weight or position might throw them down.

That thought burned in his mind as he watched his companion. She was sitting astride the branch, clasping it tightly with her legs while she used her hands to haul up the rope. She felt his eyes on her and glanced at him as she turned to fasten the line to her pack. She gave him a smile. "No use issuing any unnecessary invitations to whatever's on its way."

"No." He managed to keep his dislike of their position from his voice, but Islaen either shared it herself or else read it in the stiffness of his body or from his mind.

"Ease yourself in toward the trunk," she advised. "Set your back against it."

He obeyed and found the solid wood a decided comfort. "What about you?"

"Will you hold me?"

"Aye." His heart gave a leap when she started moving toward him at a rate he considered entirely too fast. "Slowly! I cannot reach so far!"

The woman smiled but obligingly eased her advance until his steadying arms closed around her. She relaxed against him with an open sigh of relief. The Arcturian felt the tension leave her and realized she had been as nervous as he. "We can take it easy now, for a while at least," he said to reassure her.

"That's good to hear, but I hope it won't be for too long. I can see our nest getting very uncomfortable very quickly."

He laughed. He could almost see the face she had made. "I think you have read our position well, as always." He paused, watching the auburn head smouldering against his shoulder. "We make a good team, Islaen Connor."

"I'm very glad of that." The emphasis she had put into those words surprised him. She knew it and gave a little laugh, half-embarrassed, half-defiant. "On Thorne I always regretted that fate had made enemies of us instead of comrades. I suppose I see our being able to work together now as a kind of vindication of that."

His eyes darkened. "I have no complaint against fate. She was generous in never giving you over into my power, neither you nor one of your close comrades." He felt her shudder and knew her thought. "Peace, Islaen. The War broke many besides myself in one manner or another. I must be thankful that it did not make me take the life of one destined to be my friend."

He looked into a distance beyond the screen of leaves and wood. "I must praise every god in this vast universe and beyond that it did not make a monster of me." Sogan shook the darkness from his soul. It was on their present danger that he must concentrate.

Danger it was, and close. He could sense it, taste it, in the touches he received from those things sheltering all around them. His arms tightened painfully about the woman.

"Ravagers!" He felt them now as he had felt them the previous night, but in numbers beyond belief. The first army now seemed nothing by comparison.

He fixed his eyes to the north. All remained quiet, too still, and unchanged for several eternal seconds longer. Then a dead black stain began creeping over the dark brown of the mud. Marched over it. It was a living shadow, a mass of small, moving creatures, each so close to its neighbors that no trace of ground was to be seen between any two of them.

The Commando's distance lenses were hooked to the pack she had drawn across her chest. She freed them, gazed through them awhile, then handed them to Sogan.

The things below were not large in the manner of the slugs or the serpent, but they were by no means minute. They had to be ten inches long. The distance was too great for him to make out any details, even with the aid of the sensitive lenses. The man prayed fervently that it would remain so. All the hunger of last night was present again, multiplied many times over. No creature, human or beast, could hope to oppose such a multitude. Death could be the only outcome of any contact between them.

Something above them stirred uneasily. A small twig with several leaves attached to it broke loose and fell to the ground. In the next instant, it was gone. The ravagers did not so much as break their stride while they devoured it.

Varn's stomach twisted violently, and he had to fight himself not to become openly sick. Great, warring fleets, human foes and their weapons, even that serpent, those he could endure, but this was something different. His eyes closed, then opened again. Horror seemed to compel them to remain fixed on the black, living stain below. This was life and yet scarcely life. There was no real mind, just the vast, all-encompassing drive to consume.

The incredible army was everywhere. The creatures scrambled up the roots, using them as living bridges to the trunks, blackening them in their search for still-green suckers or shoots. Would they come this high? He realized now that most of Visnu's life was considerably above them . . .

No nearer! Please, no nearer! If they started coming up this trunk, he knew he must go mad.

Sogan took hold of himself. If the trees provided refuge for Visnu's creatures, why not for two human off-worlders as well? He must make that hope suffice. He couldn't afford to give way like this. For Islaen's sake, he dared not.

Very quietly, he freed his blaster, released the safety catch. This lovely woman might know terror before the day ended, but she would never experience the agony that horde down there would bring to anything it overtook. The determination, the emotion, on him was powerful. His companion caught it and twisted her body so that she might look upon him.

Her great eyes rested on the weapon. "Let it be as you think best," she said very softly, "but, by the gods, move in time to assure yourself release as well."

Her head raised then, and when she spoke, determination rang in her voice. "Remember, though, they fear fire. We are warriors, both of us, and trained to give battle before we embrace death."

"I have not forgotten it, Islaen." The man looked upon her

in wonder, but screened the feelings gripping him so powerfully. This valiant and able woman had put her life into his
hands with those words of hers, and his heart trembled lest he
fail what had become for him an awesome trust.

That was not for now, with their enemies ravening so close
below them.

He glanced upward. "Shall we go higher?"

"There would be little use in it. If they reach this branch,
the distance is short to the others. What do our companions-
in-peril feel?"

Varn snapped his mind out. He had forgotten their fellow
fugitives. "Concern. High tension. Nothing more."

"We're probably secure. If they could have reached our
branch, it most likely wouldn't be here at all. There are no
others all the way down except those twigs just below us." Her
words came calmly, almost casually. If he could not feel the
tightness of her body against his, he would have imagined her
completely at ease.

The insects climbed higher and higher, crawling along the
ariel roots. They drew closer to Varn and Islaen. Man and
woman both stared, frozen in terror, each trying to spare the
other his fear.

Abruptly, the insects stopped. They had reached the point
where root joined trunk, and there, praise Visnu's gods! they
were halted. Clambering up on one another, they struggled to
reach the prey and the lush, gold-green foliage of the canopy,
but they could go no farther. Unlike the rest of Visnu's
animal life, these could not climb.

It was only a matter of minutes before the whole area in the
view of the two humans was cleared of every edible thing
within reach of the ravagers.

All the while, the main body of the army kept moving, ever
pressing forward into new areas ripe for harvesting. It traveled
fast as well as constantly, yet so great was the number of
creatures taking part in that march that half an hour and more
passed before the last left off their feeding and rejoined the
horde.

Neither Islaen nor Varn moved for a long time after the
dark shadow had vanished from their sight, not until the man
could report that peace had returned to the creatures around
them. Their own descent was slow and cautious. Sogan went

first, availing himself of the rope's aid. The woman then released it and came down by herself.

They stood silently together at the base of the tree which had been their refuge. Both were shaken. They had read of such things, of course, but the actual witnessing of it, the power and terror of its reality, made mockery of studied knowledge.

"This is a planet of horror," the Arcturian said more to break the oppressive silence than to state the obvious.

"She is that," the woman agreed, "but she's balanced in her own fashion.

"The ravagers and maybe other things like them rule the ground, and so most creatures have taken to the treetops or can at least flee where the armies can't reach. If they could climb, then all life would quickly be annihilated, themselves along with their victims since they would assure their own starvation, and Visnu would be left an unquickened ball."

"It is a wonder the trees survive. They must succumb to age or injury occasionally, and the ravagers must take most of the seedlings."

"Aye. Probably only those germinating and developing to the point of producing true wood in very dry years which are unfavorable to the ravagers make it. They seem safe enough after that."

"What happens to the ravagers? Surely, they do not all die off after a march."

"They could, the most of them." The Commando shrugged. "It'd probably take years of study to answer that. Maybe it's like I said this morning. They might go underground during dry times, coil themselves into living nests around their queen or queens, and hibernate. When the rains get heavy enough for the water to reach them, signaling soft ground and new growth, the wet could wake them, triggering their hunger."

"They seem to dislike rain.

"Falling on them, but perhaps not its effects. I'm only guessing, of course."

"It sounds logical at least." He glanced around them. "Shall we be going?"

"We might as well. This is probably one of the safest places on Visnu right now, but we can't stay here forever."

THIRTEEN

THE TWO HUMANS pushed on grimly, each cheering himself with the thought that they had only a couple more miles of swampland left to cross before they could begin their ascent to the plateau. Neither of them would feel easy again until they were well away from the mud and all its dangers.

They had lost a lot of time that day, and the light was already beginning to fail when they at last moved into highland territory once more. The Commando-Colonel stopped beside a small spring and gave a little sigh. There would be no real ascent now, no start on the morning's work.

Her companion came up beside her. "It is not as pleasant a site as last night's," he remarked.

"No, but there is water. We'll take as much of it as we can with us, just in case we might have to withstand a bit of a siege."

"Into the trees?"

She nodded. "Aye. We can't risk staying down here after dark, not this close to the swamp. We'll make a platform so we won't tumble off. It'll be easy enough to dismantle it come morning. We'll be cold without a fire, but there's no help for that."

Once again, Varn found himself serving as apprentice in the construction of their camp. The task was more complex than

the previous night's, but the woman's survival training was the
equal of it. The ravagers had apparently not visited the area in
some time. Underbrush was heavy, and a good part of it had
developed into wood of a size and strength sufficient for their
needs. Using supple young branches as bindings, she soon had
lashed together sections of a small platform which they then
raised with the aid of her rope and bound into place. Last of
all, she constructed a rough canopy to shield them from the inevitable rain.

Varn tested the flimsy-looking structure a bit dubiously but
found it sturdier than he had supposed. The two strong
branches to which it was anchored gave it good support, and
he felt that there was little danger of rolling off it, narrow
though it was.

The former officer seated himself beside the woman and
gratefully accepted the supplies she handed him. It was necessary to force himself to eat slowly. Islaen had promised
short rations tonight, and these were that. His body wanted
more after the exertions of this long day.

There was little conversation between them. They were both
tired, and the pensive mood he had noticed throughout their
march seemed to have settled over the woman in full measure.
Her thoughts were obviously far from the camp despite her efforts to conceal the full extent of her preoccupation.

"Is it the settlers?" he asked abruptly. "You are worried
about them?"

Islaen's head snapped toward him. "Can you now read
human minds?"

"No. It was merely a deduction."

She sighed. "An accurate one."

"The ravagers or our own kind?"

"The former."

"Rest easy. Granted, I paid little attention to the countryside around the settlement, but from what I do recall, it
bears far less sign of disturbance than any area we have seen
since leaving it."

"That may have been true in the past, since the plateau is
essentially a desolate and dry region," she answered grimly,
"but I'll warrant it holds so no longer."

The Commando frowned. "It now makes a tempting target
for any hungry horde with the crops just coming ripe. . . . And
there's the concentration of meat."

He shivered inwardly at that last but kept his mind and voice calm. "You are not concerned at all about what the developers might do? You have said that entire colonies have vanished before this."

"Prior to threatened investigation. Whatever else they may be, those men back there are not utterly stupid. They know that what they believe to have been the Patrol was here for some time, and they know part of the unit escaped. Even if the *Meteor* didn't make it through, I did. They don't know what equipment I have or what reports went out before we were uncovered. Furthermore, we had aid from a completely unsuspected source whom they can only take to be an ally, and they'll now have to beware of more of the like.

"No, they'll be very careful to avoid adding mass murder to the rest of the charges against them. They can survive or even hope to avoid the consequences of all the others, but not that."

"Why not?" he asked bluntly. "They were able to stage the attack on your unit quite easily, and you will never be able to lay the responsibility on them. They might cover their guilt in the extermination of the settlers as readily."

"They could possibly avoid legal punishment, though that's most unlikely, but the name of every one of them is known, and the fact of their guilt would be known, too. Commandos and Patrol are alike in their acceptance of danger. Our unavenged deaths would burn but would be swallowed. The wanton destruction of an entire community of helpless people, people who had already been terribly wronged by being lured into the danger and almost inevitable heartbreak of trying to settle an unapproved planet, that goes deeper. There's a horror to it which would of itself demand and receive justice."

Her eyes and voice were bleak, hard. "Word of some deeds can spread very quickly if properly seeded. Annihilation would be assured in less than a year, and all that little remaining time would be a waking nightmare."

"You would be party to that?" Sogan asked.

"I don't know. I never have been, certainly. It's rare, and I don't actually know for a fact of its ever having been used in any semiofficial sense. Perhaps I wouldn't join the effort, but that would be irrelevant. I could neither stop it nor influence its outcome."

Once more, cold anger glittered in her eyes. "Right or

wrong, I'll guarantee you that such action would do more to discourage like activities than all the conventional sentences laid down since the founding of the Federation. There's something terrifying about the rage of a people.''

The Arcturian said nothing for a moment. He, after three years' struggle to maintain the secret of his own race, was too well aware of the truth of that. ''There are other malignant forces on Visnu besides the developers,'' he said at last. ''Many of those working for them are more used to precipitating violence than considering its consequences.''

''Their bosses have them in much better hand than the attack on us would seem to indicate. They willed that, don't forget. Besides, I can't see them in that role. They're spacers, however rough, not out-and-out pirates. Men who wouldn't pause before burning down one of their own kind or a Patrol agent if they felt themselves threatened still usually hesitate before slaughtering children.''

''There could be individuals . . .''

''Granted, though I think your flame thrower may have eliminated the worst, that and flight after our escape. It doesn't really matter. A single man's rampage would be both pointless and detrimental to the interests of the others. It's not likely it would be permitted.''

Her expression darkened. ''The crews are more likely to desert, make off quickly and leave both colonists and developers to their fate.''

''That is your fear?''

She nodded. ''Aye. The Navy won't have arrived yet, and I little like seeing all those people without transport off-world when some very hungry creatures are growing ever more active no great distance from the settlement.''

The man stared at the platform on which he sat. ''What if word to hasten were sent to the Navy?''

''If transmitted in the proper code, they would comply, but I don't have an instrument powerful enough. My communicator is just for fairly close-range contact between team members.''

''A starship's unit should be more than sufficient.''

''Of course.''

He paused, still not looking at her. ''The *Fairest Maid* is well equipped.''

The guerrilla officer's eyes rested on him as if she were

weighing his words. "You're assuming she's still intact."

"If they have not turned some pretty high-power artillery on her, she should be. A spacer traveling the starlanes alone has good cause to guard himself, even without a history such as mine. I had the skill to secure myself well when I came upon the remains of a small fighter shortly after taking to space. The *Maid* has Navy-strength energy screens and voice-locks to defend her."

"And if we reached her and found her whole?"

"We would lift fast and set whatever course you dictated. You could start transmitting as soon as we cleared gravity."

"You're assuming a peaceful departure."

He lifted his head for the first time. "She can defend herself, as I imagine your *Meteor* can, and she has speed. There will be risk, naturally, but unless fate is set full against us, our enemies should have nothing to match us in either battle or race."

"If the *Maid's* defenses have been breached?".

The man grinned. "I doubt there is any ship on Visnu that we two together cannot take, and none at all that I cannot fly once she has been seized."

Islaen's great eyes fixed on him. "I'm aware of the last," she told him gravely. "I've been weighing it most of the day."

"You did not speak?"

"You've done a great deal already. I had no right to ask you to risk more, not when it's only my fear of danger and no actual emergency that's driving me. I don't think I'm too wrong in believing you would still sooner chance death than exposure, even though your peril would be far less than you'd imagined."

His eyes fell again. "That is so." Sogan forced himself to face her. "Will your comrades have betrayed me?"

"I don't know. I think not, but they'd have been proud to have had your help and proud to own it. They were with me on Thorne."

He pondered that for a moment. "It is a matter beyond our controlling, nor should it affect the question before us.

"Whether they have spoken or not, they cannot know anything of my activities since we separated. Surely, the pilot who brings a Commando off-world as his passenger is free to go his own way again once he has duly delivered her to her destination. I should not perforce have to become involved with your Navy or the Patrol because I have chosen to assist you."

"In theory, no. You should not. Reality may prove otherwise." The brown eyes held his. "I'll do my best to shield you, Varn, but I can't guarantee that will be possible."

He sighed but then nodded. "I can ask no more. If I decide not to help you, you will make the attempt alone? Has that thought also been in your mind?"

Now it was the woman who looked away. "Aye, it has."

"With what result?"

"I must—"

"Leave me to the ravagers?"

His eyes were dancing, but she did not respond to their merriment. "It'd be worse than abandoning my own self, but there are just too many lives at hazard . . ."

He laughed. His voice was tender when he spoke. "You are worthy of rank, Islaen Connor, but your resolve shall not be put to the test. I stay with you until this affair is brought to its conclusion."

"Varn . . ."

"No, Colonel, say no more. For three years now, I have lived, barely existed, without any purpose save the preserving of my own being. I had come to regard myself as a parasite on the universe, one leeching its resources and returning nothing to it. With the opportunity to be of service once again mine, I should be a fool to refuse it."

Islaen looked at him closely, then reached over and kissed him lightly upon the lips. "You are a man, Varn Tarl Sogan."

FOURTEEN

THEY DIVIDED THAT night into two watches as they had the previous one. Although there were several heavy showers, nothing troubled their rest, and both greeted the morning, a bright one, cheerfully and well rested despite their damp and chilly quarters.

They ate on the platform, then dismantled it and so scattered its parts that no one could have guessed two human beings had passed the night in this place.

Noreenan and Arcturian were alike in their eagerness to begin the day's march. There would be no returning to the horrors of the swamp. The climb ahead would not be an easy one, but they would be working in comfortable temperatures and in relative security from all but their own species. Best of all, the end of their long trek was before them. They would make camp once more, and there they would remain until they were ready to move against the spaceport.

At first, the ascent was not too difficult, merely a continuation of what they had experienced before halting the previous day. Gradually, however, the grade sharpened until they were gaining better than a foot's altitude for every two they advanced.

Vegetation was sparse, particularly on the steeper places, and such areas showed the signs of heavy weathering. Soil was scanty and hard, the stone broken and loose under foot so that both found it wise to stoop and scramble, using hands and feet alike to seek for holds.

Short-lived but penetrating rainfalls plagued them throughout the morning, making the ground slippery and even more difficult to negotiate.

Islaen clamped her jaw so tightly that the muscles ached as she clambered over the crest of yet another miniature cliff. She had gone up that one painfully on her stomach, and had believed it the last. Now she saw another, higher and steeper, rising before her.

Sogan scrambled up beside her. They lay there side by side, trying to catch their breaths before tackling that next, unexpected obstacle. "I was scarcely more covered with mud down in the swamp," he grumbled when his breathing had returned to something like its normal rate.

"Would you care to go back there?" his companion challenged.

"Not after working this hard to leave it!"

She grinned. "Oh, but the return wouldn't be nearly so difficult. All you'd have to do is roll."

"Thank you, but I think I prefer to forego that particular journey."

The woman got to her feet. "We might as well continue with this one, I suppose." She sighed. "Noreen is a nice, civilized, flat world. Sometimes I wonder why I didn't listen to my brothers and stay there."

He gave her a strange look. "I should like to have known you as you were then, that young girl you were."

"She's gone long since. Too much has happened for it to be otherwise."

"No, not gone. She has matured into a beautiful and able woman—Your kin, they are still alive? You mentioned that your parents were aged."

"Oh, aye, both of them. Noreen's race is quite long-lived."

"Your brothers?"

"Tam's a full physician now with a good practice, and Will has the farm. Both of them are wed, of course, and have wee ones of their own, a couple each. I try to get home to see them all whenever I have a furlough long enough to make it worthwhile."

"They are proud of you?"

"I've followed a road very different from the usual one, but, aye, that they are."

"I am glad to hear it," he responded slowly. "Sometimes, it is not so when a person deviates from the lifeway custom has assigned to him. I should have been sorry if that had happened to you."

"A heroine to all but my own?" Her eyes shadowed. "It might all too easily have been the case. We're a proud people and not always too tolerant of change, I suppose because we had to fight so hard for our traditions in the past. I think Mother exercised some of her power in my cause, both within our family and amongst our neighbors."

She smiled. "That would have been back in the very beginning. I'm fully accepted on my own merits now." Her chin lifted. "We've had our warrior-queens, too, or our legends badly lie, so I'm not really terribly alien."

Warrior-queen or no, the ridge was still before her and would remain before her until she had scaled it.

It proved to be the worst they had yet encountered, and only her pride kept her from asking aid of Varn.

No, it was more than mere pride. He knew she was having difficulty, but so, too, did she realize that he was struggling hard to make progress against the slope. She would not add to his battle, not while she could manage by herself.

She heaved herself over the edge at last, none too soon for her weary muscles. Whatever about her near exhaustion, there could be no rest this time, not immediately. This was the plateau, and, uncommon as they might be this far from the port and this long after their escape, they had to beware of air patrols.

She gave her hand to aid her companion, who was following a few paces behind her. Once he was up they started to run, crouching low, until they reached the trees, the outer fringe of which was set well back from the weathered rim.

Only then did they allow themselves to relax. They were quiet this time while Islaen tried to place them in relation to the settlement, drawing upon the information she had gleaned during the exploratory excursions she had made with Jake.

In the end, she smiled at her companion. "We're in luck, I think. If I'm not really off in my calculations, the cave I want is not very far. If we make that our headquarters, we'll be within a couple of days' march of our target, near enough to reach it easily and still so distant as to be able to consider ourselves reasonably secure.''

"It sounds good to me." The man hesitated. "What will happen to them?" he asked. "To these settlers?"

"They'll be taken off with all possible speed and maintained until they can be resettled on some other world of their choosing. There are just too many possibilities for disaster to leave them on Visnu during the testing period, even were there much hope of her getting colonization approval."

"Will they have the resources to begin again? From what I understand, these are not wealthy folk."

She nodded. "Aye, if they still have the heart. They'll be compensated for all they lost to this in a material sense, but there's no way to restore all their labor, all they put of themselves into their homesteads here." Her lips tightened. "I only hope we'll be able to evacuate them before anything does happen."

"Is that true concern or your fear of Visnu?"

She frowned. "True concern, or so I believe.—Varn, my every sense screams danger. It's not a warning I can ignore."

"No, you cannot. One who has lived long with peril and commanded others in its shadow must become sensitive to it. I do not have your knowledge of Visnu and do not share your native dislike of her, but I, too, feel disaster's shade upon me. Whatever we do or do not, I believe speed to be of the essence both for ourselves and for those others dwelling here."

FIFTEEN

THEIR JOURNEY DURING the next several hours was almost pleasant, except for the rain that kept their clothing soaked and the need to remain ever on the alert for patrols. The ground was fairly level and not difficult to travel despite the relatively heavy cover of undergrowth—proof that the ravagers did not visit up here with any great frequency. They were able to maintain a brisk pace, fortunately so, for the trees were widely enough spaced to permit good play to a wind as cold as any they remembered from the port.

They stopped only once to eat and rest, and by early afternoon they had reached their destination. The Commando-Colonel called a halt some distance from their target. She and Jake Karmikel had discovered it early in their exploring, marking it in their memories as a potential bolt hole. Others might have as well.

"I'll slip in close and see if anyone—or anything—seems to be about."

Sogan made her no answer. The danger was not great, he knew. He could detect any animal presence, and any human would have to be remarkably skilled to conceal himself from Islaen's trained senses. Even were that not so, he could offer no protest. The test had to be made if they would use the

115

place, and he lacked her ability to approach it with the
necessary stealth.

The possibility of trouble was so slight as to be almost
nonexistent. He realized that, and yet still he cursed himself
for his uselessness. He would be right glad to get back to the
port where he could assume an equal's share in their work
—and their hazards.

While these thoughts were roiling her companion's mind,
the guerrilla officer was creeping forward toward the dark
opening in the side of the low hill. She lay concealed, studying
it intently, for what seemed an eternity. All appeared to be in
order, yet something inside her said it was not vacant.

Her mind went out. Islaen's heart leaped. This was a pattern
she well knew! Her fingers tapped out the recognition code on
her communicator. Surprise! Delight!

"Islaen Connor!"

"Here, Jake!"

"Right! Now, don't burn me when I show myself!"

"No fear of that!"

The red-haired man stepped out into Visnu's light. Scarcely
had he done so than she was in his arms, kissing him wildly
in her joy. When he at last freed himself, he was grinning
broadly. "Such unmilitary fervor, Colonel!"

"Never you mind, you big space tramp. I'm happier than
you'll ever know to see you intact." She eyed the plastitape
covering his temple. "Almost intact, anyway.—You're all
right?"

"Sure thing. It's only a surface sear. I've left this on to keep
it dry. The weather's been abominable."

"Tell me about it," she said dryly. She glanced back over
her shoulder. "Wait here a minute. I'll go get Varn before he
really starts worrying." The woman darted out of his sight
with those words. She soon returned, bringing Sogan with her.

Karmikel eyed the other coldly. "You bastard," he hissed.
"You left me to die back there!"

"Jake!"

Islaen put herself between them. "Don't be a fool. He intended to take us both. That was impossible when we were
separated."

The Arcturian took a step forward. "I can speak for myself,
Colonel.—What she says is true. There was not time to pick
you both up. I believed you dead anyway and beyond all help-

ing, but even were that not so and I had been forced to choose between you, I should have brought Islaen out over you. I think that choice would have been yours had our positions been reversed."

"I would have had reason . . ."

"As did I! My people hold rank in high esteem. Hers was the greater, and so it is only to be expected that she would be the one I should save." His manner softened suddenly. "I am glad to find that you did survive and made good your escape."

The other continued glaring a moment longer, then he gave up the argument. The man had never been careless of life or a coward, and this open place was no spot in which to be conducting an involved discussion. "I believe you, Admiral, and I certainly cannot fault your choice. As you pointed out, it's the one I'd have made myself." He jerked his thumb towards the cave. "Come on inside. I want to hear about that weapon you used.—Watch your heads. The ceiling's low, and I'll vouch for the hardness of the stone."

Jake remained outside a moment after the others had entered the cave. The scowl had returned to his face, and his eyes bore into Varn's retreating back. His battle training and his Colonel's order forced him to cool his temper despite his own feelings and desire. Inwardly, he raged at the quirk of fate which had brought them together with their old enemy. Circumstances demanded that they work as a unit, and so they must, but he did not like the idea, and he did not completely trust the man despite Islaen's obvious acceptance of him. She had always favored Sogan, maybe enough to cloud her talent in respect to him.

His expression darkened still further. He would start no trouble, but let that son of a Scythian ape make one false move, let him so much as seem to *think* of making a false move, and he would rip him apart. With his own two hands, he would tear the life out of him.

Karmikel felt his fingers begin to curl and hastily brought himself under control. He shot a guilty glance toward the cave. If Islaen's receptors had chanced to be open just now, she would of a certainty have picked up his hostility. He flushed and hastened inside, resolving to keep himself in better check, at least until the Navy picked them up. Visnu had to be considered enemy territory, after all, and they could afford no divisions in their minute force.

The newcomers found the cave to be a narrow, deep chamber of gray rock some seven feet wide and twenty long. As Karmikel had warned, the roof rose no more than five and a half feet from the floor at its highest point. Even Islaen was forced to stoop.

It was damp and chilly despite the small fire illuminating the rear portion. The rest was quite dark. Varn thought that it must be a bleak spot indeed at night or whenever Brahmin chose to be less than generous with her light.

When all three were settled, Jake again asked about Sogan's fireball, and Varn described to him in some detail the device he had constructed.

While he spoke, the redhead's grudging respect gave way to open admiration. "Admiral, I'd set you at the head of the best Commando unit ever formed."

The other man smiled and shook his head. "I should be a poor candidate for that role, I fear. I have learned something of what it entails these last few days."

"You've carried yourself well through it all," the Colonel interjected. "The skills you still lack, we had to acquire ourselves—and were less quick in mastering them, I may add."

"Probably because you did not have to learn them in the field," he countered.

Jake raised his hands. "Peace! All this does me very little good. If you two would be kind enough to start from the time Sogan came tearing down that street, I'd be most appreciative. I dislike getting my reports piecemeal."

His commander laughed and then related their adventures in full, occasionally turning to Varn for confirmation of some point. The Captain listened intently. He looked swiftly upon the other man when she first mentioned his power, but otherwise kept his attention fixed on her.

When she had done, she inclined her head toward Jake. "Now for your tale."

"It's pretty bland fare to follow yours," he said as he began his own account of how he had regained consciousness on the deserted, fire-blackened street and used the chaos left in the wake of their flight to cover his own escape.

All three remained quiet some while after he had finished speaking. It was Islaen who broke the silence. "You've seen nothing of Visnu's wildlife?"

He shook his head. "A few small things have scuttled about, but nothing very dramatic. I've been lucky there from what you say."

"Lucky indeed."

"Perhaps the plateau will remain inviolate," Varn suggested without much conviction; anyone who had seen the ravagers and experienced their hunger in his own mind could not doubt that they would soon exploit so lush a food source as the highland region now was.

"We can't depend on that," Karmikel said sharply.

"No, that we cannot."

"What about the port, Jake?" the woman asked tensely. "You say you checked it out before heading for this place. Are there many ships left?"

"Some, a good few actually, but a lot did lift after our escape, and more may have gone since I quit the area."

"It's a wonder they didn't all go."

"I'd say those who elected to stay will have been promised a very substantial bonus for doing so. It's amazing what that can do to strengthen courage. Besides, they need wait only until the developers can close up their operation, grab what they want, and get out. That shouldn't be much longer now."

"The *Meteor?*"

"Safe to my knowledge. At least, she made it off-world and out of Visnu's near-space." He glanced at the dark-eyed man. "Your vessel's sound, too, or she was. I checked on her as well before making for here. They couldn't breach her guards and so just left her as she was. I suppose they plan to take care of her at some point later, when things settle down a bit."

"We had hoped it would be thus." Varn took care to keep his relief out of his voice. It was surprisingly keen, much more so than he had anticipated. His close association with the small ship over the past three years had given him a feeling for her that he had never experienced for the great fleet that had once flown and fought at his willing.

The Commando-Captain did not question his companions' intention of using the *Fairest Maid* for their escape. They would stand a better chance of success in a vessel familiar to one of their party.

He glanced at the entrance. It was raining again. That coupled with the advancing evening darkened their shelter until little could be seen beyond the small circle of light cast by

their fire. The feeling of damp had increased with the loss of
the sun-star's diurnal heat. Although they were out of reach of
the wind, all three were conscious of the cold. Each would
welcome his blanket tonight.

Jake rose to his feet and stretched as far as the low ceiling
would permit. He walked to the entrance, where he stood
looking out into the night for several minutes, taking care to
stay well behind the sheltering lip of stone.

He returned to his companions once more. "It's hard at it."

"We're lucky to be inside," the woman said with a shiver
that was only partly exaggerated.

"Maybe so, but after some of your experiences, I can't say
I'm totally happy about it. If something we can't fight comes
marching in, we could be in pretty big trouble."

"That, my dear Captain, is the problem with caves, as you
well know."

"Indeed, I do, Colonel, but I was only thinking of human
enemies when I decided to use it, not of having my bones
picked bare by an army of little monsters, or of being swallowed whole by a titanic snake."

She laughed. "Neither did anyone else, unfortunately, or
we shouldn't have to be here at all." The woman shifted her
position to bring herself a bit closer to the fire. "Be glad of the
rain, friend. It may give us a chilling, but it does seem to keep
the ravagers quiet."

"Aye, but it can stop at any time and let them get to traveling again, probably with sharpened appetites."

Varn looked beyond the fire. Almost automatically, he sent
out his mind in an active search. "There is no sign of them and
no trace of unease among the other creatures near us."

"For now."

"I can pick up a change fairly quickly. If I watch the night
through, I should be able to give us good warning of any approaching trouble."

"No!"

There was command in that, and he turned to face the Colonel. "You object?"

"I must. We've had none too much sleep as it is these past
two nights, and you above all of us must be fully alert tomorrow and the next day. You'll have to get us into the *Maid* and
then bring us off-world and through to Horus."

Both men straightened. "You plan to move so soon?" Jake

asked in surprise. "I should have thought a couple of days' rest . . ."

She shook her head. "We can't risk it, not when it's only a matter of time until we're attacked. If we don't get out of this cave, we're asking to be trapped in it. Your concern is all too well founded."

"Islaen is right," the former Admiral agreed, "though I confess I would prefer a little more time before starting off again."

Karmikel sighed. "I haven't been quite as active as you, to put it mildly. I'll take the first watch and make it the longest."

Varn thought the Colonel would be quick to protest that, but when she merely nodded her assent, he held his peace as well. Apparently, the needs of a situation took precedence over mere pride or fairness in her unit, as was reasonable enough in such work.

"Can your power function in your sleep?" Jake asked him suddenly.

Sogan's dark eyes watched him speculatively for a moment. The readiness with which this strange ability of his had been accepted by the other amazed him. Karmikel's familiarity with his commander's gift would have helped make his seem less incredible, but still, he had not imagined it could be taken quite so naturally, as if it were nothing more than exceptionally good vision. These Commandos were a unique breed in more ways than one.

He regretted that he was unable to give any kind of definite response. "I do not know. It has never been put to that test." He glanced at the woman. "What about yours, Islaen?"

"Sometimes. When the provocation's very strong. Try to keep your receptors open as you drift off, and we'll see what happens." She smiled suddenly. "We'll be taking our chances in point of fact, but it's no more than we've had to do until now. After all, our more commonplace skills haven't deteriorated with the waking of yours."

The three discussed their upcoming mission, set their plans as far as they were able, arranged alternate targets should all not be as they anticipated, and laid out emergency procedures in case fortune willed to take a hand against them.

After that, the two not on watch were well content to curl up, Varn in Karmikel's blanket, and put the cares and efforts of their day away from them.

SIXTEEN

IT SEEMED TO Islaen that she had been asleep only a moment when she felt Jake's touch. She was surprised when her eyes opened to find the cave still in heavy darkness; she was scheduled to have the last watch, and the first spark of dawn should be readily noticeable by then.

"So soon?" she muttered none too happily.

"It's not your time yet."

The guerrilla officer frowned. "What's wrong?"

"Don't know. Did you take any injuries during your escape?"

"No, none. We were fortunate there."

"I'm not so sure. Sogan appears to be in pain. His guards aren't strong enough to cover it completely while he's asleep." He frowned. "If he's not able for what must be done . . ."

"Varn wouldn't pull that! He wouldn't let us get into it if he couldn't handle his part!"

She slipped over to the place where the Arcturian lay, moving as quietly as a spirit traveling apart from its body. Even by the poor light of the fire, she could see that the former Admiral's face was pale and strained. He moaned softly as he shifted position, but his sleep was deep, and he did not wake.

The woman closed her eyes and emptied her mind of other concerns as she strove to enter into his thought-ways. She did

123

not quite succeed—it was as if he had a wall around
himself—but he seemed receptive to her touch despite that.
She quickly learned enough to satisfy herself.

Her fingers darted out instinctively, but she caught herself
before she had touched him. He, too, was on the alert for
possible trouble, and any such contact was certain to rouse
him. It was rest that he needed now, not pointless sympathy.
Islaen returned to her companion. "It's all right. This weather
bites at his back."

The other said nothing for a moment. He felt his own flesh
tighten. "It's very bad?"

Her eyes closed. "Aye."

"How could he have survived it, Islaen? Maximum sentence
on one ship, perhaps, or even two, but the whole fleet . . . "

"I don't know. There's no way if he did receive the full
sentence, but the Empire is to be credited for this, that its ex-
ecutioners are never those warped men in love with pain and
death but rather soldiers assigned the task and trained for it as
a duty. Unlike the judges, most of them would've seen action.
They would have had a warrior's respect for their enemies and
love for a superb commander, and, above all, they would have
understood that Admiral Sogan had preserved the honor of
the Empire itself by doing as he had. By the same token, they
were but enlisted men, and the code of sacrifice, particularly
that of personal will, wouldn't have been as intensely drilled
into them as into their officers.

"They were all well trained with their implement, and it's
not inconceivable that each might have chosen to lay only the
first few strokes true to bloody their whips and Sogan's back
and then to go easy with the rest so that relatively little damage
would be done.

"Even at that, his injuries would have been awesome, more
than dramatic enough to satisfy any official witnesses." She
shook her head. "I can't think of any other explanation for
his having come through it."

"He did have the affection of the ranks, enough to account
for their sparing him as much as possible, even without the obvious rightness of his decision."

"Too bad his aide didn't share it," she said bitterly.

"An officer's sense of duty, perhaps combined with a shade
of jealousy. I wouldn't have put too much trust in that one
myself." He glanced at the sleeping man. "You think he never
availed himself of a renewer?"

"Not by the look of that back, but how could he? Dorita's hospital is no more than an aid station. I doubt they have a renewer yet, much less at that time, and he's been afraid to seek treatment since." Determination firmed in her eyes. "I'll see to it that he gets under a ray as soon as we're out of this, even if I have to kidnap it and run the thing myself."

Her comrade smiled. "I think a requisition will be sufficient to get us both ray and physician, Colonel." He sobered. "Will it do any good after all this time? That scar tissue's well established by now."

"Aye, but minutely slow healing does take place for years after major trauma. I'd say the ray won't undo everything, not now, but it should help a lot. He should get a good bit of ease both of movement and from pain, and enough cosmetic improvement that he'll need no longer fear ready identification if he should have to bare his back before others for any reason. At the least, it should no longer be necessary to shun medical personnel. One who lives by roaming the starlanes is bound to need their skills at some point."

Karmikel's eyes lowered. "What a life for a man like that. I wouldn't have had his part for all this universe has to give. I doubt my sanity could have borne the half of it."

"Fortunately, he has his caste to carry him," she said. "An Arcturian war prince is trained from birth to endure without breaking, whether it be the hardships of combat or the vile throws of chance. I'll warrant he's been close enough to it at times, but he has the resources to sustain him. He may be an unhappy man, but he's a man all the same, and he's never allowed that to fall from him."

"He's proven it many times over these last days."

He stared gloomily into the fire for a short space, then a thought struck him, and he turned to look at his companion once more. "You were never able to read anyone like that before, Islaen."

The woman's breath caught. "No! Nor anything even close to it." She concealed her excitement. "Maybe my power has deepened or a new aspect of it wakened under the pressures of the past few days."

Her eyes closed but opened again after a few minutes. "I can get no closer to you. The readings are sharper, but nothing more. I guess Varn's ability made contact easier, especially with his being unconscious of my effort." She shrugged then, dismissing the question for which she had no certain answer.

Jake glanced at his timer. "My tour's out. Will you stay up or wake Sogan?"

"I don't know. I'll decide in a minute."

"Well, while you're thinking about it, I'll go keep that blanket company. I've been cold long enough." He paused. "Bear in mind that our friend over there isn't likely to take kindly to any special favors on our part."

Her eyes sparkled. "I know. He's great Commando material—stubborn as all hell."

She put a mock stern note into her voice. "Go off to sleep, and let me put my thoughts together. You owe me a bit of peace after rousting me out like you did."

"Aye, Colonel."

The man wasted no time in rolling himself in her abandoned blanket. Even as he settled down, his breath began to come deeply and regularly. Islaen smiled softly. Jake was proof that Federation guerrillas could sleep just about anywhere at any time.

Her heart swelled inside her as she continued to watch him. It was so good to be with him again, to be able to be with him, and she knew how much she would miss him when he left the unit.

She sighed. At least he would be demobilizing, going to the life he had chosen for himself, not entering into the next. That knowledge should make their parting the easier when the time did come. She had known enough of grief to recognize the difference.

Her attention shifted to Sogan. His breathing was much lighter than Karmikel's, although she judged his sleep to be as deep.

It would have to be, she thought. Was that not the body's, no, the whole being's, foremost and essentially best restorative? She wondered if his muscles were as sore as her own and knew in that same moment that they could scarcely be otherwise. His body was hard but in a different way, and the demands recently put on it were not those of space. If she, with all her training in surface work and her previous experience with Visnu, felt the strain, so also must he.

For a moment, she weighed permitting him to sleep through the night and taking both watches on herself, but she soon rejected that idea. It would be a false kindness to unnecessarily reduce her efficiency with battle facing them.

Varn turned to his side. She saw his body stiffen in protest. The woman winced and once more had to restrain herself from reaching out to him.

Her heart seemed to leap from her breast as a thought came to her with the force of a blow. She might not be limited to physical touch in the offering of comfort, at least not with this one.

Jake had said that she had never been able to use her power as she had a little while ago, but she realized in this moment that she had never tried to do so before. She had never attempted to use her gift to do more than receive impressions. Tonight, she had sought and succeeded in getting more specific information. It might just be possible to go still farther, to transmit thought or at least something of the feeling within herself, to offer him the hope and the promise that his discomfort was drawing to an end.

Perhaps she would succeed, perhaps she would not, but she was resolved to try. She sent her mind out from herself as she had so often done since first recognizing her talent, but it went shyly, timidly. She was striving to enter another person's inner thoughts, his feelings, an entry that would, perhaps, open a major part of her own self to him. It was a terrifying concept, and did she not believe his need was real . . .

Her heart beat rapidly. Was this for nothing? Would she be able to join with him? The Commando froze as another consciousness touched hers. Almost breathless with excitement and fear, she tried to clasp it, as a friend would clasp the hand of a troubled friend.

The Arcturian was aware of her, fully aware and not merely subconsciously as she had expected. For that first instant, he made no response at all, and she was certain he would refuse speech with her, but it was only surprise which held him. That went down and Varn Tarl Sogan welcomed her with pleasure and a readiness astonishing in one so close-guarded.

Islaen Connor told much and learned much during that incredible micromoment of initial joining. There was all the expected pain and anger, the expected shadow, the inevitable dread of the species which had given him such anguish and the resulting dread of much of life itself, but there, too, was a spirit so fine, so high and bright and clear, that it was as a flame in a universe otherwise utterly dark.

The woman cringed in shame. There could be no equaling

this. He must be reading her even as she did him, and she
shrank at the thought of how feebly her own soul stood beside
his.

A laugh, unmistakably Varn's but soft and gentle in a way
she had not heard before from him, came to her, not through
her ears, but directly into her mind. Words followed it, again,
distinct, but known rather than merely heard.

*I find in you all that is good, as I had imagined should be
true. It is I who needs must bow down before a lady so noble.*
He paused the briefest moment. *What have you done, Islaen
Connor?*

It was strange, this speech that no other could hear, but she
exerted herself to respond in kind. *What you did with the serpent. I hadn't thought to succeed to the point of rousing you.*

Why make the attempt, then?

So all was not instantly revealed when mind met mind. She
was glad of that, glad to know the spirit kept its integrity even
in the intensity and intimacy of such contact.

Her mind chose its reply carefully. She did not think of
reverting to verbal speech. This seemed the more natural and
easy now that she had begun, but she knew that she must give
her answer correctly or risk injuring this already wounded
man. His pride could not bear pity.

*You were in some discomfort, and even if I could bring you
no immediate ease, I did want to promise you my aid if the
fates will that we both lift from Visnu again—and, mark me, a
high-ranking Commando officer's influence is considerable. I
would hardly have been justified to wake you for so little
cause, so I decided to try this.* She made a wry face. *I seem to
have done that anyway.*

He smiled. *Did you really think my mind would be as lax as
my body?*

*I didn't know, Varn. I'd never attempted anything like it
before. I suppose I imagined so.*

His fingers brushed her cheek. It was the first time either of
them had made any physical move toward the other since their
mental conversation had begun. *No matter, Colonel. I am
glad you did. I had wanted to try it myself, but my fear was
too strong.*

Islaen nodded. *It was hard, the not knowing how deep such
communication might go.* Her eyes went to his. *I think we're
not very different in many ways, Varn Tarl Sogan.*

No, he agreed with equal gravity. *That was apparent even before this night.* He lowered his head, then raised it again. *You were daring to attempt this thing, Colonel.*

And you to permit it, she countered.

Sogan shook his head as the wonder of what they had accomplished gripped him. *Only days ago, I should not have believed this was possible save in the minds of storytellers.*

Storytellers have often been seers. Her expression grew solemn. *We still have so much to learn about our powers.*

Aye, but at least we now know communication is possible without violating either's privacy. Even in that first unguarded moment, I discovered something of your soul but not what you thought.

Thus it was with me.

It could be otherwise with force or conscious effort . . . Loathing lashed up in him as he spoke. It joined with that radiating from his companion. *No, never that,* he vowed. *Not between us. Circumstances forced us to oppose one another in violence once, and the gods so blessed us that disaster did not come of it. I, for one, shall not try their favor a second time.*

Islaen nodded slowly, grateful in every fiber of her being that he agreed so emphatically with her in this. Another worry rose up almost immediately to prick her. *What about Jake?*

What about him?

He's a private person, Varn. He'll be very unhappy if he thinks that we can read his every thought and feeling.

Especially me, the former Admiral agreed a trifle grimly, *but why should he be concerned? He is safe enough, or he is from me at any rate.*

From me, too. I've been trying to contact him the way I did you and have failed completely every time, whether he's been awake or asleep. The impressions I get are sharper, aye, but that's only the result of my more active seeking. In essence, it's no more than I've always been able to do.

You believe you can speak thought-to-thought only with someone who himself possesses this talent?

She nodded. *At this point, aye.*

The woman was suddenly powerfully thankful that this was so. Her soul, if not her consciousness, had been laid open during that first conversation and more strongly before it, and she found that she did not wish that yet another should know her as Varn now did. She sighed, then began speaking again lest he read that last despite the shields that seemed to guard their thoughts.

I don't know that he'll entirely believe us.

Why tell what we have done? her companion asked. *Islaen, we know almost nothing about it ourselves. Would it not be better to test our powers, discover their extent and their limitations, before discussing them with anyone else?*

The woman nodded and then smiled. *You're right, of course. I've been making things complicated when they should be simple.* Her eyes narrowed very slightly. They fixed on him. As much a novice as she was with this kind of communication, she could still sense that he had raised guards about himself.

Islaen was not long in guessing why. Of all the thoughtless fools let loose in this universe, she had to claim a stellar place among them! Varn had eased her minor concern, and all the while, he was afraid himself. How could she not have realized it sooner? They had made one of the most exciting discoveries in Federation history, certainly the most exciting in modern times, and the news of it would utterly strip away his anonymity. There was no hope in all the galaxy that she would be able to screen him once word of it got out.

Despite that knowledge, he held quiet, making no plea or protest or threat. She marveled at the courage of the man, at his silence and the pose of normalcy he forced himself to maintain. Her head raised. He would have to endure no more! She would end this matter now, without embarrassment to him.

The Commando remained quiet a little longer, as if she pondered something. Her lips pursed. *Admiral, I don't think you have any more desire than I do to spend the rest of our lives in a lab, which is precisely what'll happen to both of us if we're dumb enough to open our big mouths about this.*

You would be willing to keep quiet?

You're joking? I never said anything before. She paused. *It's very personal, this joining of minds. I don't want it . . . dissected.* Islaen felt Sogan's relief, or some of it. She believed that he was concealing the greater part of it behind those tight shields.

He smiled. *I agree most willingly, Colonel.* The Arcturian shivered slightly. The damp added fangs to the bite of the night chill. He glanced toward the mouth of the cave. *I suppose I had best take up the watch. It is my turn.*

Shall I stay up with you?

He hesitated a moment. He wanted her company and he wanted to work longer with this new facet of their talent, but in the end he shook his head. *You had best rest. We may have small chance for that tomorrow.*

Islaen was soon wrapped in her blanket, but she did not permit herself to sleep at once. She wanted to go over their discovery again, that and the conclusions they had reached.

They had chosen correctly, she decided. She might tell Jake later, when she herself knew and understood more. Right now it was all too new to her for her to give either explanation or assurances. She would do well to wait until they were alone anyway. Karmikel could and would work with their former enemy since circumstances had thrown them together and need demanded cooperation, but he took no pleasure in doing so. . . .

The woman's breath caught, and had her reactions been under a looser rein, she would have sat bolt upright. Was he jealous? Was that what was feeding these surges of hostility? She recalled now how he had seemed to relish every victory over the Arcturians on Thorne, every time they had succeeded in outsmarting Sogan, as if it had been a personal conquest. By all the old gods, had he guessed even then, recognized the feeling that might have been her death and certainly would have shattered her influence with the Resistance had it become known? None of the others had—of that, she was certain—but Jake was from her homeworld, and he had been with her so long.

She forced her body to relax. Maybe it was so. She would have to try to be circumspect, but at the same time, her confidence in her comrade remained firm. He would never betray them or their mission. All the same, Islaen Connor was very glad in that moment that it would all be over soon, that it would not be a great many more hours before they would lift from Visnu and the seemingly ever-mounting stream of perils she sent to try them.

SEVENTEEN

VARN WOKE ISLAEN when his watch had ended, dropping asleep almost as soon as he drew her blanket over himself. The guerrilla officer settled as comfortably as she might, for what she had every reason to hope would be a quiet watch. Sogan's report had been of stillness in the world around them, with only their own presence to ruffle its perfection. That would hardly have been the case had either ravager column or any more of their own kind been around.

She would have no difficulty in remaining awake. She was too well schooled in her grim work to treat her task lightly merely because present signs were good. She had learned in the past that conditions could change with a speed deadly to the unwary. The cold helped her vigilance as well. Her post was right at the entrance of the cave, just behind the shielding lip, from which she could keep the best possible watch on the area outside, unblinded—and unwarmed—by the fire.

As she hoped, the last portion of the fading night passed as peacefully as had the rest. The slow hours went by unmarked until the ever-strengthening predawn light brought a welcome change to the world beyond their small shelter. Gradually, color and detail sharpened, and some warmth crept into the night-chilled air. The heavy rain slackened and then stopped altogether.

The woman gave a sigh of relief. That should raise the temperature even faster. She smiled. Human beings were strange creatures. They cursed the heat in one moment and the cold for which they had longed in the next. It was a wonder such fickle entities had ever managed to find their way into space at all. Still, Visnu was a decidedly more pleasant place when her sky was clear and her lands bright with Brahmin's light.

Islaen's attention turned to her sleeping companions, or, rather, to Varn. Her expression grew tender as her receptors opened enough to feel the stream of his power as it swept outward to scan the planet's wildlife. She gently withdrew lest the touch of her mind wake him a second time. With such a one to stand beside her, she could almost believe that she had nothing to fear even on this world of terrors.

Darkness shadowed her thoughts. The finest shield could be shattered under too great stress, and the keenest blade could not throw back every foe. They, too, could be tried beyond their power and strength.

When dawn had done with its glory and faded into mere morning, she called Karmikel, leaving the other man to a last few minutes' rest until their breakfast would be ready.

"All quiet?" he asked.

"Aye. A right dull watch, actually."

"I doubt that sent you into deep mourning," he said dryly. He glanced at the Arcturian. "I wonder if he senses anything?"

"He's still searching," the Colonel replied carefully.

In the next moment she stiffened as a surge of fear suddenly smote her, not a coward's terror, but the natural response of a man to known danger.

Sogan came to his feet even as she turned toward him. "Ravagers!"

"Relax, friend," the Commando-Captain told him calmly. "Dreams can be too real at times."

"I would that were the case now." Sogan's voice held no resentment. The other had not meant that as a taunt.

Islaen's eyes were on him. "It was no dream, Varn?"

"No. I feel them still." The frown marring his features deepened. "This is different than before. They are as flecks on an ocean, not a powerful tide in their own right, and the frenzy, the hunger, is not with them, only excitement and something that might become triumph in creatures with greater intelligence.''

"Are they near?"

"I think so."

Can you help me join with them?

That last question sounded in his mind. *We can try it, Colonel,* his thought responded.

The woman allowed his consciousness to flow into hers. It was strange, most eerily strange, to thus share herself with another being, and she had to school herself not to draw away from him or throw up shields about herself. The Arcturian battled the same desire to flee, but he, too, succeeded in countering it, and scarcely a moment after their effort had begun, they were fully united in mind.

Islaen's lips parted in wonder as she experienced for the first time the richness of the life around them, felt touches marvelously alien, utterly different from anything she had ever known from her own species.

She frowned. All were equally new to her. How was she to know which . . . She concentrated, seeking the traits her companion had described.

There!

For a long moment, the Commando explored these nearly mindless contacts before suddenly darting from the cave and all but casting herself on the ground just before its entrance.

The two men followed after her. At first, Sogan's surprise equaled the other's, but then he realized what had happened. The woman, with her greater knowledge of nonhuman creatures, had been able to place the touches more accurately than he; she had found the beasts.

He went to his knees beside her and stared curiously at the things moving purposefully through the creeper plants in front of him. There were seven of them. They were large, a good ten inches long, and deep black in color. The bodies were fairly thin. They were divided into four distinct segments, the foremost being the longest by a considerable proportion. Three antennae, all set well back, constantly twitched and shivered as they sampled the signals Visnu sent to them.

He grabbed at the rearmost one, caught it. The thing moved with astonishing speed, twisting its body literally back upon itself and opening wide the four mandibles comprising nearly ninety per cent of the head area. They clamped down on his hand before he could react rapidly enough to drop it.

Jake's response was faster. Scarcely had the Arcturian taken hold of the ravager than he lashed out with the butt of his blaster. It struck true and hard even as the thing fastened itself.

The huge insect's grip never broke, and blood flowed from the man's hand as the force of the blow ripped the creature from his flesh.

"Don't ever try such a stupid thing—"

"Shut up, Jake!" his commander snapped. "Go after it. You *know* to do that." She turned to Varn, who was already applying pressure to his wrist. "Let it bleed! It'll help clear out any venom." Her voice was tense, sharp. Sogan could feel the fear on her and knew a moment of wonder at the realization that it was for him.

The woman closed her mind. She could not quell her dread and did not want to infect him with it. He had enough worry on him without having to bear hers as well. Sogan read her motive easily enough. His eyes closed. If he were to die now because of his rashness, still he must bless the gods that he had been permitted to know so intimately one of such inner glory . . .

Are you ill?

The question was soft in his mind. *No. I am all right.* He roused himself. "If there be poison, its action is not instantaneous." That was spoken aloud, and she regretfully answered in kind. Their seeming silence would appear abnormal.

"There should be none. I think animal prey must form only a tiny part of their diet, and as a rule ravagers should have little to fear from predators themselves. I can't imagine anything's trying to face down a column. I'm chiefly concerned about microlife at this point." She looked up to see her comrade returning. "Jake'll be able to tell us pretty soon whether there is any or not, if he succeeded in finding his victim."

"I did. It's quite dead." He went to his pack and took a small case from it. The Commando-Captain freed the flesh still pinned to the mandibles. He would begin his testing with that. "They have an impressive bite. I'll give them that. How's the hand?"

"No worse than I deserve," the other answered bitterly, much embarrassed by their attention and the delay his carelessness had cost them.

"Ah, forget that. You don't pick up this sort of thing in a week. We got our training with burnweed, and a good many of our class spent several miserable days with stinging fingers, myself among them."

Islaen began to work on the wound now. It was a surface one involving a considerable area, but the bleeding was readily stopped. She carefully washed and disinfected the tear and applied a large plastitape patch. It was the best she could do for the moment. He would have a full range of movement, as full as the unavoidable soreness would permit, and the injury would stay clean and closed. Only if something untoward developed would she have to immobilize the hand.

"That should hold you for the time being." She looked up at him. "No heroics. I want to know about it if that starts to heat or really hurt."

"You will know," he promised.

The woman got to her feet and went over to the place where Karmikel was working. He was deeply absorbed in the dead insect. "Have you found anything, Jake?"

"No. We're lucky, I think. It doesn't seem to be carrying any passengers. It's an interesting little bugger, though. Have a look."

Varn joined them. "So that is why they cannot climb."

Like the bee he and the woman had seen earlier, this creature had six pairs of legs, but only the rear four were used for locomotion, and these were very rudimentary in form, lacking any barbs or threads which might have aided an ascent. The front pair were joined and flattened to form a sharp-edged shovel.

"Adapted for life below ground," the Colonel said. "We were right about that."

Sogan smiled. "You were right, Islaen. The theories regarding Visnu's wildlife are all yours, and I have yet to see one of them proven wrong."

She smiled herself at the compliment but then turned to

Jake. "You mentioned seeing some creatures out here. Were there any more like these?"

He nodded and answered without hesitation. "Aye, quite a lot of them, in fact. They're often around either alone or in groups up to maybe a dozen in number." He frowned suddenly. "That's odd . . ."

"What?"

"This is the first time I've seen them going that way. They were always heading inland before."

Islaen Connor made him no answer. She held herself very still with her great eyes fixed on the distance, so still that for a moment neither of her companions realized there was anything amiss with her.

It was the Arcturian who first recognized that something troubled her. His hand reached out to touch hers, calling her back to them. "What is it, Colonel?"

"Scouts. Varn, they're scouts!"

"I do not understand . . ." Then he did, and his fingers tightened their grasp.

Karmikel looked from one to the other of them. "How about telling me?"

"The plateau has been explored and found desirable. Now, the advance parties are returning to transmit their reports after the fashion of their kind."

He, too, became quiet. This ability of otherwise low-intelligence creatures was too well known and too common throughout the universe for him to doubt the ravagers' possession of it. They had to have it to exist in such numbers as his companions had described. "You say they can't climb," he countered feebly after a space.

"Trees or sheer cliffs. There is nothing terribly difficult about most of the plateau wall. They'll have a lot less trouble than we did, as a matter of fact. They're so light and their center of gravity's so low that they should have almost no problem with falls or footing going from them, certainly nothing to discourage them from coming after the rich resources up here."

"So you did read the danger alright," Karmikel said glumly. "We can expect a column, and probably fairly soon."

"I would that were all."

Both men looked sharply upon her. This time, Sogan was

unable to guess her meaning. "What new horror is upon us?" He could have sought her mind, but that would still have left Jake unenlightened, and so he confined his questioning to normal speech.

The woman's eyes swept the trees around them. "This is but one very small area, yet Jake reports a large number of sightings. Multiply that over all the perimeter, or even over only this hemisphere."

"You think there could be several columns involved?" Karmikel asked.

"There could be a very great many columns involved. Varn?"

The Arcturian's expression was hard, set. "I am no one to judge, Colonel, with but a few days' contact with wildlife behind me." He straightened, as if in preparation for war. "Based upon what we have observed, I do not see how it could be otherwise. It would be asking too much of coincidence to imagine that we have accidentally found ourselves in the single point of entry for all the explorers. For one thing, even if they came up at one place only, we are far enough back from the edge that the parties should have spread out."

His voice grew bleak. "No, Comrades, we are dealing with several columns, or else one so huge as to defy sane imagination. An army many times the size of the one that treed us would not require the number of scouting parties Captain Karmikel observed, not to mention those we know he must have missed seeing. If reason has any sway in this situation, then this plateau is facing multiple assault, very probably by enormous numbers, and we off-worlders with it."

"So do I see it," the woman agreed.

Sogan seemed not to hear her. "We cannot think of lifting now, Islaen."

Jake stared at him, but the woman's head raised. Her eyes were glowing like twin stars with her pride of him. Her voice gave no indication of it. "That's obvious, I fear. Since we can transmit just as well from the surface, our leaving now would be little better than abandoning the people here to their fate."

"What would you have us do?" the redhead demanded in exasperation.

"Evacuate the populace, of course," she replied evenly.

"We can't! Even if no other ship has lifted since I left the port, there wouldn't be enough to take half those people off.''

"All the more need for our being there. Panic or confusion would finish everyone. We'll send as many as we can to Horus and arrange for the defense of the rest.''

"Defense? Islaen, a force such as you've described cannot be fought!''

"That is irrelevant,'' the Arcturian's cold voice interjected. "The ravagers *have* to be fought. We have no choice. No help is likely to reach us from Horus in time to remove everyone before the port is attacked. Those who stay will have to be protected until rescue becomes feasible.''

"How? I have no wish to see people die. Just tell me how we are to see that they do not.''

"Ravagers fear fire. We can defend the port as long as our supply of fuel holds out.''

"Which it well might not if the attack comes too swiftly and is pressed too persistently, as mindless creatures are wont to do.''

"Active battle will only be a supplement to our defenses. The buildings in the planeting complex are large and are sheathed to protect against damage in the event of a landing mishap. They should be more than strong enough to hold off insects accustomed to mud and dried soil.

"Gather the people and livestock along with supplies to maintain them and whatever goods time and strength permit them to take. They should be able to sit out a siege until your Navy comes with flame sufficient to release them.'' He smiled. "It will be no easy time, certainly, but are you Commandos not always adept at turning the like to your advantage?''

Karmikel smiled in response. "That we are, friend. It just might possibly work.''

"It will work.''

"*If* we can get the developers to cooperate,'' the Commando-Colonel told them. "Without their help, we might as well pack it up as far as saving everyone's concerned. Unless they're reassured real fast, most of the pilots will lift as soon as we reappear or,'' she added, "try to kill us again, probably with better success this time.''

Jake spat out a sharp oath. "Nothing like complications to keep a mission from getting boring.'' His jaw jutted out in a stubborn gesture straight from the pastures of Noreen. "Well,

we know pretty much where to find them. That crowd has the
nerve to stick to their offices, do what they can with their
books—which is plenty—before the authorities arrive, and
maybe rake off a bit more for themselves in the process. All
we have to do is collect them for a little unscheduled manage-
ment meeting."

She nodded grimly. "That's all indeed. If there wasn't such
need for speed, I'd be sure of our success. Reason is with us,
and they'll be willing to bargain. My rank's such that they'll
be sure any deal I make will hold. Once they realize we're
serious, they'll be only too glad to get themselves off with light
sentences. The hard part will be convincing them that there is
real danger in time to do anything about it."

"Why should that be such a problem?" Varn asked. He
knew the answer even as he spoke. Those men did not believe
there was any actual danger on Visnu; they would never have
remained on-world so long if they did. To them this incredible
threat would at first seem no more than a bluff to terrify a
confession out of them. Doubtless, Islaen Connor would be
able to convince them otherwise, but whether it would be soon
enough, only those ruling the future could answer.

He felt anger rising within him. Once they did believe, the
developers would bargain, knowing the Commandos were
pressed for time and could not act effectively without their
aid. There would be no jailings now, no fines, little penalty or
no penalty at all for the evil they had wrought here. . . .

He gripped himself. They had not won through to the settlement. Let them concern themselves with that for now, that
and the not inconsiderable problem of gaining access to those
they must see. "We would do well to concentrate on getting
into the port before judging ourselves defeated," he said
somewhat sharply.

The Federation woman gave him a rueful smile, and mis-
chief danced for a moment in her brown eyes. "Wise counsel,
especially considering the number of times we've changed our
goal since we set out on this jaunt. Sure, we might have
another set of plans entirely before we ever reach the settlement!" She made a wry face. "You must consider us as
unstable as a mote in a strong gale."

He chuckled. "The mote but responds to changing circumstances. I have never heard of any storm succeeding in

destroying one. May it prove the same with us."

Jake Karmikel glared at his old enemy. "Of what concern is all this to you, anyway? The people on Visnu are small-scale tree farmers or else rag-taggle spacers, rankless menials to an Arcturian war prince. Why should you risk yourself for their sake? Three short years can't have wrought that much of a change in you."

Sogan stiffened but compelled himself to answer quietly, if in a voice frigid with tightly reined anger. "Three years can be the equal of many lifetimes, Captain, but as it so happens, there is no alteration of thought at work in this."

The dark eyes were cold, haughty. All the centuries of royal breeding were plain upon him as he spoke. "Like most people in your ultrasystem, you have judged us according to your own conception of us. As is usual in such cases, your conclusions are false.

"It is quite true that all other castes exist only to serve the Empire's warriors, but we fighters, in turn, are deeply obligated to them. There is not one of us, no, not the Emperor's own heir-son, who would not lay down his life without question to defend the meanest hovel on any one of our planets. That service is not so terribly different from what is required here, the more particularly since these people quite obviously have no little courage of their own and are, thus, more worthy of a warrior's aid than are abject slaves."

Islaen glared at Jake, waiting. He reddened and lowered his head. "I ask your pardon, Admiral. You've never led us to believe less of you, and I shouldn't have questioned you as I did just now."

Varn Tarl Sogan quelled his resentment. "It is but natural that you should question, considering who I am." His face tightened. "I deserve no credit in any of this. I am quite without choice. Either I battle these ravagers and win, or I myself must feed them."

His fingers brushed the grip of his blaster. "Islaen and I, we have seen those things march. We have seen what their coming brings to the land over which they pass. I, we, fear them as no one not yet cursed by that experience can."

He raised his bandaged hand. "I do not want to confront those creatures again. I do not want so much as to race against their certain coming." The hand fell again, closed into a fist.

"None of it has any significance besides this, that I shall never while I live allow any sentient being to fall into the jaws of that black horde! Now, Comrades, we waste time. Let us start for our target and make what plans we might as we go." Without looking again at either of them, he turned on his heel and began striding in the general direction of the settlement.

EIGHTEEN

SOGAN DID NOT go far before he slowed his pace. The emotion on him had cooled. He had succeeded in getting the two guerrillas moving, and now he waited for them, knowing that they, and not he, must claim the lead.

Karmikel, he being the most familiar with the country between them and their target, took the foremost place. The Colonel matched her pace with Varn's. The three of them traveled in silence although each was aware that soft conversation was no danger to them at this stage of their approach.

The Arcturian was sunk in thought. He was ashamed now of having put so much into speech and ashamed as well of some of the things he had not said. It had become important to him that the Commando-Colonel should realize something more than stark duty or personal fear was moving him.

I saw two children, a girl of about eleven and a boy much younger, playing at ball in one of the fields near the port, his mind said suddenly. *That field will soon be bare soil, and those gay little ones will as surely be bleaching skeletons if nothing is done to shield them. I cannot remember their laughter and then think to walk away from this battle.*

It is not in you to flee from any need came the soft reply. There was a pause, then her mind touched his again. *Don't be angry with Jake. Ours is a profession that breeds suspicion, and he doesn't have our gift of mind to help him read others.*

I am not angry, not now at any rate. Total acceptance, or seeming acceptance, would cause me much greater concern, that being the more illogical.—Be still a moment!

She felt the surge of his power as it went out in active search and then the ebbing of it again a few seconds later. *All is well. I felt uneasiness back there, but our own passing had merely startled some ground feeder.*

The woman's eyes flashed to the trees about them. *Between us, my friend, we should be able to duck any party the developers send out to find us.*

Land-based, aye.

She nodded slowly. A flier could come too fast for the alarm to reach them before it was within sighting distance, and the very trees which concealed them could act as a sound baffle as well. That last was a real danger, but she did not believe the trees were closely enough massed to confuse their senses too badly provided they kept themselves very much on alert, the more especially since they knew very few patrols came out this far. If they did not guard themselves well, if they lapsed into any false sense of security, then they might all too soon find their enemies sweeping down upon them.

The land left them free for their watching. This part of the plateau was flat, so much so that it seemed almost a work of conscious purpose rather than of nature's wild hand. It was well drained despite that, and its relative dryness did not encourage a great proliferation of growth, as would have been present in any similarly unravaged section of the lowlands. The trees were tall and full with little crowding either at foot or crown. Undergrowth, though present everywhere, formed a serious impediment in only a few spots.

Islaen Connor remained some time with the former officer, then moved up along their trail until she was beside her comrade.

He raised his hand a trifle in greeting. "You two were very quiet back there."

"Varn is keeping watch," she replied evasively, pitching her voice low, as he had done. "He says we're a rather disturbing influence around here."

"I'll bet we are! It's no more his fault than ours, either. He's surprisingly good at this business."

"He should be after the schooling he's had these past few days. This is like an amble down some inner-system nature walk by comparison." A frown creased her face. "I just hope it isn't so easy that he gets careless again. He must concentrate firmly on moves that are natural to us."

"I doubt he'll make a slip. Sogan doesn't strike me as a man who requires a second such lesson very often."

"Aye. That business with the ravager could've been nasty."

"It still could. Whatever his assurances, our Admiral won't be quick to whimper if his hand starts acting up."

"No fear. I'm monitoring him for that."

He gave her a fixed look. "Doubtless you are."

The woman sighed. She chose to misread that. "I'll have to start watching for more than that. We've been depending so heavily on his talent since we discovered it that I've been neglecting to use mine." Her eyes shadowed. "Sad, isn't it? With all we have to face, we must still fear our own kind most intensely of all."

"Aye, but that's always been the way of it, even in pre-space times, wherever humans or their equals have risen up. It's a curse on intelligence, I suppose."

They were silent a good while, then the man looked to her again. "It's strange, that power of his."

"No more so than mine."

"But why should it wake now?"

She shrugged. "Who knows? We discussed it some but to little effect. Maybe it was always there but without anything to which it could respond; Arcturian officers give little thought to low-intelligence life forms. The pressures of the situation could well have sparked it, too, as those of Navy life woke my own."

Her voice sharpened. "Don't ride him about it, Jake. Varn's not like me. He's a practical man and is forcing himself to accept what is proving to be a very useful ability, but I feared he would try violence against himself in the first few minutes after his discovery of it."

"A nice compliment to you," he said dryly.

"I couldn't be angry with him, Jake, not then."

"No," he conceded. "I suppose you couldn't. You—you were upset yourself, weren't you?" The man asked that last hesitantly. He had never spoken to her about the first awakening of her talent, but he realized now that the experience could not have been other than traumatic.

"I didn't know whether I was going mad or should destroy myself as a monster," she replied simply. "Fortunately, I had a practical turn of mind, too, and was able to come to terms with myself—and the new dimensions of my fellow creatures opening to me—fairly quickly."

She smiled a little grimly. "One in the midst of Commando training has precious little time for personal agonizing." Her eyes softened. "I'm glad you gave so little reaction when we first mentioned it. That seemingly natural acceptance meant much to him."

Karmikel frowned. "It was natural. The surprise didn't come until later." He paused a moment. "I'm glad I didn't hit him with it, too."

The woman glanced at the sky, patches of which were visible through the branches above them. It was bright blue, free of clouds. Perhaps the rains were over for a spell. Too bad they had not ended before rousing the ravagers. . . . But it was not the weather that interested her now. "How often do the patrols actually come out here?"

"Very rarely. They searched all over for us the first day but now seem to be concentrating on the areas nearer the settlement, or so I believe. I guess they figure we'll eventually be heading back, and they don't really have the manpower to beat the bushes for us. Needless to say, they've not involved the colonists."

"Fliers?"

He nodded. "Aye."

"Low altitude or high?"

"Treetop. It's a proper search, right enough. They want us and want us dead. To judge by even the little I've seen of them, they've sent the worst of their kind after us. Any movement at all, the flash of a branch in an odd breeze or some strong shadow below, sets them blasting. If Visnu had anything much in the way of wildlife, there would be a good bit of it slaughtered by now. The settlers don't come out as far as the patrols, so they're all right."

"For that, we may give thanks, at least."

He looked swiftly upon her. The Federation officer's lips were curved in a smile that held nothing of warmth or humor. He had seen its like on her before, and the heart within him chilled for those against whom her mind was set. The Captain knew better than to disturb her now. He held his curiosity until her silent nod and the look of satisfaction on her gave him the opening to voice it. "What are you thinking?"

"Of how we might win through to our targets.—Let it rest for now, Comrade. I must see one of those fliers before I can know whether I'm navigating on course or not."

Karmikel was forced to content himself with that. She seemed to wish to play her ideas a little more, and he withdrew into his own thoughts. They were bleak and had been since this latest turn had come into their mission. If he gave them rein, they would sweep him into a morass of depression deep enough to cripple, and yet he was unable to block or deny them. . . .

Gentle fingers brushed his arm. He looked up. "I'm sorry." He had forgotten she could read this in her seeking for their foes. The hand returned to her side. "Jake, what is it? You've been down almost since our return."

The man shrugged but then sighed. Why hide it? "You brought a considerable change to our mission." He shook his head. "I was enjoying it before that, the challenge of it, the expectation of victory, aye, and even the possibility that I might not actually be around to witness that triumph. Now the stakes are too high. Too much depends cn us."

He glared at her almost fiercely. "It's always been that way. Had we erred badly on Thorne, Thorne's populace could have been burned off, or we could have released Sogan's fleet against ours, possibly to our ruin in the Sector. On our last assignment, the blackmailers could've freed that plague as they threatened. Before that . . ."

He spread his hands helplessly. "I can't take this kind of responsibility anymore, Islaen. I love you terribly, but I must be glad you decided against me, because I doubt I could keep faith with the agreement I tried to use to win you. Any connection I retain with the Navy is going to have to be a marginal one."

"I'd never ask more of you than you could give, Jake," she said softly.

"No, but you'd rightly consider yourself pretty foully used." He mastered himself with considerable difficulty. "You don't like this constant bearing of worlds on your shoulders either, but at least you seem to have the strength for it. You'll stay with the Navy?"

"I have little choice if the stars are to remain open to me."
She gave him a wry smile. "I have neither a brother willing to
accompany me nor the skill to fly alone as you do, my
friend." The brightness left her features. "The gods fit us for
what fate decrees. I suppose it's ours to bow down to that and
make what we can of it."

The Commando-Colonel allowed herself to drop back a few
paces so that she walked between the two men. Her conversation with Jake had depressed her in turn, and it was to a
decidedly barren future that her mind now turned.

The stars she had to have. That she knew. She had known it
from the moment she had first lifted from Noreen and found
herself out amongst them, the stars and the countless realms
they nurtured, the countless life forms to greet and intrigue
her. A planet-bound existence, even if she could place herself
where she might do work of some worth, would be a prison
for her.

She did love Noreen and even more her family and the farm
on which she had been born, but there most certainly could be
no returning, not permanently. She could never again fit herself into the mold of a woman's place there, as she must if she
went back. Otherwise she would be viewed as an eccentric,
however accepted her present state might be. She had no desire
whatsoever to assume the role of an eternal anomaly amongst
her own, one deeply honored and respected, aye, but ever set
apart by her strangeness.

She was another of the War's many casualties, Islaen Connor thought, one of the countless rootless ones rendered unfit
for life in a universe at peace, doomed to wander with no place
to claim them and no work to which they might give both hand
and heart.

Her chin lifted a little. That was not entirely accurate. The
gods had been far kinder to her than that. She still did have a
home, a true home despite the fact that she could not make it
her residence, and the work she did was of no little importance. Unlike so many others equally worthy, her place in the
drastically reduced peacetime Navy, with the Commandos,
was secure. If the pressures on her were at times awesome, she
knew it was needful, imperative, that someone bear them. Her
eyes closed and stayed so for a moment before opening again
to spy out where she must set her feet.

Aye, purpose, and high purpose, was hers, but was that

enough in itself? Life held so much. There were a multitude of relationships and experiences apart from those born in the waging of war, be it against military foes or criminals. Some she had tasted. The rest . . . Would she never truly share in that vast bounty, that richness whose wonder she recognized and for which she longed with so little hope of fulfillment, now more than ever in her life before this?

NINETEEN

ONLY A TRACE of the shadow still remained with Islaen when the three settled into their first rest break several hours later. There was too much to concern her at this point to permit the luxury of any such wallowing in herself.

None of them said anything at first. As easy as the country was, they had traveled far, and both Islaen and Varn were feeling the strain of the continuous guard they had been keeping with their minds. It was not until they had swallowed a few mouthfuls of their rations that Sogan broke the silence gripping all three of them.

"There is a change in the things around us. They are more nervous than those we encountered earlier, and they seem to be keeping well below the upper canopy." Even as he spoke, he opened his mind so the woman might experience with him what he described.

She pursed her lips, listening with him for several seconds while she appeared to ponder his words. "The patrols must come over here fairly regularly. We'll have to be more conscious of staying under cover. Some of these trees are widely enough spaced to expose us to a sharp eye if we're not careful." She got to her feet. "Let's go. This spot suddenly seems a bit open."

Sogan's thought came to her as they started out once more.

His touch seemed timid, and she turned slightly to acknowledge it even as she opened her mind to welcome him.

What would you have, my friend?

*Your confidence. Some shadow lies over you. I would know
its cause that I might lift or lighten it.*

A personal matter. I had no right to let it sweep me at all.

Of course not, Lady Goddess, he replied with teasing sar-
casm.

I'm very far from that, I fear.

*A fact for which I must give fervent thanks. I should be
hard-pressed to work with the like.*

The Federation woman smiled despite herself. *Very well,
Admiral. This truly is not the time for it, but if we survive and
you still want to know, I promise to give you the information
you now ask.* Her head tilted a little as she studied him. *Although I wouldn't bother if I were you. It's no great story, and
there's really nothing much that can be done about it.*

*In so speaking, you are trying to deny me what you have
already granted. Let me judge both, Colonel. An Arcturian
war commander is trained to accomplish much even where all
is deemed lost, and that I remain although the privileges of the
state have been reft from me.*

Once again, she smiled. *All is hardly lost, Admiral.*

The Commando-Captain slowed his pace, and she quick-
ened hers to join him. "You're looking pleased with yourself," he commented when she reached his side.

"A few pleasant thoughts go far toward brightening the
mood. What's happened?"

"Nothing, but we should be running into patrols anytime
now. It might be a good idea to put your sensors or whatever
you call them into high gear."

"Will do. Thanks, Jake."

Karmikel was right. The nervousness Sogan had detected
earlier had intensified in the creatures inhabiting the forest
around them. It was not true fear, certainly not terror, but the
feeling was strong enough to be uncomfortable for one receiving it over an extended period. Varn strengthened his efforts
despite the ever-growing weariness continuous use of this new
sense caused him. His persistence bore fruit at last. About an
hour after Jake had given his warning, he felt alarm and sudden movement in the trees above. Sogan hissed a warning. As

he did so, the whine of a flier broke through the silence, but the three had already dived into the deeper shadows that lurked around the trunks of the trees. The two guerrillas followed their training and flung themselves away from one another lest both be destroyed in a single strike, but their companion went down beside Islaen.

He kept his mind tightly closed. The trees were widely spaced, and chance just might betray them to the hunters for all their care. If so, well, the thickness of one human body should be sufficient to shield a second from any weapon the flier was likely to carry. He was determined to serve the Federation woman so should the need arise, but he doubted Islaen would permit it if she read his plan. It was fortunate indeed that as their ability to communicate one mind with the other increased and deepened, so, too, did the strength of their shields.

The machine passed near them, almost directly over them, a small, cargo-class civilian vehicle whose like they had seen operating around the settlement on more mundane tasks. The Commando-Colonel's eyes slitted as they fixed upon it, and her mouth tightened into a hard, merciless line. Her powers had strengthened since she had fled the port, and she picked up and read what its two occupants were transmitting without difficulty.

Their feelings were easily deciphered. They were bored on what was to them but another of the seemingly interminable series of sweeps they were required to make over the treelands. Both were longing for some living thing to show itself that they might burn it to relieve their tedium.

This boredom and the fact that they expected to find nothing made them careless in their scanning of the ground below, what tiny part of it was visible through the leaves. They failed to see anything of their quarry and soon brought their craft out of the fugitives' sight, and then their hearing range as well.

Islaen Connor waited until Sogan told her that all had returned to normal in the forest before giving the release signal. There was purpose on her, and she spoke almost as soon as they were on their feet and together once more. "Jake, am I right in believing that flier will return shortly by the same route?"

He nodded. "That seems to be their usual pattern. They

keep sweeping the same area over the same course. I think they
believe one or the other of them is bound to pick us up when
we try to get back in, no matter how we make our approach.
This'll be the last time for today, though. Since they can't see
beyond their lights after dark, they apparently pull back and
tighten their defenses around the settlement at night."

"That would be their logical course."

Her head snapped toward the former Admiral. "If that
thing were brought down, could you set it flying again? We're
no novice mechanics ourselves, especially Jake, but I have a
feeling you're our master in that."

He eyed her somberly. He did not question how she intended to take the vehicle with only their antipersonnel
weapons to aid her. "I am good, Colonel, but I cannot
perform miracles. If you turn its systems into rubble, there
will be little I can do, no more than I was able to repair that
other flier."

Jake Karmikel strained to peer upward into the leafy crown
of the tree above him. "If we can crash it into the branches instead of letting it tear straight down, the damage shouldn't be
so bad."

His commander picked up his idea as he spoke it. "Brilliant,
Jake! They're flying low. If we can lure them down only a
little farther, we could pick them off from the topmost
branches."

A closed machine would end that hope, but they would not
have to contend with that. The flier had been requisitioned for
this task, not converted for it. It was a labor vehicle only and
lacked not just a weapons system but even the fittings to
receive one. Whatever firepower it had must be provided by its
occupants themselves, and they could not discharge any
weapon while sealed inside their transport.

The Captain's eyes still ranged the treetops. "There look to
be several good perches up there, but at best, it'll be long-
range shooting."

"Not for pellets."

He gave her a quick, sharp look and then lifted his pack to
the ground. "No, not for them."

Varn Tarl Sogan watched the two Commandos draw out
and check over their pellet guns, small-scale versions of the
weapons that had seen such heavy on-world service on both

sides during the recent War. Whatever the reduced size of these, he did not imagine they lacked anything in power or range or in the deadly effect of the tiny, electrically charged missiles they fired.

The Federation soldiers made their preparations quickly and in almost total silence, working together so smoothly that they seemed more extensions of one being than individual fighters.

He began to feel something of the awe with which even their own forces regarded the elite guerrilla troops. Seeing them thus, observing the precision and coolness with which they prepared to execute their incredible plan, he could begin to comprehend how their small units had been able to accomplish so much. To the like of these, what lesser soldiers would call impossible was merely a testing of their mettle and ingenuity.

The Arcturian kept well back from the pair so as not to distract them. That, he thought with an infinite misery, was all he could do. Whatever his will or his courage or even his marksmanship, this was their work, and he was no match for them in it. He knew too well from recent experience how clumsy and slow he would be if he tried to go up with them into the trees. He was all too painfully aware of how much he had to learn before he would be able . . .

The Commandos' preparations were now complete, and Sogan moved in nearer to them. He might at least know their plans even if he could have no part in them. Both had unfastened their belts as Islaen and he had done when they had climbed to escape the ravagers.

The Colonel studied several of the trunks around them, weighing the advantages and disadvantages of each potential post. After a short while, she slapped her hand against one of the great emergents, those trees towering well above their mates.

"This one, I think, for me. You take one of the others to my left. We'll stand a better chance of at least one of us being able to get off a good shot if we separate somewhat." Her head snapped toward Sogan. "Varn, you'll be decoy. . . ." She stopped. It was not hers to order him thus.

He grinned. "Go on, Colonel. I dislike a spectator's role."

She nodded and handed him a small tube she had taken from her pack. "We want to draw their interest, bring them down a bit. A little of this signal dye should do the trick, but it

can't just be sitting there in a bright orange blot, or they might
be too suspicious for us to work our will on them. I want it to
leap suddenly to their attention so they'll react instinctively to
it, as if they'd just sighted something moving below.''

"I am to wait until the flier is nearly overhead before pouring it out?''

"Aye. A few drops will do, but you'll have to move fast.
They'll come in blasting.'' She paid his courage the compliment of not offering him the chance to withdraw from the
mission.

He gave her salute. "It shall be done, Colonel Connor. Just
see to it that you do not miss when I bring them in for you.''

"We won't.'' She signaled to Jake to begin climbing and
snapped her own belt around the trunk she had selected.

Islaen went up quickly. This highland tree was neither as
thick around nor as smooth-barked as those she had scaled
earlier. The lessened strain on her arms and improved grip for
both belt and shoes helped her immensely, as did the fact that
the branches started much lower down, sure evidence that it
had indeed been long since the ravagers had last visited the
plateau.

Her eyes clouded. It was a bleak testimonial for her kind.
All that time, the insects had found this place dry and too bare
to bother making the effort of the climb. Now, humans had
come with their farm crops and their own bodies, and the old
balance was gone.

The plateau was undesirable to Visnu's wild creatures, and
it had not been so long inviolate that special adaptions had
arisen to enable the various species to colonize it more heavily,
so at least there was no wealth of animal life to die in the invaders' jaws. All the same, she was in that moment infinitely
grateful for the service provided by the Settlement Board, not
because it protected potential colonists but because it guarded
the planets they thought to make their own, worlds that might
crumble under the impact of an invasion which their delicate
ecosystems could not handle.

The Commando officer's mind returned to her immediate
mission as she gained the crown. She was not long in finding a
thick branch granting both good cover and a clear view of the
rest of the canopy well below. She settled herself so that she
might sit securely, and then once again inspected her position
with a practiced eye.

There was need for care. This tree, topping the others around it as it did, was both very exposed and likely to draw the eye. If she failed to see some bare place or misjudged the response of the branches to the breeze, she would be quickly exposed.

She soon saw that there would be no such problem. She had chosen well. The gold-green leaves enjoyed the full benefit of Brahmin's light. They were large and thickly grown, providing her with ample cover. Jake's post was equally well screened. She knew the tree he had claimed for his post but even so could not find the place from which he would fire.

Almost automatically now, she sent out her mind in search of him. The woman found him readily enough. She could feel the battle fire rising in him, the excitement, the tension that always preceded combat. Of his thought, she could learn nothing. Islaen sighed in her heart and turned her attention downward, to the ground and the one waiting there. She touched momentarily with Varn and returned to the work before her.

That would be the last contact between them save for warning of the flier's approach until the ambush was over. With both facing considerable danger, it would be best not to weaken the concentration of either with the reminder of a sharing which might never be experienced again.

The waiting was hard, as it always was. The guerrilla checked her weapon once more lest it had suffered some damage during the climb, but after that there was little more she could do to further their chance of success.

She might at least hold watch. Her mind ranged far, as far as she was able to send it, seeking for any hint of the unpleasant souls that were the machine's crew.

Perhaps it would not come. Jake reported that these patrols usually seemed to follow identical paths during their sweeps, going and returning by the same routes, but his experience with their patterns was not great, and no law insisted that they always do so or that they should come by that same path now.

She began to feel the madness of this attempt. Even should their target be only a little off, its occupants would probably be beyond the range of both her gun and her comrade's. If the crew had any indication of trouble at all, they would most assuredly alter their course. . . .

Islaen drew a sharp breath. There! The contact was very

faint, but it was a true one and strengthened even as she became aware of it. Her warning flashed to Sogan. A moment later, he was able to confirm it. Visnu's creatures were again moving, fleeing the flier's approach.

It came on. She could hear it now and braced her gun so there would be no flash of movement later to betray her. The vessel swept into view, almost exactly on its predicted course.

It was nearly upon them. Varn must act soon, or all was lost! The machine was too high to provide them with acceptable targets. She held her mind firmly in check. The timing, the decision, were the Admiral's and must remain his. Only he could rightly judge when to release the dye.

A river of glaring, incandescent orange seemed to run across the ground below her!

Fire answered it, a roaring curtain of it from out of the suddenly banking flier.

The Commando's heart went dead in her breast. A long-range blaster set to killing strength at the widest possible beam. How could Sogan hope to avoid that, following as it did so immediately upon the release of the dye? Her fingers whitened on her weapon. Soon, the bastard who had fired it would die as well.

She crushed her anger, forced it back out of her conscious mind. Such emotion could interfere with the accuracy of her performance.

The machine dipped down to investigate the glowing orange streak, so patently alien to this realm of green and brown.

Soon now. Only a little closer . . .

Islaen took aim. The man she wanted would be Jake's target, but no matter. Her comrade rarely missed, and if he did, the death of the pilot would ensure the destruction of that one as well.

The familiar soft, eerie hiss sounded as she released her pellet. Bright scarlet covered the temple of the man nearest her as his head jerked back under the double lash of impact and electric charge. He was already dead.

The other died almost in the same moment as Karmikel's missile pierced his forehead nearly at its center. A third pellet flew. The Colonel did not hear its discharge, but she saw the drive rod quiver and drop into idle position.

Momentum and gravity had a strong grip on the machine, and its descent did not stop, but most of the force had gone out of it. There was still some breaking of branches and a loud crumpling of metal when it struck the canopy, but it held where it first hit without any drive to push itself farther down.

The flier had come to rest nearer to Jake's position than to hers. He began to make his way toward it while his commander kept her weapon trained on their victims lest one of them be only shamming death.

The man moved very slowly once he had left the trunk behind. Visnu's trees were not large, and branches thinned rapidly the further one got from the central stem. They trembled and shook beneath him with every move he made, shivered so even at their mid length that he could only pray they would continue to support him at their tips, where he had to cross from one to the next tree.

It was a long, tense time before he reached his goal, but in the end he won through to the stalled vessel. Jake approached and boarded it gingerly, not wanting to upset what might be a very tenuous balance.

The vehicle held steady under his entry and weight. He gently eased the dead pilot aside and took hold of the controls, first picking out the embedded pellet from the drive rod with the point of his knife so he wouldn't get a shock from it. The charge could remain active for some time in the damn things.

The rod had been deformed by the blow. He struggled with it for several minutes before being able to wrench it back onto its track and into active position.

The engine responded sluggishly. That was hardly encouraging, but it was good enough for his present purpose. He sent the battered craft down in more of a glide than true flight, carefully guiding it through the interlacing branches until he at last was free of them. His work was easier then, with only the trunks against which he must guard, fortunately so since the flier was giving him greater trouble than he had anticipated when he had begun his descent. Jake brought it to rest on the forest floor with only a gentle bump to show that all was not completely right with it.

Only when he had stepped from it and waved to indicate he had made the landing safely did the Colonel begin to come down. There was no feeling of triumph on her. Her heart was heavy, leaden and lifeless in her breast, but she gave thanks Karmikel had come through without injury. She had been aware that he was having trouble with the vehicle and knew

she might easily have lost both her companions on this wild
venture.

Islaen kept her eyes and mind fixed on the rough bark. She
did not want to look at the charred place below. Death was
part of her work, affecting both those officially assigned to it
and any others who joined with them. That dire fact must only
be acknowledged and accepted, yet the destruction of a comrade was ever a bitter blow, and this more numbing than
most. . . .

Had her control been less, she would have cried out when
she reached the ground and turned at last. Two men awaited
her there, one already bent over the engine, the second standing beside it.

"So you did survive." Her voice was harsh. She had to
make it so or let it vent the emotion that swept all her being.
Only now, with Varn standing living before her, did she realize
fully what this man's loss had meant to her. What she had
known that first time was nothing to this. . . .

Sogan's head raised in response to her tone, but then he saw
her face and the huge, too brilliant eyes.

He had reached her side in a moment. Had they been alone,
he would have taken her into his arms, but now he merely let
his fingers brush the too-pale cheek before withdrawing his
hand once more. "Islaen . . ."

She looked into his face as if still not believing he did live.
"I was so sure you were dead," she whispered.

"You should have known from the past that I am not easily
slain. I leaped even as I released the stuff. There was little time
to spare, but it was enough."

He felt her wondering touch as the shields around her mind
were lowered. *Would my death have made such a difference?*

Varn had asked in thought, and her own replied, *It would
have come through your aiding us.* She stopped. *It would have
mattered, aye. It would have mattered.*

But, Islaen, could you not sense me?

I had closed my mind.

Would he understand this, that she could not bear to find a
void in place of the vital soul she had known? Perhaps he did,
for he nodded slowly, and his mood turned somber. *I should
not will to lose this thing we have gained.*

Jake Karmikel thought they had merely fallen silent and
looked up from the flier. "Let her look you over, Admiral.

That power of hers can ferret out injuries that one isn't even aware exist."

The Arcturian glanced back at Islaen. She smiled at him. "With your permission, Admiral?"

"I am quite at your service, Colonel Connor."

He started a little as she began her examination. This was different from any of the other contacts between them. Her touch was like to that of gentle fingers probing all his body for traces of pain or weakness.

She soon withdrew from him again. "You're sound out," she told him.

"Good," Jake said. "Now, would you mind giving me a hand here, Sogan? This thing took a worse beating than I'd thought it would. Civilian craft aren't as tough as service ones, I guess, not these anyway." He gave the stubborn drive rod a disgusted crack with the wrench he was holding. "My pellet didn't do much to help matters, either."

"What I can do, I shall, Captain."

Islaen left the two men at it, knowing another hand was not needed in the cramped space of the flier's engine case. She turned her attention to the two bodies Jake had taken from it. Working swiftly, she stripped them of their gear and outer clothing. It would be best to look as much as possible like their victims when they tried to breach the port's defenses. The longer they could avoid detection, the better their chances of success.

They were fortunate it would be dark when they reached the settlement, she thought. Both tunics were badly bloodstained, too much so to pass through in full daylight.

The marks might be noticed now, but there would be enough shadow to conceal the extent of them, especially with the crumpled nose of the vehicle to serve as explanation. Accidents did happen, and she imagined they must occur here with some frequency, for most of these men really knew little about maneuvering in and around a strange wilderness. Such incidents were likely to be messy but not serious. Jake's bandaged head would add credence to the supposed mishap, as would Varn's injured hand.

The guerrilla quickly went through the salvaged equipment and small store of personal belongings but, as expected, found nothing of interest. She rose to her feet and stood for a mo-

ment looking down at the dead men. Her face was bleak and
drawn. She had known what they were, yet they seemed different in death, still and vulnerable.

Sighing, she took a collapsible shovel from her pack and
locked it into position. She didn't suppose burial would shield
them from the ravagers, nor would that really matter now, but
time was hers, and she might at least give to their bodies the
final shelter she had been raised to believe was due to any
human.

The Colonel had finished with her digging when she felt a
movement beside her.

Sogan.

He said nothing as he bent to help her place the corpses and
then took the shovel to cover the graves. At last, he stood
erect. He did not draw away but remained beside the woman,
looking somberly at the shallow graves.

"You would have tried to spare them had they been men of
another sort?" he asked suddenly.

"Do you judge me, Admiral?" she snapped in reply, ver-
bally although he had expected her answer to come directly
into his mind.

"How should I dare, I who have slain and commanded men
to slay, I who have ordered men to their deaths? No, I do not
judge."

"We couldn't have spared them. The distance was too great
for any hand blaster, much less one set to stun."

Her brows creased, as if she were under the lash of sharp
pain. "I would have tried all the same had I known less . . ."
She shuddered. "I didn't realize it at the time, but I dared to
set myself above these men, to judge whether they merited life
or death."

He caught her to him, not in body but in mind. She desperately needed comfort, support, and he strove with
everything that he was to meet that need, knowing all the while
that nothing save his true belief in her would serve. Anything
less would wound, maybe to the point of destruction.

He felt her soul relax in his hold, felt her self-loathing begin
to melt. Only then did he dare open himself to her. *There can
be no guilt where there was no intent. Your gift, too, has
broadened, and this was a danger you did not recognize. You,
we, shall know now to beware such influence in the future lest
some tragedy rise out of it.*

The woman sighed. *You argue well, Varn Tarl Sogan. Again, it is mine to thank you. You—your strength has been my support more than once since fate threw us together.*

He made her no answer, for Jake had finished stowing the tools they had used and was coming toward them with his brisk stride. This conversation was too personal for the hearing of another. At the same time, the quiet of mental speech was too unnatural not to rouse suspicion, and neither of them was yet ready to admit this ability of theirs.

Karmikel came to a stop beside them. "Thanks, Sogan. I hate to admit it, but you're about the best mechanic I've ever seen, myself included."

"My pleasure, Captain. I much prefer the idea of flying to walking any farther through this wilderness."

"I second that," the woman said with considerable feeling. Jake glanced at the crew's clothes. "Let's get into these things and take off. It's late as it is. Sogan and I should wear them, I guess," he remarked to his commander. "You're too small. You'll just have to scrunch down in the back when we're passing the sentries."

"Good enough. You take the controls. We'll get a couple of hours' sleep, and then Varn can relieve you. It'll be best to have our powers working at full as we near the settlement."

Both men nodded and then hastened to prepare themselves for this, the most uncertain phase yet of their ever-more-complex mission.

TWENTY

IT SEEMED THAT no time at all had elapsed before the Commando-Captain called Islaen out of an oblivion as deep as intergalactic space. She sat up, vowing to herself that she would sleep for at least a month when this was all over.

She glared at Varn in response to his silent laughter but then opened her receptors fully as she sent her mind out in active search. She withdrew it again after a couple of seconds. Nothing yet.

"Are you receiving anything?" she asked Sogan.

"Not much of interest. The creatures here are very uncomfortable with our presence, but that is all." He was quiet a moment. "There is more activity. All the day creatures are gone, and the night supports both greater numbers and a larger variety."

The woman chewed on her lip. Tension swept through her like waves of a hidden sea. It was dark now—the flier's lights had already been activated when she woke—and soon they would be at the settlement and facing the first of their confrontations there, confrontations that must end in defeat even in their success.

A soft touch reached into her mind. *Do not dwell upon loss, Colonel. That can well bring it. Concentrate instead on saving the lives of these people, and see how the rest works out.*

He could feel her smile. *First, we must think about getting into the port,* she told him. *It will be guarded, you know.*

Hardly a problem for a pair of Commandos, Colonel.

Life is full of problems, Admiral, she retorted. *That's what keeps it interesting.*

No more than ten minutes passed before Islaen stiffened. She opened herself to Varn so that he might know what she had detected, the distant jumbled babble of many minds, each engaged upon its own concerns.

The woman softly called to Jake and then squeezed herself into the deep shadow behind the front seat. As she did so, she heard the gentle whir of the canopy closing.

Would it be enough, the night and the glare created by the sentries' lights on the transparent covering, or would their ruse be detected? This was a risk she had faced times without counting, but it never became easier. Fortune was fickle and could betray at any moment, and this time, they had one not Commando-trained with them.

She hated her own passive part. Even to be up front, playing that dangerous role, would have been something. . . .

Was she so helpless? There was yet something she might try to aid their cause.

Certain patterns were increasing in strength. They were almost upon the sentries now. Slowly at first and then more strongly, she began beaming her thoughts outward.

. . . The front of the flier was all crumpled . . . Scant wonder the fools were late getting back . . . Must have been drinking . . . Boring, this endless sweeping over these infernal trees . . . Why bother them? . . . Too late to exert oneself now anyway . . . Tired . . . Bored . . . Indifferent . . .

Over and over, she broadcast those thoughts and others like them, reinforcing them with feelings of weariness and boredom and that false sense of security which had betrayed so many guardians throughout history.

The vehicle slowed but picked up speed again without ever quite coming to a full stop.

Islaen Connor did not allow herself to relax. They were inside the settlement area, but that was a far sight from having attained their goal. There would be more guards to face before they gained entrance to the port complex and then the eyes of the countless passersby, any one of whom could detect something amiss with them.

. . . Only one flier among many . . .

She strove to stress their anonymity, to render them, in effect, invisible. The strain was incredible, so terrible that the woman felt she must shatter if she maintained it much longer, yet she dared not ease off. She didn't know how much effect she was having or if she were having any effect at all, but they had drawn no attention thus far, and she could not chance reducing their guard at this stage.

She could not hold!

Varn was with her, supporting her, pouring his strength into her.

Islaen's power surged forward, once more steady and sure. With the Arcturian to brace her, she knew she need not fear breaking or weakening. She felt the machine change both its speed and direction. The lights died abruptly.

Hang on, Islaen, Varn whispered in thought. *We are concealing the machine now, and then we must walk to our enemies' stronghold. That will be the hardest part of all.*

The guerrilla's response came in a redoubled outpouring of power. She scarcely felt the flier come to a halt in the black alley that had been its goal.

The others got out, but she was incapable of doing so, incapable even of responding to them. All her strength, her energy, her concentration was fixed upon the thing she strove to do, to create and maintain a wall of invisibility that would stand, if necessary, against every eye on Visnu.

Strong arms lifted her, and once again, a stream of power flowed into her, power and something else, a warmth that was glory itself.

She was aware because she had to be aware and because Varn kept her aware of what transpired around them.

They quickly crossed the hundred-odd feet separating the alley from the rear entrance of the building the developers had chosen for both their living quarters and working space. There was a tense three minutes while Jake worked with his clutch of antilocks, then the door swung open. They darted inside, swiftly pulling the barrier in behind them even as they crouched low. Karmikel covered the room with a blaster set at broad beam to kill.

The door was no sooner shut than Islaen snapped her mind into active probing. The tension left her body, and she allowed her head to drop against Sogan's shoulder. "Safe," she murmured. "We made it undetected, and there are no guards here."

A few seconds were sufficient to restore her, and she asked Sogan to set her on her feet although she was glad to retain the support of his arm.

Jake was staring at her in open awe. Apparently, Varn had told him what she had been doing and perhaps something of its intense difficulty, for there was sympathy on him as well.

She managed a rather shaky smile. "It's amazing what you can do if you only set your mind to it."

Her fingers closed on Sogan's hand. Time was not theirs to waste. "We're in luck. Five of the six apartments are still occupied. Their owners are all peacefully asleep, and they have no sentries posted. They haven't a fear of anyone's trying to reach them."

"Let's go collect them." Jake hesitated. "You're all right?"

"Aye. The energy seems to be restored quickly, at least after a relatively short-term effort."

She glanced at the ramp leading up from the entranceway. "There's that conference room on the second level. I think we'd better make for that. We'll want lights, and it's an interior chamber."

The three gained entrance to it without mishap. It was a functional, Spartan room, as were all the others in the building. The men using it were professionals. They preferred to maintain themselves quietly during such work and reserve their wealth for their inner-system residences and pleasures. That both reduced the need for guards and gave them added credibility with those they duped, as if they, too, were seeking to build their lives on this first-ship colony world.

Varn Tarl Sogan's dark eyes were cold as he examined the place. He walked over to a desk standing against the wall to his right and looked at it pensively. Its surface held paper, letterhead and blank sheets, and pens but no written or printed material.

"You go up. I shall await you here."

Karmikel looked at him in surprise. He had come to believe

the Arcturian would take part in all their activities, but he
shrugged in the end. It was better this way. One not schooled
in a Commando's work could too easily give them away.

Islaen, too, regarded him curiously, but he offered no explanation. "As you will, Admiral."

The guerrillas slipped up to the third and final story as
silently as animated shadows. Each went to the entrance of
one of the apartments, nullified its locks, and glided inside to
awaken its sleeping occupant. After that, the Federation
woman left their prisoners with her comrade and, drawing
upon her talent for added guidance, brought out the other
three in quick succession.

The five men shuffled down the ramp to the second-level
conference room, each trying to keep his body as far as possible from the blasters in the hands of his captors.

They were not cowards. They had risen high in a profession
in which risk was inherent, and they had succeeded in a great
part through their ability to read others. They took courage
that they had not already been slaughtered and from their
recognition of the intruders. If these people were indeed
Patrol agents, then they were not murderers. All was by no
means lost.

The leader of the five straightened his considerable frame.
"What do you mean by this intrusion?" he demanded in Basic
laced with a heavy Albionan accent.

Jake regarded him with patent distaste. He flashed his service badge. "I'm Commando-Captain Karmikel. Commando-
Colonel Connor here has decided to convene an emergency
board meeting."

Islaen stepped forward. "Stress the word 'emergency.'
Visnu is facing total disaster." She detailed the peril threatening the port community and colonists alike. "Summon your
pilots and the settlers' representatives. It'll be best to get the
evacuation started as quickly as possible."

There was no yielding in her opponent, however stunned he
might feel at finding himself facing Commandos instead of
mere Patrol agents. "I think not, Colonel. It's our business to
know Visnu, and we simply do not believe that any such danger as you describe exists here."

"Call it a drill, then, if it makes you feel happier. Just get
moving."

He shook his head. "These colonists are Amonites. They

hate the confusion and needless effort inherent in official life.
That's why they chose to throw their lot with us on Visnu instead of going through your Settlement Board. Such a pointless exercise as you suggest will accomplish nothing but getting
them irritated with us."

"I'm afraid you have no choice. You have named yourselves planetary officials and as such cannot refuse full
cooperation during a death-peril emergency, as I formally
declare this matter to be. To do so would be a grave criminal
offense. With the Navy on its way, I doubt you want any more
charges on your heads."

"Aye, that's your game, and I well know it. The Settlement
Board has little liking for sharing its profits with private individuals. You want to trap us in some sort of violation and
then ruin us, all because we helped these poor people get
homes for themselves several years before the Board would
have done."

The hypocrisy of his speech both sickened and infuriated
the woman, but she held herself impassive.

She had been trying to wield her power as she had outside,
but either these were of sturdier mind or else the importance of
the issue to them rendered them immune to covert influence.
She began to gather herself to strike at the developers' wills.

A sudden warning seared into her mind. *Beware, Islaen!
Think what you would do!*

The guerrilla caught herself sharply. Despise them though
she might, her prisoners were human. She could not attempt
the abomination she contemplated and retain that title herself.
Even if she must allow them to escape punishment entirely,
she could not violate their wills and with that their humanity.
If she did, she would make the Federation she represented less
even than the Empire they had fought for the sake of freedom.

Thanks, Varn, her thought responded softly. *That danger is
past.*

The Albionan continued speaking smoothly, unaware of the
peril he had so narrowly escaped. "No, Colonel. This plot of
yours will serve only to disrupt the entire colony and upset
people who are content with Visnu—and do it, I may add, at
great expense. Before we'll be a party to it, we want a signed
and voice-sealed pledge from you absolving us of any violations you may invent with respect to Visnu and her colonists.
We will not help you destroy ourselves."

"The ravagers will do that quite nicely—and at no expense at all," Jake growled.

"Ah, these ravagers of yours! A most picturesque name. Presumably they have a more scientific one as well."

There was triumph on the man. "You stress the need for hurry. I suggest giving us our assurance now so we can begin. If you wait too long, our crews will learn of your presence here. You will not be attacked again.—That was a most regrettable and, of course, quite spontaneous incident—The ships will merely lift."

"Leaving you to face the ravagers," Islaen pointed out.

"And all those innocent people with us. I think you will not risk that, Colonel Connor."

She quietly raised her blaster.

The Albionan laughed. "Burn us? Come, Colonel. I know something of you Commandos. You were not chosen for your bloodlust. The Federation had learned enough from history not to loose packs of legalized pirates on already bleeding populations. I know, in fact, the opposite is true, that although Commandos occasionally escorted assassins during the War, never did one of you carry that duty himself. No, you will not slaughter helpless men, and I assure you that we'll make no move to give you an opening to fire." He grinned. "You're not Arcturians, after all."

"No, but I am." The eyes of all five fixed upon the source of that cold, measured voice.

Varn Tarl Sogan was seated on the edge of the desk. His face was as hard as an image of Death.

"We are less fond of bloodletting than your tales would have, but we do slay without qualm when necessary. The extermination of vermin in time of need gives us no pause at all."

The developers' faces had turned a sickly white. Sogan's race was apparent now, and apparent, too, was the utter contempt in which he held them.

An Arcturian, and an officer amongst them to judge by his manner of speech and his bearing . . .

"How could Commandos work with . . ." That was no attempted argument but only a horrified whisper.

The deadly eyes did not flicker. "They are practical. I have skills they can use."

The other four were ready to capitulate, but their leader was made of sterner stuff. He gathered the shreds of his courage. "You need us . . ."

"Not all. One will serve, and he need not be whole."

Stark silence greeted that pronouncement. The Albionan seemed to shrivel. "We will do what you want. The broadcast systems are in the communications center below—"

"One moment." The former Admiral felt Islaen's surprise but continued speaking without looking at her.

"A crime of the magnitude of that which you have perpetrated would earn you the death penalty in the Empire. Here, it will not, but I am minded that you shall not escape with only short imprisonment or heavy fines, which you can afford.

"You will sign this confession that I have prepared, and you will sign this compensation agreement by which you will out of company or personal funds give each of these colonists satisfaction for his or her labor in accordance with Federation standards of time and pay for all work done on Visnu."

Karmikel gasped. Those the former Admiral addressed made no response at all. To comply would leave them ruined men, hopelessly ruined.

"The choice is yours. There will be no blaster to demand compliance, but if you do not agree, I shall be forced to consider you intractably uncooperative in this time of emergency and a potential danger to the others on Visnu. That we cannot afford, and I shall be compelled to leave you here, firmly bound, while we are working to evacuate and defend the rest. Since you claim not to share our belief that the ravagers will come, you should not be too concerned about waiting for us to be proven incorrect."

"You would not!"

"Perhaps I should have stated that I was once an officer of the Empire. My role in what your Federation would term a major atrocity was displeasing enough to my superiors that I was cashiered for it."

The five looked to the Commandos in despair, but their faces were impassive.

They yielded. Within minutes, the developers had placed their signatures and voice-seals on the documents along with those of the witnessing Federation soldiers.

Sogan took up the papers and, after carefully folding them, gave them over to the Colonel. He turned once more to the shattered prisoners. "Do not imagine to fight these documents later. As you mentioned, your would-be victims are Amonites. Should you escape Federation justice, be assured that you will find yourselves on Amon with your names and your deeds known to all there. That is a populace with little liking for and less patience with delay or dainty dealing. Your deaths will be less agonizing than those the ravagers will bring in the event of their victory here, but they will be equally certain."

He looked toward the Commando-Colonel, bowing his head very slightly to signal the return of initiative to her. She gestured lightly with her blaster. "Shall we go, Gentlemen? You have transmissions to send."

TWENTY-ONE

THE ALBIONAN RETURNED the mouthpiece to its place. "There's nothing more we can do. We've called our crews together, but it's up to you to keep them here. I wouldn't stay and risk the kind of death you describe," he added viciously.

"No, you would not," Islaen Connor replied. "But the danger to them isn't really great, and I've found that most spacers are essentially human."

She nodded to Jake. "Take them back to the conference room and bind them."

The woman saw their look of horror. "No, you won't be abandoned there, but you must pardon me if I put little trust in you."

Once the Captain had gone, taking Varn with him lest his prisoners prove foolish enough to attempt to overpower him, the guerrilla officer at last sent her call out to the commandant on Horus. She explained the urgency of the situation facing Visnu and asked him to send help as quickly as possible, ships to carry away humans, animals, and cargo, ships which were prepared to win through to them should they be found in the midst of a heavy siege.

Sogan returned as she was requesting that renewer rays and the personnel to operate them accompany the rescuers.

"All's well?" she asked him when she had closed the transmission.

He nodded. "Aye. Karmikel will be down shortly. He wants to make doubly sure of our prisoners' bonds."

"Good."

"Thank you for your support. Had you seemed to gainsay me, it would not have worked."

She studied him closely. "You'd been thinking about that move for some time?"

"Even so, but I had to watch their responses to you to know if it would work. That is why I did not give you forewarning. I hope you are not angry that I took over as I did."

She smiled, and her great eyes looked directly into his. "Varn Tarl Sogan, you're probably the best thing that's ever happened to me!"

He grinned. "At another time, I might take advantage . . ."

"Never you mind that!" A cloud settled over her spirit. "If you hadn't acted as you did, we would have failed badly here. That's a sad confession for a Commando officer to have to make."

"Why so? It could really have been no other way. You were never sent to Visnu to enforce Federation law, remember, only to gather evidence. The other is the work of the Patrol, and they themselves would have been hard-pressed to succeed in this case. As for you Commandos, mere rule does not out-weigh life with you, whatever your willingness to sacrifice your own. As long as any kind of bargaining were possible, you could not slay, not even the likes of those you opposed here. The developers knew that and realized they could profit by it, as they knew I was not so bound. Have I not read it aright?"

"You have, Admiral."

She looked to the ramp as Jake called down a greeting to them. "All secure?"

"Aye." He joined them. His eyes went to the transceiver. "You got through to Horus?"

"The Navy's on its way. They'll be here in three days, less if nothing goes amiss to delay them."

"Excellent!" The Federation man turned his attention to Sogan. "They'll have a real prize, thanks to you."

The other shrugged. "A bad reputation is not always an evil thing," he replied with a smile.

"Our friends above wouldn't agree."

"I suppose they would not." His mouth hardened in

distaste at the mention of the developers. Islaen had kept her mind open during the interview so that he was aware of all she knew of them. Such creatures were beneath the ravagers in his estimation.

Karmikel had no greater liking for them. "I'm glad you proved their master," he said with sharp feeling.

"It could not have been done had you intervened. I have already thanked Islaen and must thank you even more warmly. She had her power to tell her how far I would go."

The redhead gave him a look of mock disgust. "I may not have the good Colonel's talent, Admiral, but I'm not quite an imbecile when it comes to reading my fellow creatures, either. I'll admit I wasn't all that sure of you when it came to burning them, and I was weighing how soon I'd have to act to stop you if you tried it, but I knew very well that you'd never leave anyone to face the ravagers' jaws."

Varn smiled faintly. "I am grateful all the same."

He saw Islaen's head snap toward the door. "The spacers come?"

"They do."

She sighed. "I only hope I don't lose what you've gained for us."

TWENTY-TWO

THE CROWD OUTSIDE gathered quickly and in an orderly fashion despite the strangeness of the hour. They had been expecting the order to lift, and believed that their employers had merely decided the time to evacuate had come.

The Federation Commando waited until she was fairly certain that all were present, and then stepped outside the building.

The sudden appearance of this lovely, slight woman whom some of them had so recently tried to kill froze the spacers. It was for an instant only, but the officer well knew the type of people with which she dealt and used the chance given her effectively.

She stood perfectly still, as if sure of both herself and her audience. Her eyes swept the crowd so that she seemed to measure each individual, then she raised her head.

"I am Commando-Colonel Islaen Connor," she said in a voice that carried to the outermost shipman. "I have a proposition for you that should prove to your benefit. I ask only that you hear me out and give due consideration to what I have to say."

She bent a grim smile upon them. "It will cost you nothing to grant me that. My blaster and those of my comrades inside are not sufficient to bend so many to our wills, and we do need you all."

No one moved, and she gave an inward sigh of relief. Curiosity held them, and more strongly the mystique of her unit, that and the high rank she had gained within it; they knew no minor deed had won that for her. They would at least hear what she had to say.

She explained the danger facing the off-worlders and once more fixed her eyes upon them. "All I'm asking is that every ship represented here lift with as great a number of people aboard as she can carry and take those people to the Navy base on Horus. In recompense for this, each crewman will receive a third-level heroism citation and, of course, the credit reward that accompanies it.

"I don't cheapen the award in offering it this way, although it isn't normally granted as freely. I don't anticipate danger to any of you, particularly if you remain near your ships, but chance and foul fortune can always work ill, and it'll be necessary for you to wait here until your passengers can be chosen and readied. That will take time, and I simply don't know how much of it we have."

She saw a shuffling within the crowd. "I'm aware that some of you may not welcome any close contact with either the Navy or the Patrol, but be assured that you shall not come to grief because you choose to help us. I've been granted authority to nullify any violations currently standing against either your vessels or your persons and do so absolve anyone taking part in the evacuation of Visnu upon the delivery of their charges to Horus."

Now, the spacers stiffened. Islaen knew that last was more valuable than any credit reward, for it opened more legitimate and, for the greater part, more profitable and less dangerous work to them. Most of those who did carry indictments against themselves or their licenses had earned them for relatively minor cause, and the chance to be rid of them was as a miracle. The others, well, they too would be glad to be rid of the shadow of more severe punishment.

Islaen hated that these ones should escape, but the need of the settlers had to rule, as it would have ruled with the developers themselves had Varn not intervened. If they would help, they must be allowed to go free. Her head raised almost imperceptibly. She knew even without the readings she was receiving that asking for their decision was but a formality. She had won.

* * *

The Commando-Colonel returned to her companions. Varn
Tarl Sogan stepped forward to greet her. "You were magnifi-
cent," he told her quietly. More than that, he thought in his
innermost mind, infinitely more than that. He had been aware
of her loveliness and her bravery almost since their first
meeting, but tonight, her beauty and courage had been terrible, for she had stood as the champion of a people.

Jake Karmikel offered her his congratulations as well, but
already his mind was racing ahead to hurdles yet to be cleared.
"Sudden emergency is part and parcel of a spacer's life, but I
wonder how the colonists will react when they find out what's
ahead, especially when they learn that less than half of them
can be taken off."

"Amonites are not given to panic." Her face hardened in a
manner new to Sogan's experience. He wondered at the
change until he realized she had assumed the cloak of command. The feelings of the woman and former agrarian were
swept aside as she took on responsibility for the safety of the
colony. "If they do, it shall be quelled before it rises beyond
controlling."

"If it cannot?"

She looked at the Captain bleakly. "Then the ships shall lift
empty. The crews have responded as men, and I'll not sacrifice
them to disorder."

"We'll know soon enough. The settlement representatives
should be gathering shortly if they come as readily as the port
people did."

Islaen Connor faced the Amonites as she had the spacers,
save that now her two companions stood beside her. She had
no need of cover with these.

For the third time that night, she described the approach of
the ravagers and what their coming would mean for anyone
taken by them. To her relief although not to her surprise, her
news was accepted calmly, at least at this stage. After Amonite
custom, the head of their Directing Council spoke for her fellows.

Gaea of Amon was well suited for the task ahead of them,
the Commando decided gratefully, a woman in her race's middle years, strong of will and mind as was usual with them, and
apparently with a long history of public service behind her.

She would not be quick to crumble.

Her first words gave evidence of that and that she had been weighing the guerrilla officer as well and had not found her wanting. "Very well. How do you propose we move to protect the people?"

"We evacuate as many as possible. I suggest sending infants, children, and young people under sixteen first along with any sick or injured you might have and any pregnant women in their third trimester. Some able adult supervision will be necessary, and the last can serve in that capacity. Send also any medical personnel required by the ill.

"Let lots be drawn for the remaining places after first excluding any who choose to remain behind."

The older woman lowered her head in assent. "You reason well thus far, Colonel. Our people are a disciplined folk and will cooperate fully. The Council will, of course, remain, all save one who must go to guide those slated to be our successors. They are named already, and so there should be no disruption of government."

"Excellent. We'll try to make certain that their duties will be very temporary."

"There is hope for those who stay behind?"

"Aye, definitely. The buildings in the control complex can be defended actively with fire. Even without it, those walls should be proof against creatures never opposed by more than mud and soil in their natural state."

"But they are burrowers."

She nodded, her respect for the Amonite rising even higher. "They are, and for that reason, I'm not as certain of the floors although I did examine one of the ravagers and don't think it was so equipped as to win through to us.

"As a precaution, we'll gather in the control tower complex. The fuel reservoir runs under that and is as secure from below as it is from above."

"What if they get through some crack?"

"If they do, it'll have to be a fairly big one. They're not small creatures by any means and should be seen and stopped if they find a chink large enough to admit them. There will be several lines of defense at the various levels to bar any such entry."

"The animals?"

"None can go, obviously. They'll be brought to the warehouse nearest the tower and penned there. It's part of the complex, and guards can be set over them."

"Sleep gas? They would give no trouble then."

Islaen shook her head. "No. We don't know how fast we'll have to move when the Navy comes or under what conditions. We'll set canisters to be released if the ravagers win through so that the poor beasts will pass easily from life, but we'll have to withhold it otherwise. That building is tightly sealed. They shouldn't become aware of the fires or their danger if their guardians don't transmit fear to them."

"We'll pick steady watchers," the other assured her.

"There'll be room to store whatever goods you are able to salvage as well. Ships can return for those later should they have to be left behind during the evacuation."

"Our crops are lost beyond saving?" There was scarcely a question in her voice. That was fairly obvious from the Federation soldier's description of the ravagers' work in other areas.

The Commando-Colonel met her gaze steadily. "Those were lost anyway. Visnu doesn't have colonization approval."

For the first time, a stir ran through the assembled settlers, a low, angry rumble. "This is the truth you tell us?" Gaea demanded.

"It is," she responded evenly. "My unit was sent here to investigate the unusual amount of activity centering about Visnu. You may praise the Spirit of Space that we were. If we hadn't discovered this danger facing you, it is doubtful anyone would survive its coming."

"If the ravagers do come."

"If they don't now, they will eventually."

"These openers of homesteads, where are they now?"

"Inside, bound and under arrest."

"They stay! They called themselves colony officials. Let them now take that part!"

"That's your decision and one with which we hold. It's to your benefit to guard them well, however." Islaen had the pleasure of explaining the agreement which had been forced upon the developers.

"A harsh judgment and a just one," Gaea said after a moment. For the first time, she turned to her companions and consulted with them in their own language. After a brief discussion, she faced the Commando once more. "Aye, we shall guard them. A more direct revenge would give us nothing for all we have put into this world.''

Her eyes narrowed. "You represent the Federation. How were you able to gain all this? I doubt their hearts were moved by repentance or pity for us.''

Islaen's smile was cold. "My kind can do much, Councilwoman. Don't doubt that. However, it's my comrade here whom you must thank. They yielded to his will as they would not have done to mine. Gather your people now. I want the ships to lift as soon as they can be loaded. My comrades and I will meet you at the control complex. We've work waiting for us there if our defenses are to be ready in time."

The two Commandos and their companion labored throughout the night to prepare their stronghold for the assault they knew was coming. They worked, too, to ready fliers for battle service, so that they eventually had three set to cast flame.

They felt secure in leaving the first stage of the evacuation entirely in the hands of the Amonite leaders, and were rewarded by the sound of ships lifting with reassuring regularity.

When the time came for the second phase, the choosing of those who must remain on-world, they did join the settlers. There could be no delegating of responsibility in this, and the deciding must be Islaen's if some disagreement arose.

None did, and the actual lottery was smaller and less painful than might have been the case. A good number of colonists had volunteered to remain. To the Colonel's surprise, no few of the spacers had joined them, those whose skills were not essential for the run to Horus.

Scarcely had the choice been made than the loading of the starships began again, and those fated to remain turned their hands to the work before them, the gathering in of the stock and goods and the supplying of the areas in which they would take refuge until their rescue. Soon, most of the ships were gone.

Varn Tarl Sogan seemed completely absorbed in his own hidden thoughts during this last phase of the evacuation, and it was with apparent effort that he roused himself to address his companions.

"You take the *Maid*. My power may prove of use here."

"You must be joking," Karmikel retorted.

"We can no more leave Visnu than can the Council members," Islaen told him. "Besides, it's a Commando's nature to fight a war one way or another, not flee it."

"Were the soldiers of the Empire ever less?"

"Varn, we can't afford to keep that ship here. We may well lose this battle, and people would then die who should otherwise have lived." Their eyes locked, but there was no yielding in her, and the Arcturian turned away in the end.

A few of the spacers who had given up their places to the colonists were still standing nearby after having watched their own vessels lift. His attention settled on them now. "Can any of you fly a ship?" he demanded suddenly.

One stepped forward. "I can, sir."

The dark eyes fixed on him. He was a Sirenian, young but with an air of competence about him. His instinctive response to the former Admiral and the straightness of his body proclaimed recent Navy association.

"You are licensed?"

"Fighter pilot."

"Experience?"

"Plenty during the last phase of the War, Sir."

"You will take the *Fairest Maid* to Horus."

The younger man gave him a sharp look. A spacer captain did not release his vessel into another's hands. Islaen felt both his surprise and his growing distrust.

"Captain Sogan has skills we need here," she explained, then asked, "You were left without a place when the Navy cut back to a peace-time level?"

"Aye, Colonel, and with no place outside it. The market's glutted with men with a lot more years of flying behind them. I was lucky to get a berth as a cargo hand on this flight."

"Bring the *Maid* and those aboard her through, and I guarantee you an assignment more in keeping with your training." She hesitated. "It'll probably have to be at the apprentice level at first."

"No trouble there, Colonel!!" he said with an excitement that required no use of her gift to detect. "I'm more than good enough to make the run to Horus and probably a lot of others, too, but I also know enough to realize I've nothing like the experience necessary to keep a ship in the starlanes, much less

beyond them, for any length of time. It was an apprenticeship
that I had wanted.''

"Go with Captain Sogan, then. See if you'll have any problems with the *Maid*. If you think you can take her, return to
me, and I'll give you the orders you'll need.''

"Aye, Colonel Connor. Don't worry. I'll deliver the *Maid*
and her passengers safely, the Spirit of Space willing.''

"Of that I have no doubt.''

Sogan aided the young pilot in the loading of his starship
and computing her course. When all was at last ready, he took
his leave of him and returned to the Federation woman's side.

Together, they watched the *Fairest Maid* lift. His eyes
stayed on her, straining after her, until every last spark had
vanished from the black sky of Visnu's moonless night. At
last, his head lowered. His work was now in the brightly il-
luminated spaceport. What happened amongst the stars lay
with chance and the wills of those beyond his knowing.

Islaen's mind brushed his. *You chose well, Varn. He
wouldn't betray you even if I made him no promise, and I
fully believe his skill is more than equal to the task set to him.*

As do I. What now, Colonel?

*Check that our defenses are correctly placed and try for
some sleep. Visnu's gods alone know what daylight will bring.*

He sensed rather than heard her sigh. *What is it, Islaen?* She
hesitated, and his head raised. *Have I lost your trust?*

No, but I may spark your anger.

The man frowned. *Speak, then. At least, give me the benefit
of the testing.*

She smiled. *No testing, but I do heartily wish that you'd
gone. Jake and I, we represent the Federation and were bound
to stay, but that wasn't true of you. I—I don't want to see you
dead.*

*Islaen, do you know me so little? Strength itself brings re-
sponsibility, as does this power I have. Had I chosen to assure
my life by going, I should have rendered myself unworthy of
it. I could no more leave these people than could you, and
never could I leave . . .* His thoughts retreated behind tight
shields.

"I know it is fear for me that makes you speak so,'' he said
at last, "and not any doubt of my worth in the battle to
come.''

"I should doubt the beauty of the stars before I doubted that," she whispered fiercely.

"Let there be no more talk about our lost chances, then." He grinned suddenly. "After all, there is a matter to settle between these ravagers and me." He raised his bandaged hand. "They bloodied me. The honor of an Arcturian war prince demands a stern accounting for that."

TWENTY-THREE

THE COMMANDO-COLONEL and her two companions set up a command post in an office near the spaceport's main control room. They gave orders that they were not to be summoned until the middle of the following morning, barring unexpected developments. The five hours of sleep they would gain would be no answer to their bodies' demands, but it would be enough to restore them for whatever lay ahead.

No time at all seemed to have passed when the sound of a soft tap drew them back into the waking world. One of the settlers, a young man, was visible through the transparent portion of the door. He was holding a tray in his hands and was trying to peer into the darkened room. Islaen got to her feet and hastened to admit him, switching on the light as she reached for the door.

"A fair morning to you," the man said. "Gaea thought you would prefer to eat and wash in here."

"Thank the Councilwoman for us. She's most thoughtful."

"I am sorry that there is only washing cream, but she felt it best to conserve the water."

"Rightly so. We don't know how long the siege will be." The woman took the tray from him and set it on the desk. "Anything to report?"

"No, Colonel. We sent scouts out once the sun rose as you ordered, but none have called in yet. They would have had they discovered anything."

"We should be able to at least eat in peace at that rate. How are the prisoners surviving?"

The Amonite grinned. "They do not like that they were left here."

"They're in good company in that," she said dryly. "See that they're not too uncomfortable, but keep them tied. I don't put the same trust in their nerve as I do in your people's, not with an enemy such as this. Panic could be disastrous."

His head raised at the compliment she had given his kind. "That we shall do, Colonel, and with great pleasure." He took his leave of them so they could eat and discuss their plans out of the hearing of those who were their charges.

Jake Karmikel was frowning. He had watched the Amonite during his conversation with the Colonel and realized the man was far from easy with them, particularly with their dark-haired companion. His eyes had kept flickering from one to the other but had settled most consistently on the former Admiral, as if it were taking all his will not to stare openly at him.

When the young settler quit the office, he was quick to follow after him. "Hold up, friend!" he called as soon as the closing of the door had shut off the sound of his voice from those inside.

The Amonite turned, surprised, and came back to the Captain. "Aye, sir?"

"Something was troubling you in there. Is it that we're Federation-connected?"

"No! We are not so narrow-minded."

"I didn't think so, but what is it, then? It is us and not the ravagers."

"It is not you. Not you Commandos." He looked away. "The prisoners claim your comrade is an Arcturian."

"That man stayed when he might readily have gone."

"But they say he took part in some atrocity . . ."

"The part of preventing it, and for that he has paid and pays each day a price the like of which I hope no other need ever have to give!"

He eyed the youth with open contempt. "Aren't you the credulous race? First, you allow those men to lure you here, take nearly all you had saved or could raise, and come within an eye's blink of abandoning you, and now you believe them again?

"That Arcturian forced heavy concessions for you from them. Do you not imagine they'd like to see his life ruined for that—or, better still, have him slain? Most of their fear of fighting that agreement would vanish if he were gone."

The colonist flushed hotly. "I had not considered . . ."

"Well, consider now, and make sure your fellows consider as well. Sogan was never less than a man, and he's a man now. It's right that he be treated as such."

"Aye, Captain. He shall suffer no hurt or insult through us."

The other was gone from sight before Jake realized someone was beside him. His head turned. Islaen. Her step was ever light, and he had not heard her approach in his anger.

She watched him gravely. "Thank you for that."

"Ah, it was nothing. I couldn't see the Admiral wronged. You knew, too, then?"

"Aye. I sensed his discomfort and its focus, but I couldn't just walk out, or Varn would've realized as well."

"How did you get away?"

"I told him we'd wash first and then eat." She sighed. "He knows I realize he doesn't like to bare his back before others and didn't question our leaving."

Her lips tightened. "I wasn't about to let that challenge go unmet."

"We succeeded, I think."

She nodded. "Aye, or rather you succeeded. That one should straighten out the others. These Amonites may not be a particularly cheerful people, but they have a straightforward sense of justice and the belief that one race is essentially as good as the next. They'll not abuse him because of his birth, especially not in the face of their debt to him."

Jake gave a cold smile. "I think our developer friends may well find themselves gagged as well as bound after this."

"My heart bleeds for the poor things."

The woman had brought their share of the washing cream with her, and the two guerrillas now separated, each taking possession of a room.

Islaen stripped quickly. She rubbed the cleansing substance over herself and followed with a brisk toweling. It was efficient, that cream, she thought as she dressed once more, but in this, as in so many other areas, Federation science supplied little in the way of real comfort. She longed for a shower or, better still, for a hot, scented bath. Even a dip in one of Visnu's frigid streams would have left her more content.

That could not be helped, however, and she was well aware that she should be right pleased to have been granted this much time for luxury in the midst of such an emergency.

Islaen and her companions made short work of the rations they had been given.

Varn's eyes went to the door. "No word yet."

"No," Karmikel said. "Perhaps they won't come until we're all off Visnu."

"They might not come at all," his commander remarked hopefully. "Our theory's based on pretty slim evidence even if we didn't dare ignore it. We've actually seen only one column, after all, and a few scouts, and we don't know but that the plateau may be too high and too arid for their liking."

"Like it or no, they have visited it in number before this," the Federation man said firmly. "The look of the vegetation proves it has been raided in the past, if not very recently."

She gave him a quick smile. "Granted, yet still I'm hoping we may escape without any test of fire."

"As do we all." the Arcturian interjected. He shook his head slowly. "Somehow, I cannot believe we shall. Fate seems determined to stage a battle here, or else it is Visnu's own gods who have set themselves against the idea of any human settlement. The desires of such opponents are rarely thwarted."

"A gloomy assessment but accurate, I very much fear," Islaen said.

The Captain got to his feet. "We're finished here. Why not join the others and see if any reports have come in?"

The Amonite settlers had gathered in the big control room, those whose duties permitted them to be there. Most were still working frantically to salvage what they could out of their homes.

It was a sad task. The animals had already been secured and made comfortable with food and water, but much, so very much, remained that would probably soon be destroyed. It was no easy matter to abandon the fruit of so much work and so much hope.

Gaea saw the three and hastened to join them. She gave them greeting and then briefly outlined what had transpired while they had slept. What she reported was no mean accomplishment for so short a span of time, and Islaen was quick to acknowledge it.

"You have our congratulations, Councilwoman," she said gravely. "Your people have responded with both courage and wisdom."

It was no idle compliment. Most races did follow their own leaders better than aliens in times of crisis, but these had displayed a calm efficiency from their first summoning that would have been the envy of any military command. Whatever their dislike of Federation authority, they respected completely the authority of those they had set over themselves from their own ranks. That bond of trust and discipline had held against many trials during their parent world's long history, and she believed it would hold firmly now, whatever was to come.

Her brown eyes sought out the planetary transceiver. "No word yet?"

"None. Maybe these ravagers will not come until after your Navy has taken us off."

"I hope they don't, and there's really a pretty good chance that they won't." She sighed. "The ships'll be here soon. In the meantime, we can only wait."

"That we can do. We are known as an impatient people, but it is usually at human stupidity that we bridle. We see it as pointless to roil ourselves over the blows of chance, which are beyond any man's commanding."

They remained within the control room, Islaen's party and the Councilwoman. The scouts had been ordered to explore along the rim area when they reached the plateau's edge and only then to report back. They should be receiving the first of those transmissions shortly.

It was another fifteen minutes before the operator announced that a call was coming through.

"Put it on room intercom," Gaea ordered.

The voice of a man, who identified himself as Izaak,

sounded from the loudspeakers. It was steady, but obviously so only by the strength of his will. The words came tensely and with some slurring of the precise Basic normally characteristic of an Amonite's speech.

"It is beyond credence. Below me is one solid black mass moving up the wall and over the ground until it disappears into the trees. I cannot see where it begins. All the lower slopes are covered as near as I can tell." His voice caught a little. "There is no break in them. No stopping. No end . . ."

Islaen's eyes closed. Ravagers, and everything she had feared they could be. She gripped herself.

"Izaak, this is Colonel Connor. How wide is the column?"

"I do not know, Colonel. I flew six miles in both directions without seeing any lessening of it at all." His voice gained strength as he spoke. His own terror and awe were submerged by the weight of his responsibility to report accurately.

"I have contacted the others. Every one, every single one, makes the same report. It was decided that I should call in for all and thus save you the delay of waiting for each individual transmission."

"By Her Who rules all space! Are such numbers possible?"

The Commando-Colonel did not hear Gaea. "So they are coming up along the entire rim?"

"Aye, Colonel. We have checked the whole of it, and no place on it is free of them."

"How far in have they advanced?"

"Far, but I cannot say exactly. There were dark patches to be seen where the trees thinned better than ten miles inland."

"My thanks to you, Izaak, and to all your comrades. Return to the port as quickly as possible. Note if you can how far they've penetrated, but don't delay or risk yourselves in any way to find out. We'll learn soon enough."

There was no hesitation on the Federation woman. War was upon them, and it was hers to command the waging of it. She turned to the Councilwoman. "Call in your people at once. No one must be outside with that black tide approaching."

"It shall be done, Colonel." The older woman seized the transmission mike and, after adjusting the controls, began speaking rapidly in her own language. Her composure had returned, but that came as no surprise to Islaen. She expected courage from her.

Those inside the building complex moved quickly and in a

grim, almost total silence. They checked again their stocks of
food and drink and made a final test of the seals on the por-
tals, those leading from the exterior and those within. The
guards who were to stand beside each one clad themselves in
protective garments and confirmed that their blasters were
functioning and held full charges.

The Commando-Colonel studied these sentries critically
when their preparations were done. They were brave, she
thought, every one of them, and she prayed with all her being
that they would not be called upon to put their courage to the
ultimate test.

"You're as well set as you can be," she said to them.
"You're armed for this war, but remember it's our hope that
you shall never be forced to use your weapons, that the
buildings will be strong enough to keep the ravagers out. It's
only because we realize no fortress is utterly impregnable that
we deem it necessary to guard every door. Your assignment is
to close off passages and carry warning if necessary, not to
engage the ravagers or try to fight them off in the event of a
major breakthrough.

"In only one instance will sacrifice be demanded of you. If
flight would open this chamber and those inside it to the
ravager horde, then you must be prepared to remain where
you are and accept the fate inevitable to that stand."

Her eyes met those of each volunteer in turn. "These insects
are vulnerable individually, and a small crack can be closed or
held fairly easily, but you cannot keep them back if they come
in numbers sufficient to get around your blaster fire.

"Don't give them the opportunity to surround you. If any
of you are seriously pressed, go through a door and close it
behind you. Your clothing will give you some protection, provided you move quickly. Bear in mind, though, that those
garments are not armor. They were designed to shield the
human body from fire or vapor or corrosive liquid in the event
of an accident in the port, but they're still fashioned of cloth
and will not hold long against countless tearing mandibles,
probably no more than three to five minutes. It'll be up to you
to use that time well.

"Go now. Rest if you can, but be ready to respond at once
when the command to take up your posts is given."

TWENTY-FOUR

NOTHING REMAINED BUT the waiting. Islaen and her companions did not leave the crowded control room again but contrived to find a spot against the rear wall where they might sit somewhat apart. The woman's eyes were closed so that she seemed almost to sleep, but her mind and her nerves were fully alert.

She hated this. Patience had never been one of her great strengths. She was all too aware of the way prolonged idleness, especially when coupled with anticipation, could sap both strength and control. She would need her resources intact later, and she owed it to these people to hold herself calm and still before them.

There was little else she could do for them at the moment, she thought wryly. The Amonites were very well organized and had both settled and secured themselves in the control room without any need of assistance from her party.

When the scouts returned, she questioned them, but they were able to add nothing to their initial report, save to state that the invaders had not yet reached the farms; the heavy canopy had prevented them from seeing how far they had advanced beyond a few unconfirmed glimpses that seemed to indicate a penetration of at least fifteen miles.

After thanking and dismissing them, the guerrilla sat back

once more. Fifteen miles? No, the insects would have come farther than that, she decided. From what she had seen of them, they moved fast when marching, and there just was not enough vegetation near the edge to cause any major part of so huge a number to delay their advance. Some would stop and feed as they had below her tree-refuge, but the rest would keep right on going.

She felt Varn's agreement. Their minds had been lightly linked throughout the afternoon, each drawing a quiet comfort from the contact although neither had been very much inclined for actual speech. Now, however, she had opened her thoughts to him, and the Arcturian had roused himself to respond.

"The farms may slow them a little," he said aloud, "but not much. Their scouts must have been too efficient in spreading the news of the food supply up here and have drawn too many."

Jake turned his head. "All the worse for us. They'll be hungry and more determined than ever to break through to us."

"So do I see it." Sogan fought back the desire to shiver as he recalled the night he and Islaen Connor had spent in the lean-to with that column all around them. Those insects had been afraid, and there had been ample food nearby to draw them away, yet they had stayed so long . . .

Suddenly, his body went rigid. The color drained from his face. Islaen recoiled as a fist of panic rammed into her mind with all the force of a physical blow. She braced herself against it. *Varn, take hold of me!*

She felt his consciousness grasp hers, and she herself relaxed. She had expected worse. He was a strong man. Some surprise had swept him, but already he had the stark terror under control. A moment more, and he was himself again although he neither released his mental hold nor that which he had taken on her hand.

"They are here," he whispered. "That single-minded . . ." He opened his thoughts so that she might know what he was receiving.

The Commando gasped. It was a primal force that blasted into her, a hunger not driven by conscious intelligence or planned action but only a desire to feed and to move on to food, that and an equally mindless awareness that food of the highest and rarest order was near and in bulk. She sickened to

realize that the prized goal of all the great horde was animal
protein.

Now it was the former Admiral who held her, supported her
until she could regain her balance after the initial impact of
that blind horror.

Karmikel was watching the two of them. "What is it?" he
demanded, keeping his voice low so that those around them
should not realize anything was amiss.

The woman forced her voice to answer steadily. "The
ravagers have come into Varn's range. They'll be on us very
shortly now."

"How far off are they?"

"I do not know," Sogan replied. "Their numbers might be
strengthening their transmissions enough to considerably ex-
tend my ability to receive them. They are still outside the
farms, I think, but they—they are already aware of us."

"Their exact position scarcely matters now," the Colonel
said. "It's enough to know they're very near. We'd better get
set fast." She got to her feet and swiftly crossed the room to
the intercom controls. "Guards, go to your posts. We're
under full alert. You will be informed of further developments
via the intercom."

The volunteers quickly left their places amongst their fellows and hurried from the room. Gaea gave the Commando a
hard, searching look but did not question her order. Her eyes
turned to the viewer screen focused on the large, paved saucer
that was the planeting field.

A full hour passed and half that again without any change.
It seemed to those around them that the Colonel's order was
premature, and the Councilwoman suggested at last that they
recall the guards for a while.

Islaen only shook her head. "When they do come on us,
they'll come fast."

She was not yet prepared to reveal the source of her certainty. She had no will to reveal it at all, not unless these
people forced her to do so.

Soon now. Very soon. Varn's ever-more-nerve-wracking
contacts told that the ravagers were on the farms, passing over
each one in a matter of minutes, devouring in those few
minutes the labor of long and weary months and the hopes of
a lifetime.

A dead and horrified silence fell abruptly over the huge

chamber. A black shadow poured over the lip of the saucer
and remained poised there, as a mighty army would pause to
gaze upon a fertile plain prostrate before it.

Still, it did not move.

Of course. This hard, alien barrenness was something beyond the insects' experience. Perhaps it would be enough to
baffle them, convince them nothing of interest to them existed
here. . . .

No. They had sensed life from afar, and they sensed it more
powerfully now. The vanguard of the nightmare host flowed
down to cover the dark surface of the landing area with their
own blackness.

Their advance was not silent. A clicking hiss accompanied
it, the tapping of countless legs against the hard pavement, the
rustle and rubbing of their bodies one against the other almost
into infinity. Within seconds, they had reached the base of the
buildings sheltering the refugees.

Very quietly, the Colonel activated the intercom. "The assault has begun," she told the guards waiting throughout the
complex. Islaen Connor did not move. Now was the first and
probably the major test of their defenses. If the walls failed,
they would die.

Her fingers went instinctively to the knife at her side, and
she knew without having to move her eyes from the screen that
it was a gesture repeated many times over in the control room.
Every man and woman here knew what the failure of their
plans meant, and each one had obeyed the command to provide against that dark eventuality.

Five minutes passed. Ten.

She drew a deep breath and released it. The insects could
make no impression on either the landing surface or on the
even more important walls. That last meant that they would
not be able to penetrate the reservoir and enter from below
should they attempt to burrow in from beyond the port area.
The refugees had been granted at least the hope of life.

The Federation officer activated the interstellar transceiver
and broadcast the news that the colony was under siege, giving
her assessment of the situation as it now stood. The fleet's
response was quick and concerned.

"As of now, it looks like we can hold out," she assured

them, "but just hustle your burners, and when you get here, come in blasting fire."

"Will do, Colonel. Hang on."

"We'll try. You can count on that."

The woman signed off. She turned to Gaea. "They'll keep the frequency open. Report each hour or whenever any change whatsoever takes place."

"Aye, Colonel."

Islaen glanced over her shoulder. "Where are our mechanics?"

A half-dozen people, all suited in defensive coveralls, stepped out from the mass of their fellows. "Come on, then." She bent a sudden smile on them, all the more dazzling because it was unexpected. "It's time we outsiders began to do our part."

The small party ascended one level to the flier hanger that was part of most such installations. The machines used by the scouts were there and three others with them. On the nose of each of these last was mounted two deadly looking objects —deadly indeed to those who could identify what they were.

Varn Tarl Sogan had spent long hours working with those vehicles. They could cast flame as had that one he had used to rescue Islaen, but more efficiently so that there need be no opening of the passenger area to the hostile world outside. They bore artillery-class blasters as well, weapons he had removed from the *Fairest Maid*. They would be well armed even should their supply of liquid fuel be exhausted.

It was necessary that they keep the roof clear. The refugees and their animals would probably be evacuated from there, and, of more immediate concern, only one floor, one major line of defense, separated it from the people below.

Her plan of action was simple. Two of the fliers would stay in the air at all times, circling the buildings, guarding the several places where the roofline or the various service appendages dipped to within a few feet of the ground. The gods of these people were to be praised that none actually reached it.

Because this would be a long-term assignment, each of them would rest three hours in turn, during which time their fuel and ammunition supplies would be replenished and their vessels serviced.

The fire-armed fliers should be effective in the event the ravagers found some way up, but they would have to depend on these three. None of the other vehicles Sogan had adapted had been designed to protect their occupants from the effects of ship emergencies while working close to them, and only these would defend their passengers should they have to come down in that mass of living death outside. The others provided so many openings to creatures of that size as to present no opposition at all.

Besides, she would not have liked setting any civilian behind Varn's unorthodox flame throwers. She was not overly pleased at being forced to handle one of them herself. Quelling that thought, the woman resolutely squared her shoulders and headed for the flier nearest her.

"That one is mine!"

She turned sharply in time to catch Sogan looking away in obvious discomfort. "Admiral?"

"My apologies. I . . . had a feeling for this one . . ."

Shrugging, Islaen gave him an amused smile. "It's yours, Comrade. Fly well."

He nodded his thanks and took his place inside. "Is my door seal tight?" he inquired of the Amonite standing near the vehicle to perform that check.

"Aye, sir."

The Colonel stopped beside her own flier. She knew that voice. It was the youth who had challenged Jake about Varn's past. She looked full upon him, probing with her mind as she did so. There was no distrust on him now. His expression and the emotion he radiated held only a kind of dazed awe which still remained as he came to assist her.

"He faced what lies out there once and still stayed to face it a second time?" he whispered more to himself than to her. "And you stayed?"

"No one has ever seen its like," she told him. "What we witnessed was less than a shadow of its shadow. But, aye, he remained and would have remained even had he known the full of it. As my comrade told you, he's a man."

She boarded her own vehicle. "Draw back out of the hangar," she told the ground crew, "just in case something unpleasant's waiting out there."

Her fingers hovered over the button controlling the release

mechanism which would open the hangar door. *Ready?* her mind asked.

Silence greeted her query for a moment, then his thought reached her. *I knew it would be thus even when we first began our march for this place.—Islaen, I have faced blasters and pletzars and the fury of my own race and would face them all again, however little I might enjoy doing so, but I have no will to go out against that horde.*

Nor do I.

He sighed. *Let us begin, Colonel.*

TWENTY-FIVE

THE BIG DOOR drew back to reveal a blessedly clear roof and the two fliers rolled out. Below and beyond the limits of vision, they could see only one vast, black ocean of seething life.

The Arcturian's vehicle stopped. He sat rigid at the controls, seeming to stare at the horror before them. Islaen could feel the power surging out of him. It stopped abruptly, and he slumped forward.

Varn!

She could not reach him, then his touch reassured her, and he pulled himself erect. *I tried to convince them that we were not for the eating, but there are too many. I am all right now.*

You're sure? You don't want to crash into that mess.

Perfectly sure.

The next time you want to try something like that, ask for a back-up. I wouldn't have let you exhaust yourself as you did.

I shall do nothing while in the air. I could not maintain the necessary concentration. Shall we fly, Colonel?

They circled the buildings several times, only firing once, when Sogan thought the creatures were pressing too eagerly toward a low point.

He brought his flier up again once he had driven them off,

matching its speed and altitude with that of the woman's so
they flew wing to wing.

How are you managing?

*Fine. The course is certainly easy to keep, but the scenery
does get rather boring.*

The Arcturian laughed and pulled away from her. His post
was opposite hers on the wide circle that was their route.
Several turns went by without any change to mark their passage. Both found they had to set themselves against the mo-
notony of their work lest they grow careless. Thus it was that
they welcomed the diversion when their transceivers suddenly
activated.

"Colonel?"

"Go ahead, Councilwoman." The Commando frowned.
There was a tightness in Gaea's voice that she did not like.

"I had best let Izaak speak. He is the scout . . ."

"I remember him, of course. Put him on."

The man must have been standing at his leader's side, for
his voice followed almost with the next breath. "Thank you,
Colonel. Once again, I bring you dark news."

"Let's hear it, Izaak."

"I am a master builder, Colonel Connor, not a farmer, and
I know the materials comprising these buildings. I should have
realized sooner . . ."

His tone firmed. "The crystal in the viewing ports will hold
against anything, but not so the sealant strips binding them
together and to the wall. That stuff can take heat and the
shock of great impact and individual blows from even razor-
keen shrapnel, but not constant worrying by countless strong,
sharp mandibles. What is worse, nearly every portal inside is
held to the walls by an even weaker variant of the same
substance. Once those ravagers gain access to the interior, and
they cannot be far from achieving that now, they will be . . .
feeding within two hours. There is no way the guards will be
able to contain them."

Her eyes closed. No fortress is utterly impregnable. Had she
not said that in her pride and confidence?

A weakness was not defeat. "It's up to us to make sure they
don't get inside—how much fire can those windows take?"

"A great deal. They were designed to withstand enormous
heat both in sudden, violent blasts and under more prolonged
exposure."

"We'll keep the ravagers away from the windows. You do what you can to get them blocked. Find metal pieces, furniture or whatever you can locate that will hold up under possible contact with high heat and flame, and drag them in front of the viewing ports. I doubt you'll be able to stop the ravagers completely if the sealant is broken, but you might be able to reduce the numbers coming through enough to contain them."

"What we can do, we shall." That was the Councilwoman again. The tension was still on her, but so, too, was strong determination. If the Federation party saw hope in combat, her Amonites would wage the war.

Islaen was relieved to find no sign of panic. "Contact the fleet. Let them know of this new development."

"Aye, Colonel."

Scarcely had the contact between them been broken, than Jake's voice sounded over the transceivers. "Shall I come up? You'll need help."

She thought for a moment. "No. It could be two days yet and maybe longer before the fleet reaches us. We'll have to maintain ourselves and the fliers throughout it all. Let the original plan stand."

The battle which followed was as grim and harrowing in its own way as any the three warriors had experienced during the War.

They would spread liquid flame onto the walls and the pavement around them, incinerate the insects crawling there, drive their more distant fellows back, but gradually the fires would die, the ground would cool, and the black horde would move forward again only to draw yet another burning stream down upon itself.

Brahmin's setting added a nightmare quality to the struggle as the harsh, unnatural brilliance of the spaceport lights and the glare of the ever-burning fires cast a surrealistic aura over a scene already too full of horror.

Islaen had to fight herself not to openly flee the field when her turn to retire from this eerie terror came at last. Even the aching weariness of her body and mind was nothing beside the weight crushing her spirit.

She brought her flier down smoothly and guided it into the hangar. Scarcely had it come to a halt and the great door

closed once more upon the threatening world outside than the
Amonite mechanics swarmed around it. She was lifted to the
ground and hastened into the corridor beyond where food and
drink were ready for her and a campbed prepared for her use.

The woman ate quickly and lay back. She felt safe, secure in
the knowledge that she would find her vehicle refueled for battle and in top functioning order when she woke. This was the
first time she had experienced something of the legendary
bond that developed between pilots and their support crews
under combat conditions, and she felt a little stunned both by
the intensity of it and by the speed with which it had come into
flower. Of course, the circumstances currently ruling life on
Visnu tended to foster a sense of immediacy, if nothing
else. . . .

The three hours passed quickly, and the woman resumed
her work in the air. She flew in a quick sweep over the entire
port before settling into her assigned course, returning with
dry lips and deepened pallor.

Every other building in the community was alive with the invaders. They were visible on the roofs, through every window,
and she knew as fact that several of them had been sealed as
was the complex she guarded. Only the rain of fire provided
by the Commandos and their ally was holding the colonists'
refuge inviolate.

The day passed slowly into yet another evening, and still the
siege continued until the eyes of the three pilots were red and
sore with the strain of ever working in the glare of the fires
they created and fed.

Islaen was scarcely aware of physical discomfort at that
point. She was frowning deeply. Something was wrong. An
unease had stolen upon her perhaps an hour previously and
had increased rapidly until it was now a low, persistent clamor
in her heart. What was it?

Sogan! His mind was closed to her! It was the loss of the
soft, speechless contact they had maintained until this tour
that troubled her.

Without attempting to reach him by either mind or transceiver, she sent her flier racing toward him. Seconds later, she
was beside him.

One glance confirmed that all was indeed far from right.

His face was tense, set, his body stiffly held, his hands white with the force of his grasp upon the controls.

"Varn, what's the trouble?" She used the transceiver. His mind was tightly sealed, to guard her against the knowledge that he was in difficulty, she realized bitterly. His head never turned to acknowledge her. He gave no sign whatsoever of surprise.

"Nothing really. There is some roughness in the guidance controls."

"Return to the hangar."

She opened the circuit to those inside. "Sogan's having trouble. Jake, take over for him."

Her attention returned to the Arcturian. He had not moved from his place. "Varn, break it off! We can't afford to risk you."

He abandoned his pretended lack of concern. She would know all too soon, whatever his will. "I cannot," he said quietly. "The controls are jammed in place. I have been trying to release them but to no avail."

"Can you reduce power?"

"No, or I should have asked you to draw me in. The engine is seizing even now. If I tamper with it . . ."

A violent shudder passed through the machine. Sogan fought to retain control of it and for a moment seemed to succeed, but then it swerved sharply to the right, in toward the building he had been defending. The man threw all his strength against the frozen control rod. If he could raise the flier only a little, he could try to come down on the roof or else leap out as he passed over it. . . .

No good!

The wall loomed near. Within a matter of seconds, he would strike it, hopefully to be slain in the first impact or in the explosion certain to follow when his fuel and ammunition ignited—anything but to be cast still living into the rending hunger below.

With a last, desperate surge of energy, he flung himself against the rod, not upward but to the left. It gave! For a fraction of a second, that victory seemed empty, but then he was slammed against its side as the vehicle tore back along its course, away from the doom that had been but three feet distant.

The shock and strain proved too much for the troubled

engine. A long, hollow whir issued from it, and after that, nothing. The controls were now loose in Varn's hands. He manipulated them carefully, bringing his vessel around in a smooth curve so that it once more faced the threatened building and into the wind.

He tried to keep the craft high, to glide it onto the roof, but realized almost from the start that he would not make it, would nowhere near make it, and so he set himself to bringing it down gently wherever it would land. Any break in the hull . . .

The flier had come far out over the planeting field before he had been able to turn it, and it lost altitude rapidly despite all his skill in nursing its glide along. It would ground very nearly at the point over which he had flown since beginning this mission.

The seething blackness drew close, closer. The flier's wheels touched ground, skidded on the crushed insect bodies.

Sogan played the controls. There must be no crash now, and he must hold to the direction he had faced in the landing. The machine slowed and finally stopped altogether. Well before its motion had ceased, it had blackened under the countless living creatures crawling on it.

TWENTY-SIX

ISLAEN CONNOR WATCHED the Arcturian's struggle in an agony of horror and helplessness. She saw him land, marveling at his skill even as the heart quailed within her at the thought of the doom waiting to receive him. She knew full well that the flier's low, gently sloping form presented no barrier at all even to wretchedly poor climbers like the ravagers.

She flamed the area around the machine, but she dared not bring her fire too close. The flier's defenses would hold, right enough, but not its deadly cargo. The fuel feeding the flame thrower would ignite in a blast that would rival the very heart of a star in its fury.

A myriad beyond counting of the savage insects were inside the fiery circle, each in a frenzy of excitement as it struggled to reach what was within that thin metal shell.

They had not succeeded, not yet. Varn's mind screens had gone down in the intense effort of these last endless seconds, and she had shared his dismay and his courage. If the ravagers got to him, she would know his pain as well.

The woman had not tried to contact him while he had fought, first to escape and then, more successfully, to preserve his life and the fragile shield sustaining it.

Now she called out to him. Her mind called, for she did not know if his flier's transceiver was functioning, and she did not

want to leave him sealed in that awesome isolation even long
enough to make a test of it.

To her infinite relief, his response came instantly. *I am all
right. I took no injury, and they cannot get through the flier.*

I'll try to drive some more of them away from you . . .

You have a mission before you, Colonel Connor.

Varn, I can't leave you!

*You cannot help me, and I am in less danger at the moment
than those inside whom we are sworn to defend. Now go you
to your work and leave me to mine.*

Your work? She could almost see his grin as she felt it,
strained, perhaps, but still real.

*Am I not sitting here with ample fuel, facing my target and
at optimum firing distance? I have enough play with my hose
to keep spraying a goodly area even if my enemies are pressing
me so thickly that I cannot see the effect of my labor.—I shall
have to depend on you to redirect me as you fly over if my aim
should wander a bit.*

Tears stung the Commando's eyes, but she blinked them
clear and took her machine up to its former level. She circled
him once more while confirming that his communications
equipment did work and pulled back onto her course.

His thought reached her again. There was a trace of uncer-
tainty in it for the first time since they had reestablished contact. *Remain with me, Islaen. I shall not break, but it would
mean much to have you near in mind while these things are
like to a living tomb around me.*

A great surge of warmth filled him as her reply came to him.
All you would have of me is yours.

An idea struck her. *My eyes feed my mind. Can you draw
on the information they send?*

She felt his seeking touch and the rush of his excitement.
*Aye! It is strange, not quite sight, and the perspective is
against all my other senses, but no longer am I blind. You are
quick of thought, Colonel. You have my thanks.*

*Remember that if the ravagers begin to get through to you. I
have an idea, dangerous in the extreme but perhaps able to
give you life if all other hope is gone. Don't wait until it's too
late to put it into action, until I must endure the pain of your
dying with you.*

No, came the slow reply. *My trust is in you, Islaen Connor.
If I sense an increase in my peril, you shall know it.*

*   *   *

Tears once more clouded the woman's vision as she returned to the battle. He trusted her, and all she had to offer him was a plan so dire that it was in reality but a passage into the very doom it would strive to avert.

She struggled to conquer her pain. Varn might not be of her service, but he, too, was a warrior and was bound, indeed, had been bred, to the warrior's code. She could not expect less of him or give him less now.

She was granted little time in which to master herself. Karmikel opened contact with her nearly as soon as she had resumed her former course. "Islaen, what's happening out there? I heard you exchange signals. Is he . . ."

"Varn Tarl Sogan is a stubborn, arrogant fool!"

"Meaning he's in one piece and more or less secure for the time being," the Federation man translated. "What do we do?"

"Continue as we have been doing."

"What?"

She sighed, and her eyes closed. "Varn's right. We can't help him, not really, and the colony's our responsibility."

There was a moment's silence. "I'll be up in a few minutes."

"No, stay where you are. He'll keep the front covered."

"Through what power of sorcery? They're so thick on that flier that they've effectively blinded him."

The Colonel almost smiled. "He's facing the building. It's a target hard to miss."

Her eyes went to the ravager-covered vehicle below. At this distance, she could barely distinguish its blurred form from the ground. "His transceiver's working. Talk to him, Jake. He'll be glad to hear a human voice now and then in place of their infernal clicking and scraping."

TWENTY-SEVEN

NIGHT CLOSED IN once more on the embattled colonists and flowed slowly by, dark, grim hours that varied little from each other.

Toward dawn, the character of the Arcturian's fire changed. His supply of liquid fuel was gone, and he activated the blaster. This weapon was not so simply handled. It required care to lay his bursts, great care, for now there was danger of causing severe damage to the building he was trying to protect.

Even blind, he proved himself an inspired gunner, but he was not forced to function thus for long. Islaen took to the air shortly after he had abandoned his makeshift flame thrower and opened her mind to him. Once he had adjusted to the difference in perspective again, he was able to refine his aim and technique almost as if his own eyes were bringing the information to him.

A feeling of satisfaction filled him. He would have the routine well enough set in his mind by the time she retired once more that he should require no more direction than an occasional minor adjustment from Karmikel.

It was about half into the woman's tour when Jake's voice came suddenly over their transceivers. "We've just gotten word from the fleet! The Admiral sent his fast fighters on ahead of the rest. They'll be here within the hour!''

Silence greeted his excited announcement. The Captain stared at the transceiver in complete bafflement. Why did these two alone fail to share the jubilation sweeping the hangar and the control room below? The answer came to him, and he leaned, almost sagged, against the side of his flier.

Sogan's machine was scarcely discernible even from the altitude at which they were operating. Those fighters would not see him at all. They would come in blasting a sea of flame . . .

Even if they were given his location, it was very unlikely they would be able to spare him. The fires they sent down would either engulf him directly, fires whose terrible, all-consuming fury his flier's defenses had no hope in the universe of withstanding, or else they would ignite whatever trace of fuel was left in his weapons tanks.

Islaen's voice snapped out like the crack of a whip. ''Jake, get into the air. You'll have to give us cover.—Varn, I'm going to drop a rope to you. It'll mean venturing right into the middle of them, but the way I see it, you have no other chance at all of surviving this.''

''What would you have me do?'' The former officer's question was quietly spoken. Only the fact that his mind was tightly sealed gave evidence that her suggestion troubled him.

She matched her tone to his. ''Jake will keep most of the ravagers back. You concentrate on those that remain, convince them your flesh isn't for their taking.''

''I cannot influence so many, nor could I maintain concentration of that magnitude and be able to make any move at all to help myself or to aid your efforts.''

''Do the best you can with those closest to you. I'll put the rope down as near as I can to the driver's door. When I tell you to move, break off your efforts if you must and race for it.'' She paused. ''I'll get you off the ground as soon as you have hold of it, but they'll swarm over you unless you succeed in discouraging them. Some are bound to get on you whatever you do, maybe too many.''

''That is understood.''

''Varn, you can refuse to do this.''

''No. I would as soon die trying to save my life as be crisped sitting here.'' His mind opened into hers. *If I go down and cannot rise again, you will burn me?*

Aye.

Begin, then. My courage is high now. It may not remain so if I am given too much time.

Varn, don't cast up shields, whatever happens. I don't know what I might be able to do for you if ill chance befalls, but I must know how it is with you, exactly how it is, at all times. Do you understand?

I do, Colonel. He activated his transceiver again, for he wished to reach Jake as well. "I am about to set my mind against the ravagers. It would be best if you did not contact me again until Islaen is ready to make her move."

The Commandos circled the crippled vehicle as closely as they dared, pouring rivers of fire onto the insect-covered pavement below. Leaving Karmikel to keep any newcomers from crossing their blazing barrier should the flames die and the ground beneath them cool too rapidly, his commander darted toward its center.

She lowered the rope slowly, carefully, ever so carefully, lest it brush against the machine and thereby become a bridge for the creatures she was seeking to thwart.

It was down at last. The loop at its end swung a bare two feet from the ground, an easy step for a groping foot, but even from here, it looked to be desperately far from the flier.

There was no help for that. Any closer, and its swaying would bring it into contact with the ravagers. At least, they no longer seemed to press around the door quite so thickly. Sogan's own fight had succeeded that far.

"Now, Varn!" Her voice and the mental command which had preceded it pierced the Arcturian's concentration. His hand hit the release mechanism on the door, and he flung himself outside.

The first ranks of the insects held away from him, deterred by his false warnings, but there were many, so very many others, immediately behind them whose minds he had not been able to affect. They were famished and as near to angry as such insentient creatures could come after their long effort to reach the man, and they all but leaped at him now. He had only a few steps to run, no more than a half dozen in all, but in that short time, they blackened his legs nearly to the knee.

He caught hold of the rope, jammed his right foot into the loop waiting for it, and lifted himself off the ground. Before he could secure the left as well, he could feel himself being drawn swiftly upward.

Sogan tightened his grasp on the rope. Well had it been realized that there would be no time for maneuvering a loop over his body, but the lack of such support left him totally dependent upon the tightness of his grasp and on his own balance.

Fire tore his legs. His survival suit had protected him thus far, but now the ravagers were through it and ripping the flesh beneath. He could feel them climbing higher, some shredding the tough material, others moving up under it, but most stayed where they were, feeding. . . .

Some reached his trunk. Tears of agony blinded his eyes as he set his will to clasping the slender cord that was his hold to life. His legs were useless. That they still supported him was little short of a miracle, and he could not even venture a guess as to how much longer they would continue to do so. He did not know if anything much remained of them. There was no sensation below his thighs but an infinity of pain more intense even than that which he had endured under the lashes of his people. All depended upon his arms, and already a few of the insects had found them. Soon, they, too, would go.

Islaen Connor ignored the torment ripping into her mind. She fought to strengthen Sogan, poured her will into him, supplying what pain and shock and the immense loss of blood had destroyed of his own. If only those things did not eat through his hands! Once they went, there was nothing more she could do.

The roof was below them. She dropped almost too rapidly toward the tight group of figures standing there. The woman waited until she saw Varn lifted down and then brought her flier up again, still dragging the blood-soaked line. The assault on the buildings continued, and Jake could not carry the war alone much longer.

Two eternal hours crawled by before Islaen was at last able to bring her machine back to its hangar.

It had scarcely ceased moving before she leaped from it "Where is he?" she demanded of the white-faced mechanic who had hastened to her side; she lacked the courage to ask how Sogan fared.

"In the corridor beyond. Dr. Kurmut set up right there."

Tears rushed to his eyes. "He is like to lose the legs . . ."

"Not a chance!" the Commando snapped. "There are renewers with the fleet." So intense was her relief that she was not even aware that his nearly equaled it. There was little danger of death, or the Amonite would not have spoken of this other thing first, not without also expressing the hope that release would come soon.

Her spirit rose higher still when she passed from the hangar into the area beyond. The colony's chief physician was there but withdrew to the end of the hall when he saw her, and that he would not have done if he had any immediate fear for his patient.

Unless . . .

The guerrilla's new-born fear vanished when she knelt beside the low cot on which Varn lay. She knew the look of dying men all too well, and it did not blight him. That he was gravely injured was obvious, but his condition had been stabilized, and the blood he had lost was already being replaced.

Sogan was under heavy sedation—his eyes were glazed from it—but he was conscious and managed the shade of a smile when he saw her and felt her gentle probing.

There is no pain, my comrade. His words came directly into her mind; she doubted he was capable of verbal speech.

She slipped her hand into the one he had opened to receive it. It was bandaged only on the back, and she was surprised at the strength in his grip. He wanted this contact with her badly enough to struggle to maintain it. Her fingers twined in his, and she felt his relief as he relaxed once more.

You were my strength out there. I could not have lived . . . The horror of that time swept him and, because he was unguarded, her as well, even as his pain had swept her during those terrible minutes of the ravagers' attack.

Islaen mastered it. She forced herself to respond quietly and lightly. *Nonsense. Everyone knows Arcturians are damned hard to kill.* She fixed him with a penetrating look. *You were less than certain of that flier, weren't you? That's why you insisted on taking it yourself.*

The smile was a little stronger this time. *Of course. I could not risk you. Never could I risk you.* His face suddenly became as a mask. He turned his eyes from her and fixed them on the ceiling. *I heard them say that my legs . . .*

You're going to have to stop this eavesdropping while people think you're unconscious, she told him sternly. *Your legs will be fine. All Navy ships that are even moderately large are outfitted with a renewer and you heard me specifically request them on this mission. You'll be under treatment long before night falls again on this part of Visnu.*

The battle? How goes it?

It's over. Whether it was through their fear of fire or some concession by that collective intelligence we mentioned earlier, I don't know, but the ravagers have withdrawn from the port and its immediate environs. The fighters are keeping watch lest they return, but right now we're anticipating a completely uneventful evacuation. Even if we're wrong about that and they do attack again, the fighters have proven they can force them back and keep them there.

The pressure of her fingers increased slightly. *There's no further need for worry. Just relax and wait. You'll be the first one taken out and the rest of us will follow fast after that.*

Islaen laughed to see him frown. *No use protesting, Admiral. That's the unalterable prerogative of the wounded, of which you are our sole representative apart from those who took a few nips while beating the little monsters off you.* She gently disengaged her hand. *Sleep now. When you wake again, you'll be free of pain, without need of any chemicals to keep it from your awareness.*

TWENTY-EIGHT

VARN TARL SOGAN was waiting in the Commando-Captain's office when Karmikel returned to it. He rose swiftly to his feet and stepped forward to greet him. "I need not ask the verdict by the look of you."

"Victory, my friend, total victory for us and, more importantly, for the Amonites. Those developers will be old and very poor men when they finally get out of prison."

"Excellent.—And the colonists? Have they chosen yet?"

"No. All three planets are extremely attractive."

"I must admit I am surprised everything is moving so quickly for them," the other said slowly. "I had understood it to be a lengthy process."

"Especially for those who tried to bypass the Settlement Board?"

Sogan nodded. "Even so."

"Normally, it would be, I suppose, but the Amonites' story is now well known, and the Board is eager to set them up as an example of what can be done for colonists in the hope of averting future disasters. Besides, everything that's happened to them, the way they responded and the fate that so very nearly befell them, all of it has won both high respect and sympathy for them on every level. The circumstances are seen as extraordinary. Nothing apart from actual safety re-

223

quirements is being permitted to delay them. Of course, money is no problem at all to them now.''

He smiled. ''My first job in civilian life will be acting as general Federation liaison and post-settlement explorer for them.''

''My full congratulations, Captain. It is no small task, but you are the equal of it and more.'' His dark eyes measured the redhead. ''I had thought you intended breaking with Navy work.''

''So did I, but I find the idea of accomplishing something of worth to others as well as my own self has taken a rather strong hold on me. I'll no longer bear rank after this week or be in any sense connected with the military, but I have let it be known that I'm available for tasks such as this.''

''A worthy decision,'' the other man said gravely. ''I hope it shall bring you all you seek in life.''

Jake's eyes fell for an instant. ''That it cannot do.'' He looked up again. Noreen's sons were able to accept what must be, and so he had accepted this. It was now his to go beyond that.

''I should hate you, Varn Tarl Sogan.''

The former Admiral stared at him, completely taken back by the quietly spoken statement.

''Why?''

''Islaen Connor is an incredibly strong woman. I've seen the sign of tears on her only twice—when Morris Martin was killed and when we received word that you had been executed.'' He sighed. ''It's preferable to be bested by a living man, I suppose, rather than by a ghost, but either way, I never had a chance.''

His blue eyes fixed somberly on the other. ''Perhaps you've become such a fool in these last three years that you'll lift from Horus alone, but I should be a thousand times greater fool if I didn't recognize that there's a bond between you two that no other can share.'' His brows drew together slightly. ''Maybe more than one bond. Those times of seeming silence back on Visnu, they were something very different, weren't they?''

Sogan lowered his head in assent. ''They were.''

Jake's breath caught for an instant with the wonder of that admission, but then he released it once more. ''I hope we shall meet again, Admiral, the three of us,'' was all he said.

"I think that we shall, aye, and perhaps meet frequently. There is much to be done in this war-roiled universe, work to draw all our talents, whatever individual courses we choose to follow."

Islaen Connor's office was small and businesslike, military in its appointments and possessed of the quiet order that was the mark of its occupant.

The Commando-Colonel was seated at her desk when Sogan entered the room. She was scanning a sheaf of documents she had just removed from a safe-lock portfolio beside her and seemed oblivious to his presence.

His eyes darkened. Her expression was pensive and solemn, as if some harsh weight were pressing down upon her. Did she labor under the depression that so frequently followed battle?

"Islaen?"

She looked up. Her face and eyes brightened gloriously, and she rose swiftly to her feet. "Varn! You look wonderful!"

"I should, after nearly four weeks of renewer treatment. I was beginning to think they would never release me."

Her eyes ranged his face and body critically. "Not bad at all," she told him.

The gray-and-black spacer's garments he had chosen fitted his slender, firm form well, and the fashionable semi-military look of them was suited to the man. Beyond that, he looked good, in his face, in the deep brightness of his eyes, in the familiar, easy grace with which he carried himself.

"How are the legs?"

"They might never have been damaged at all."

Islaen steeled herself. It had not been the ravagers' ghastly work that had given his physicians such trouble. She had their reports, of course. They were satisfied, or nearly so, but some scars twisted more than flesh.

"Your back?"

The smile he gave her was natural, with no trace of his former strain. "There is no longer any pain or stiffness, and if it is still no thing of beauty, neither could it now be used to terrify the timid of heart—I owe much to your people, Islaen Connor."

He glanced toward the papers she had set aside. "I understand from Jake that we have something to celebrate."

"Conviction and maximum sentence on every count," she

replied triumphantly. Her head cocked to one side. "I don't know how pleased I should be. It's not very flattering to me that you sought out my Captain first."

He chuckled. "Merely an example of my good sense, Colonel. With the verdict due, I figured you might be delayed in the court, and my impatience would brook no greater delay than necessary in discovering the result." He grew serious. "Thank you for keeping me out of it."

"It was easy enough to do. There were witnesses in plenty without calling in yet another."

"I had thought the developers would pull me in to weaken your credibility or, failing that, to avenge themselves on me by exposing my background."

She smiled coldly. "Oh, they tried, right enough, but I just testified that you had indeed made that claim before them and had achieved great effect by so doing."

"That was accepted?"

"Why shouldn't it be?" the guerrilla countered. "Your testimony was not required, and your past was of no significance to the case. Even if there had been no personal interest in you, Navy tribunals do not take kindly to the introduction of extraneous matters or to delaying tactics of any sort. Maybe that was part of the Patrol's plan, too, when they called us in. They knew they were giving the military jurisdiction by so doing. A civilian trial does take far longer."

Her smile softened. "There was more to their consideration than that, of course. These people look upon Jake and me with respect, but you, they hold in awe. There is not a man or woman in this base who would hurt you, including those serving as tribunal judges. They certainly would not permit a pack of criminals to twist their court into an instrument of vengeance against you." Her eyes fell, and for a moment, it seemed that her mind had slipped into another universe.

Sogan's fingers brushed her arm. "Islaen, what troubles you?" She had tight shields up, and he could gain no access at all to her thoughts.

The woman recollected herself. "I'm sorry." She sighed. "It was your mentioning of Jake just now. He'll be demobilized by this time next week. I—I'll miss him."

The man studied her for several seconds. "You gave me a promise on Visnu. I would have you redeem it now."

"Promise?"

"You were shadowed then, and you are shadowed now. Tell me what cloud is on you."

She shook her head and pressed a graceful hand to her eyes. "I have no right to this," she said more to herself than to him, "not when I've been given so much. My comrades are alive. The people for whom I fought through all the years of the War and since are free and safe, and I may rightly claim my little part in securing their safety. I have success . . ."

"And still you hunger for the life you have opened for me?"

Her head raised, and she looked sharply upon him. Once more, his hand reached out to touch her, but he only smiled and allowed it to drop back again, its mission unfulfilled.

"Do you imagine, Islaen Connor, that I can return to my former way, crawling along the starlanes like some rodent through the walls of a hovel?"

"You never . . ."

"Perhaps, perhaps not, but what served these last three years will serve no longer."

Fire, determination, flashed in the dark eyes. "You once described a course one in my position might claim. Well, I will to have it and have it in connection with your Navy, with the Commandos. I am bred and trained to fight, and I will fight again—with purpose and in a manner and cause consistent with my honor."

Varn drew a deep breath. "Come with me, Islaen. It will cost you nothing beyond the comforts of base life and the pleasure of having a number of troops always at your command, and I think you do not seek either. Your rank would still be yours, aye, and the likelihood of quick promotion since you would frequently be acting as the Federation's representative as well as its troubleshooter.

"You would have not merely access to the stars but the opportunity to learn the ways of the starlanes and the space between and the ways of the ships that span them.

"I, for my part, would have the power of your authority behind me in my dealings with men, your battle skills beside me, the chance to gain knowledge of worlds and their ways as you know and understand them."

He paused. "And through whatever fate may choose to send us, we would have one another."

The Commando made him no answer. Her eyes were fixed

on him, their expression deep and unfathomable. Her face was pale but otherwise completely masked. She seemed in that moment the dream of a woman and no living being at all.

His head lowered. He was glad to be able to conceal most of what he was and what he felt behind shields as strong as her own. "You gave me life in place of existence and have opened for me a vision of such richness . . ."

He stopped speaking, then began again. "I love you, Islaen, enough to respect your decision and to make myself content with the memory of what I have been privileged to share with you." He would have turned to go, but the spell which had held her shattered in that moment. She seemed almost to sway, and he instinctively reached out to support her.

Incredibly, she came to him. She rested against him while he folded her in his embrace. "I've longed to hear such words from you for so many years," she whispered. "I've wanted this so much and never dreamed to have it."

She looked up at him. Her eyes seemed huge and nearly too brilliant. "Even on Visnu, with you returned from the dead and at my side, I didn't think it could ever be."

"Did you not realize I loved you, my Islaen?" he asked softly.

"Aye, but I believed you would not, could not, act upon it. Fate had so dealt with you that nothing could be possible unless the decision was yours, born only of your own self."

"I think now that there is nothing which is not possible if only we two stand and strive for it together."

He bent to kiss her, and all that she had kept concealed within herself of love and tenderness and passion rose up to receive him, and the offering of himself which he, in turn, lay open for her taking.